BALDWIN STREET

BALDWIN STREET

A Novel

ALVIN RAKOFF

B&B

BUNIM & BANNIGAN
NEW YORK · CHARLOTTETOWN

Published by BUNIM & BANNIGAN, LTD., PMB 157 111 East 14th Street New York, NY 10003-4103
BUNIM & BANNIGAN, LTD., Box 636 Charlottetown, PEI C1A 7L3 Canada

www.bunimandbannigan.com

Manufactured in the United States of America

Design by Jean Carbain

Frontispiece illustration by Joe Rosenthal

Cover illustration: Kensington Market
Roy Greenaway (1891-1972)
Oil on canvas, 30.5 x 38.1 cm.
City of Toronto Art Collection, Culture

Library of Congress Cataloging-in-Publication Data

Rakoff, Alvin.
Baldwin Street : a novel / Alvin Rakoff. — 1st ed.
p. cm.
ISBN 978-1-933480-14-5 (trade hardcover : alk. paper)
1. Jews—Ontario—Toronto—History—20th century—Fiction. 2. Immigrants—Ontario—History—20th century—Fiction. 3. Toronto (Ont.)—Fiction.
4. Young men—Fiction. 5. Domestic fiction. I. Title.

PR9199.3.R25B35 2007
823'.914—dc22
2007001458

Hardcover

ISBN: 1-933480-14-9
ISBN-13: 978-1-933480-14-5

135798642

First edition 2007

CONTENTS

To the people of Kensington Market

Kensington Market in Toronto is an area of stores and stalls.
A street market. To this day it is one of the few street markets in
the New World where immigrants—from Europe, Asia, the
Caribbean—can find solace in their ability to purchase familiar
produce; be it live chickens or live fish, fresh papayas or dry limas,
cumin or curcuma, bleached bags or chopping boards.

Baldwin Street is the main intersecting street in
Kensington Market.

I called it home.

When you are young you want to change the world.
When you are old you want the world to be more like it
was when you were young.

BALDWIN STREET

THE LOTTERY

The two full crescents of Sadie's behind wiggled and waggled as she scrubbed the floor. Sadie was on her knees. In a cotton dress. A thin cotton dress. Made from a print of yellow daisies and white tulips and green stems all on a maroon background. As her bottom swayed the flowers undulated, waving enticingly to and fro, blooms caressed by a breeze in a field. In an incongruous field of ruby-red. The sweat running down Sadie's thighs and the splashing soapy pail nearby made the dress material translucent. In patches. Variegated windows to shining skin. And beyond the dress's hemline the lush flesh at the top of her legs could be seen to end in rolled-up lisle stockings.

Leonard was watching her. Sadie knew he was watching.

She manoeuvred the pail to a new position. Adjusted the knee pad. Recommenced work at a different pace. A brown hulk of soap rubbed frantically against the wood-backed scrubbing brush. Onto the floor. Circular motions. Strong and quick. Making her body vibrate. Her shoulders, arms, upper torso, waist, but most of all her bottom, pulsating from such exertions. Rapid movements. That stopped abruptly.

Sadie leaned back on her haunches. The brush plopped back into the galvanized bucket. A splash. Sending foamy water, perhaps, onto Sadie's chest. She looked at Leonard. And delicately stroked water from her breast. The curve of cleavage slowly began to reveal itself. Sadie paused when she reached the lower curve. Holding her breast. Her eyes never left Leonard.

"How old are you?" asked Sadie.

"Sixteen," lied Leonard, adding a year to his age. He could hardly speak. His intake of breath became shorter and shorter. He was mesmerized by the sight and thought of her wet breast. The shape now clearly visible under the shimmering dress.

She turned away. Back to the chore in hand. She slopped a long rag into the pail. And once again changed the rhythm of work. This time with deliberate strokes she glided the rag over the floor to remove the layer of bubbling soap. Softly. Slowly. Sensuously. On all fours. Turning and turning. Until once again her ass faced Leonard.

<hr>

Sadie Skolnick was a prostitute. At least that's what Leonard was told. And the rest of the gang on the street-Al and Voomie and Norman and Morrie and Ape and Abe and Harry-knew it to be true. "Look at her," said Norman, "she's a whore."

The stand in front of the Abelson store was a favoured place for the boys to congregate on Sundays and holidays. Abelson's had the advantage of being at the intersection with Kensington Avenue, the crossroads of the market. And whereas most other stalls had fruit and vegetables or produce of some kind hidden under tarpaulin and could not be sat on, at Abelson's the front stand was a double level of wide shelving where goods—pots, pans, dishes, dresses, shirts, sugar bags and more—were displayed by day but taken back into the shop at night. Empty benches. Where the guys could gather. And sit. Talk. And observe.

On any given Sunday the gang could be seen lolling around the Abelson stand. To avoid the gang's scrutiny most women would cross to the other side of the street. Not Sadie.

It was her wobbling backside parading past the boys one such afternoon that confirmed her calling to Norman. And to the others. "She's a whore," repeated Norman without taking his eyes off her bouncing bottom. He spoke softly. He was not of an age yet to openly state his opinions. And would not dare to challenge Sadie.

The eyes of each boy were on the bouncing bottom disappearing down the street.

"She's got something," said Ape.

"Yeah, a lot of fat," said Morrie.

"Fat? Yeah, maybe. Plump. Yeah, zaftig, rather than fat," said Harry.

"And she's old," said Abe. "Betcha she's what? Thirty-seven? Thirty-eight? Somethin' like that."

For her part Sadie appeared oblivious of the boys. A gang of pimply faced kids was of little interest.

"Yeah, she a pro all right," said Norman, emphatically and louder now that Sadie was a safe distance away.

"How much do you think it would be?" asked Leonard.

Harry tilted his head back and roared. "Too much for you, Lennie baby, that's for sure," he said.

"How much?" persisted Leonard.

"Ten bucks," suggested Ape.

"Maybe twenty," said Abe.

"Maybe even a hundred," said Harry.

"For a hundred bucks, I'd want your sister," said Al. Harry punched his shoulder. Hard. Playful but painful enough to make Al rub the ache away.

"Whatever it is, you ain't got it," Norman told Leonard. "And Lennie Abelson, you ain't about to lose your cherry to Sadie Skolnick." Norman was supposedly the only non-virgin in the group. Or so he said. None of the others quite believed him.

"Unless of course," said Norman's younger brother, Voomie, "we hold a lottery."

"What?" asked Al.

"We each put in ten bucks," said Voomie. "Have a draw. Whoever wins gets the money. And gets Sadie."

The boys became thoughtful. Silent. Until Al spoke. "Where the hell am I gonna get ten dollars?" asked Al.

"Work for it," said Harry. "Or steal it."

"Steal it? From who?" asked Al.

"From your old man," said Harry. "When he puts down his bundle. Before he climbs onto your Maw. Sneak into the bedroom one night. Pinch it."

"I couldn't steal from my father!" said Al.

"To get laid? Sure you could," said Harry.

Conversation stopped. The young heads were filled with thoughts and visions. Of Sadie.

It was agreed that each guy would endeavour to raise ten dollars.

Sadie was still in her teens when she went off with a Spadina Avenue cowboy. A man with a mouthful of teeth and an assured smile, with a camel hair coat and a Stetson hat from Sammy Taft., a padded wallet, and easy words. Had proclaimed his undying love and took her to Montreal. For two weeks. The Mount Royal Hotel. Big time. Sophisticated. For two whole weeks.

When she returned her mother wanted to throw her out of the house. Her father intervened. "They gonna get married, right?" said Mr. Skolnick, "so what's the big deal? Eh?" But the white-toothed cowboy didn't marry her. Within weeks she saw him less and less. Then hardly at all. Then not at all. Gone.

The Skolnicks had a butcher shop. Sadie's three younger brothers, Herschel, Moishe, and Lou worked in the family shop—as did most children on Baldwin Street—from an early age. After school. Before school. During breaks. The brothers hacked meat. Carved roasts. Made bicycle deliveries. Worked. But not Sadie. As sometimes happened, especially when there was only one girl in the family, daughters were protected. Over protected. And did not help in the store. Sadie was one of those protected few.

Less than a month after Sadie was back from Montreal her father died. A stroke.

Mrs. Skolnick took over the store. She had been at her husband's side from the first day the store opened. Shortly after the marriage. Stopping only for a few hours on four occasions. When she gave birth to her children. Butchering was not new to her. Lifting a side of beef—the forepart only, for the shop was kosher—slapping it onto wooden slabs. Veal. Mutton. Lamb. Chopping out chops. Slicing steaks. Removing hearts. Livers. Lungs. Grinding sausages. A butcher.

Sadie maintained it was grieving over her father that threw her into the arms of another man. She called her mother from a cabin in Muskoka. Mrs. Skolnick told her never to come home again. But three days later when a rejected Sadie presented herself, the two women, mother and daughter, collapsed into each other's arms. Weeping. Wailing.

After this last reconciliation, there was a difference. In Sadie. One morning she went to the kitchen cupboard and selected an apron. White. Full length. Voluminous. A butcher's apron. Sadie tied the strings round her back. Checked her reflection in the striated glass of the door that partitioned the store from the dwelling area. Straightened. And, without saying a word, entered the store. To work.

Voomie's preparation for the lottery was meticulous. Sitting on the Abelson stand he measured, pencil marked, snipped a sheet of paper into squares, making sure that each one was exactly the same. He even ran a finger along the edges to ensure there were no apparent differences to be felt.

The other guys watched.

Voomie licked the leaded end of the pencil. Leaving a mark on his tongue.

"An X goes on one of them," said Voomie. "Whoever gets it, wins. Okay?" Leonard was so intrigued by the grey line on Voomie's tongue, he had to make himself listen.

"Okay?" repeated Voomie.

Okay, they all agreed.

Voomie deftly scored one of the squares. Folded carefully four times. Put into a brown paper bag usually reserved for oranges and apples. Then in the same precise manner Voomie folded the other eight squares. Also into the bag. He shook the bag. The ballot papers rattled inside. He held the neck of the bag tight. Looking inside was impossible.

"Turn your head away. Put your hand in. Pull out just one, Okay?" ordered Voomie.

"Hey, Norman, your kid brother," Harry pointed at Voomie, "is a real stickler for detail, i'n't he?"

"Yeah, that's why we let him do it," said Norman. "And what's more he don't cheat."

"He don't cheat! *Now* you tell me!" said Harry "I gave him an extra five bucks to let me win!"

"Very funny," said Voomie. "Enough talk. Let's go."

One by one the boys reached into the bag.

———— ·•◦•· ————

Sadie did not like handling meat. The offal in particular offended her. Raw liver squelching under her touch caused a shudder. As did lungs. Intestines. Hearts. Tongues. And such. As she could not help show her distaste for these items, she took more instinctively to other tasks. Laying out wrapping paper. Wiping scales. Returning knives and choppers to designated hangers. Her favourite task was at the cash register. It became apparent to her mother and brothers that she was quick and efficient at totalling the amounts customers owed and the change needed. So that was where she was usually to be found. But still a part of the family team. A small part.

Until another man came along. And another. And another. A pattern was established. A man. An escapade. Forgiveness. Back to work.

Not that, considering the years involved, Sadie had many men. And as to whether she actually sold her body or not, was a matter of conjecture and not fact. Nobody had ever seen her ply her trade. She did not walk the streets. Although Norman's father, Manny Levy, the chicken dealer, claimed he saw Sadie once in the King

Edward Hotel. No one knew whether to believe him or not. Norman was given to making proclamations to gain attention. Was his father the same? Like son, like father?

When the stories of Sadie's escapades spread, especially after she became suspected of being a professional, customers were reluctant to be served by her, and would wait for Herschel, Moishe, Lou or her mother to be free. As if food touched by Sadie might be contaminated. Mrs. Skolnick was soon aware of this and found other chores for her daughter. In the house. Rather than the store.

Those chores became more and more menial. Although nothing was said or pre-arranged, it seemed that after each adventure with a new man, the jobs sank a level lower. Sadie did not mind. In the end she cleaned the house. From top to bottom. An early riser, the store tasks mandated to her were to scrub the floor every morning, spread a fresh layer of sawdust, scour the chopping blocks, scrape the choppers and knives. All this hours before the first customers stepped into the shop. Indeed long before Mrs. Skolnick or her three sons appeared. Mrs. Skolnick was a stickler for cleanliness. She took her responsibilities as a purveyor of food seriously. Now in the mornings as she entered the shop, she sighed, regretting deeply the life that her daughter had chosen, but compensated to a small extent by knowing that in Sadie she had, at last, a cleaning woman capable of meeting her own demanding standards.

Aprons were another fetish of Mrs. Skolnick. They had to be clean and white and crisp and ironed and neatly stacked. Other butchers might be unconcerned about red blood forming Rorschach patterns on white cotton. Not Mrs. Skolnick. She disliked the blood-dominated uniforms of her trade. Her minimum requirement was a fresh apron each morning. And another apron after lunch. Some days—the busy days of Friday and Saturday— saw her utilizing more. Two or three more. To make sure of a constant supply, Sadie bought bleached sugar bags at Abelson's and had them made into aprons. Dozens of aprons. Always at hand. Piled. Starched. Crisp. Clean.

Ape smiled. Kissed the X on the paper. Smiled again.

His real name was Michael Freedman. But he was known—and preferred to be known—as Ape. Largely because of a mane of thick black hair that cascaded down his neck beyond his shirt collar. He was a good-looking boy, too pretty to be called handsome, with a small snubbed nose, long eyelashes, and thick brows. He was the tallest member of the gang. Wide shouldered. With a ready laugh.

"Hey, it's me," said Ape. "Guys, it's me! Eh?"

The others stared at him. He shuffled away from the gang still sitting numbly on the Abelson stand.

"See ya, guys. Yeah, see ya. Eh?" said Ape. He wandered off.

In bed that night Ape thought only about Sadie.

And every other member of the gang that night only had thoughts about Ape and Sadie.

———

Sadie did not often appear after dark. When she did a taxi would usually speed her away to some unknown destination. But Leonard noticed that as winter's darkness approached, on Tuesdays, regularly, Sadie sashayed down the street. One Tuesday he followed her.

The red-bricked Baptist Church on Dundas Street was where she led him. Had she converted? Surely not. But one could never be certain. Even Dolly Kurtz, whose father was orthodox—a frummer—had become a Christian recently. At the church door Leonard saw Sadie being greeted with the half-familiarities of acquaintances. She settled down. In the church hall. For a bingo game.

Leonard's doubts about Sadie being a paid lady of the evening increased. He would have liked to discuss it. With whom? The guys in the gang? No. Too much bravado and not enough thought. With his parents? *Hey, Maw, tell me, do you think Sadie Skolnick puts out for gelt?* No, not with his parents. He would have to puzzle it out for himself.

———

"Who's gonna speak to her?" The boys considered the question put to them by Norman. Looked from one to the other.

"Not me," said the first.

"Nor me," said the second.

"Not me. No way," said the third.

And so on.

Seventy-three dollars and eighty-five cents had been raised by the gang. And although short of the ten dollars per guy objective, it was decided the time had come to approach Sadie.

"It's up to me again, i'n't it? Up to me. Right. I'll do it," said Norman. The others were much relieved. "But I won't do it alone," said Norman. "You're coming with me, Lennie."

"Why me?" asked Leonard.

"In the first place 'cause it was your idea—" said Norman.

"No it wasn't," declared Leonard.

"—and in the second place 'cause you talk good," said Norman. "You're gonna be a professor or a doctor or a lawyer. Or whatever it is your Mama decides you should be. Educated. Not like us. You can do the talking."

Despite Leonard's protest, the decision was made.

The William Houston Public School fronted on Baldwin Street. The school had been recently abandoned, but the surrounds formed a playground, official, paid for by the city, and unofficial, used by some youths for games of baseball, volleyball. And, after dark, first time experiments in sexual foreplay.

The school grounds were surrounded by a formidable caged fence. But some anonymous benefactor with wire cutters had snipped a gaping hole. In fact, every season when the fence was repaired, the mysterious hole-maker would also restore his handi-work. Cutting through the school grounds shortened the route to Spadina Avenue with its more upmarket stores—shoe shop, hats, restaurants, drug store—and, most important, the streetcar stop. Local residents gratefully used this short cut.

It was late autumn. Dusk. On a Sunday. Too cold for games of any kind, including sexual ones.

Leonard and Norman watched Sadie as she ducked down

through the holed fence into the playground. And chased after her. Somewhere between second base and the outfield they almost caught up with her. Close enough. Walking behind her, Norman pinched Leonard's thigh, and head gestured towards Sadie, ordering him to speak.

"Hello," said Leonard. Sadie kept on walking. "Uh—ah!—uh," said Leonard a trifle louder.

Sadie was still walking.

Norman hit Leonard's back.

"Hello! Miss! Uh. Hello-ohhhh!" shouted Leonard. Sadie stopped. Her heels, as she turned, sprayed up the dust that a summer's playing had created on the baseball pitch. A pause. She appraised the two boys.

"Yeah? What do you want?" asked Sadie.

"Well, miss, I'm—my name is, that is—I'm called Leonard. Leonard Ab—"

"Yeah. I know who you are. You're one of the Abelson kids," said Sadie. "So what? What do you want?"

Leonard looked at her. Looked at Norman. Looked back at her. He could not speak.

"What do you want?" repeated Sadie.

Leonard's mouth moved. Lips parted. Adam's apple bobbed up and down. No sound emerged.

"What do you want?" she said yet again.

In desperation Leonard held out his hand to her. The hand displayed the seventy-three dollars and eighty-five cents.

Sadie shuffled forward. Her body swaying with each step. Nearer and nearer she came. Stopping only when the boy's extended hand was about to touch her breast. She looked into Leonard's eyes. Smiled seductively. Then glanced down at the money in his palm. Her fingers hovered for a moment above the money, poised, ready. When her fingers did contact his palm, it was a surprisingly slow and delicate movement that Leonard found pleasant. The soft fingers pranced through the money. Pushing aside the ten dollar bills, the five dollar bills, the crumpled one dollar notes. And found a quarter. She held up the twenty-five cent coin under Leonard's nose. Smiled again.

"Streetcar fare," she said. "Thanks. I got no change." With that she smacked Leonard's hand upwards. The money flew through the air. Caught in the wind. Scattered. Coins embedded in the dust. Sadie giggled. And could be heard giggling more and more as she walked away.

The rest of the gang had been watching from a distance. Behind trees. Behind the school building. Behind each other.

Ape, who had washed his hair, put on his Sunday best, was the first to break away. He bounded towards Sadie. And had to be stopped. His imagination, his visualization of what would happen between him and Sadie was so complete, so real, he was convinced all he need do was accost her and his dream would become fact. Norman and Leonard held him back.

The rest of the gang scrabbled after the money.

———•••———

Leonard asked that someone else do it. "Tell Syd to go. Or Sol," he named his brothers. Leonard was not one to shirk such a simple task and his mother regarded him quizzically. Something must be bothering her son for him to refuse her request, she knew, but she had no time to find out what it was.

Leonard," said Mrs. Abelson firmly, "do what I say."

"Okay, okay, okay," said Leonard. He struggled into his parka. Sighed. It was Sunday. A day of rest. A much needed day of rest. Saturday consisted of the five males in the family and Mrs. Abelson waking at five in the morning. Loading a truck. Driving to the family stall in the St. Lawrence market. Unloading. Setting out the goods. Selling. Leonard or his mother or both then returned to the Baldwin Street store. Ready to open by 9 A.M. In late afternoon the truck returned to be unloaded. Saturday night was the busiest time on Baldwin Street. The whole family, even the toddlers Lorraine and Sandra, served in the store. By the time goods from the outside stand were brought inside, the last customer gone, the store—interior and exterior—swept, it was well past midnight.

Syd, Sol, Ben, and his father were always out of the house soon after waking on Sunday. Syd went horseback riding. Sol would be playing snooker. Ben was with his own gang at the club, a rented room in a deserted office block on College Street. Ruth, the eldest of the seven children, sat upstairs in the living room listening to CKEY 580 AM. Loud. Very loud. Maximum volume. She sat whistling a tuneless whistle and rocked back and forth to the rhythm of the music, her back bouncing off the upright section of the sofa. She rocked so hard and so often that years ago the springs had given out and a huge indentation received her body shape. Lorraine and Sandra played in the same room, ignoring their sister and ignoring the cacophony of sounds. The only place for Leonard to read was the kitchen. That meant being under his mother's eye. And subjected to errands.

His mother reached into her apron pocket. Handed him five dollars. "Tell Mrs. Skolnick I'll give her the rest next week," said his mother.

Leonard watched his mother turn back to the crowded stove to prepare the Sunday meal. Cabbage borscht. Years later supposedly sophisticated friends would argue there was only one borscht, beet borscht. Not true. Not to Leonard. His mother's family had had a café/bakery in the Ukraine. His mother was a fine cook. And the term borscht was generic for any sort of soup, be it beet, cabbage, or—on hot summer days—iced spinach borscht. Cabbage borscht was a sweet-sour tasting broth, tomato-based, with cabbage leaves and strips of stewed steak, to be served hot and steamy with garlic bread. Russian style garlic bread. Black bread, the crust of which was salted with rubbed garlic. Cabbage borscht was a Sunday favourite. Not only for its taste. But because it could stay brewing on the stove until each member of the family wanted to eat. The Abelsons rarely ate together. Nine people crowding into a small kitchen was almost intolerable. And after the busy Saturday, stomach clocks varied with each member of the family.

After the schoolyard encounter Leonard avoided Sadie Skolnik, avoided going anywhere near the butcher shop. Easily. It was winter. The long days of darkness and the cutting cold meant a retreat indoors for Torontonians. Including the inhabitants of Baldwin Street. But now the air was lightening. In a few weeks it would be spring. Easter, Passover. People would reappear. Like actors on cue. Waiting for the warming spotlight before making entrances from the wings.

But Leonard also knew he could not avoid Sadie forever. And was dreading having to face her again. Yet here he was, shuffling over the icy sidewalk, towards Skolnick's, five dollars in his pocket, payment towards his mother's debt to the butcher. A common practice. One storekeeper to another, allowing a bill to mount up before expecting repayment. And Mrs. Skolnick had a soft spot for the hard-working Mrs. Abelson, with her seven children to feed. "Don't worry. Pay me when you can," said Mrs. Skolnick. Mrs. Abelson was grateful for any respite from financial pressures.

———•━•━•———

The blinds in the butcher shop were down. Leonard knocked. The voice he dreaded answered. Sadie.

"Come in," she said, "the door's open."

She was on her knees. Scrubbing the floor. It was *that* afternoon. The afternoon that her well formed rear orbs were deliberately projected towards him.

"My mother sent me," said Leonard. His face was scarlet. "To pay. Some of our bill."

"Wait," said Sadie.

She sploshed water onto a corner of the shop floor. Folded a newspaper. Punched his feet. He jumped to one side. She spread the paper. "Stand on that," she ordered.

It was then that she continued her display of her bottom and her breasts and her body towards the young man.

She took her time standing. Yawned. And stretched. First her neck. Then shoulders. Then arms. Upwards and outwards. Her dress strained to contain her.

"I keep the accounts in the kitchen," said Sadie. "Come through. Take your shoes off."

She led the way. On tiptoes. Leonard followed.

"How much y'got?" she asked.

"Five dollars."

"A lot less than the last time. Eh? Not seventy-three dollars and what?—eighty-five cents?" giggled Sadie. Leonard wanted to die. He had hoped no mention would be made of their last meeting in the schoolyard.

Sadie pencilled the payment into the book. Paused. Then scratched her head with the other end of the pencil. All the while looking at Leonard.

"Are you a man yet?" She used the pencil to point towards his crotch.

He wasn't sure how to reply. Was she asking if he had reached puberty or was she asking if he had lost his virginity? He said nothing.

"Well?" said Sadie.

Leonard still said nothing. Sadie smiled. And pulled at the top her dress. Leonard's eyes widened. The dress resisted Sadie's tugs. Leonard said nothing. Sadie changed her mind. Turned. Her back to Leonard.

"Help me," she said.

Leonard wondered where to begin.

"Nobody's home," she said without prompting.

Leonard took hold of the hem and lifted the dress with some difficulty, since it was wet and clingy and restricting his efforts, over her head. She was in bra and half slip over panties. She took the damp dress from Leonard and held it to her chest. Without turning, she shook her shoulders. The brassiere's clasp bounced away from her back.

"Undo me," she said.

"I can't," said Leonard.

"Yes you can," said Sadie.

Leonard's knowledge of brassieres was limited. A brief glimpse of his sister Ruth's from time to time. Nothing more. He decided it would be best if he did not touch her. Or at least make all contact with her body as minimal as possible. It was a double clasp. He reached for the top interlocking metals. Struggled. The clasp was stubborn. Remained closed. Sadie waited. Patiently. Leonard was afraid to tug too hard. Must hurt. Mustn't it? Oh, I don't know what to do. What do I do? He fluttered his fingers near the clasp like a pianist before the opening chords of a concerto. Can't keep her waiting. So do something! Leonard closed his eyes. A silent prayer. A giant tug. And the top catch was released. So that's how it's done! Another firm pull. The brassiere was undone.

Sadie's liberated back glistened.

"Help me," she said.

Forefinger and thumb pinched the straps delicately from her right shoulder. The bra fell away from her breasts. He loosened the left strap. As Sadie shrugged her ample bosom free, Leonard caught sight of budding pink nipples and some crescents of skin. Still not facing him she moved out of the kitchen through the neighbouring dining room and into the last room on the ground floor. A bed-room. The aligned doors of the three rooms allowed Leonard to see her put on a dressing gown. A flash of flesh. And her slip was off. Then she was out of sight. Hidden by architraves. Then back. Another flash. Stockings were removed. She was hidden again. Then reappeared. As she tied her dressing gown, Sadie half smiled and half laughed at Leonard. Then she was gone. The sound of shower water plopped on tiles.

Many minutes later Sadie emerged with three towels around her. A small one, turban-like on her head, she massaged vigorous-ly. Around her chest the second towel. The third below her midriff.

Leonard waited. He had not moved since Sadie left him. In his left hand the brassiere still dangled limply.

Sadie, seeing the sight of him through the distant door, this time laughed loudly.

Leonard knew he was a ridiculous vision. But could think of nothing to change matters.

Sadie stopped rubbing her hair. Held her eyes on Leonard. Threw the small towel on her head away deftly. The towel around her chest was removed more deliberately. Also thrown to the floor. A pause. She unwound the last towel slowest of all. Let it drop. She was naked.

Leonard had never seen the nude female form before. He had been warned that women seemed much larger when undressed. But that had not prepared him much for this moment. Sadie's breasts were, to him, enormous. The pubic triangle of hair appeared endless. But as his eyes ravaged her body, she was, he thought, if not beautiful, then certainly desirable. And something more. What was it? Yes. Yes. That's it. Loveable.

Sadie slid into the bed. Tucked the quilt under her chin. Waited. Leonard ambled forward. Stood by the side of the bed.

"I think you can drop that now." Sadie gestured to the bra in his hand. Leonard, now aware that it was still in his hand, let it fall. "Get undressed," ordered Sadie.

He pulled his parka open. Started to scuff off his shoes. "Slowly," said Sadie. Leonard looked at her blankly. "Very, very slowly," she ordered.

His shoes and parka were already heaped on the floor. He danced on one leg and removed a sock. Then the other. He started to unbuckle his belt. "No," said Sadie, "the top first." Leonard nodded. Pulled at his sweater. Remembered to slow down. Pulled more slowly. He paused between undoing each button on his shirt. Paused. And waited. The smile on Sadie's face remained constant. Leonard's under vest slid off easily. He finished unbuckling his belt.

Zipped open, too quickly, his fly. Stopped. Stopped abruptly. Worried. Pulled again at the zipper. Harder. Harder still. Stuck. The zipper was stuck. Immovable. Leonard lowered his trousers. With all his might he tugged downwards. Nothing. His pants were locked firmly on his hips.

"What's the matter?" said Sadie.

"Can I leave my pants on?" asked Leonard.

Sadie giggled. "Come here," she said.

With the trousers inhibiting his movement, Leonard shuffled forward to the bed one foot at a time. From under the covers Sadie reached out. Rocked the zipper. Back and forth. Until it was free.

But in doing so had touched Leonard. His erection was immediate.

He dropped his trousers. His underpants were a tent over a mast of excitement. Sadie was still smiling. Leonard's fingers loosened the elastic waist. The shorts fell.

Leonard was about to leap into bed. Sadie stopped him.

"Sit here." Sadie patted the side of the bed. "Sit here first."

Leonard sat. His back to her.

"When we finish," said Sadie, "you'll think you love me. It's not love. You'll think it is. But it's not. You'll want to call me. To see me. Don't. Don't. You mustn't. When we finish it's back to what it was before. I'm me. And you're the kid that lives a few doors away. Okay?"

Leonard was puzzled.

"Okay?" she repeated. She slid her arm under his arm and over his thigh to touch his member. He throbbed with desire. He would have agreed to any demand. He nodded.

"Are you sure?" she said.

He nodded again.

Sadie pulled back the quilt. Leonard jumped into the bed beside her.

In the years to come both Sadie and Leonard would have the same dominant memory of that afternoon. Not, for him, the moment when his aching penis was enveloped for the first time by the silkiness of a vagina; nor, for her, when her body rejoiced in being embraced by flesh so much younger than her own. Rather it was the vision, post-coital, of Leonard at Sadie's breast, her nipple in his mouth, sucking, sucking, sucking. "My baby, my beautiful baby," said Sadie over and over and over again.

This continued for some time. Madonna and child. More than an hour later, Leonard, waking, saw Sadie looking at him softly. She slid her head along the pillow, closer to his. "You'd better go now," she said, "get dressed. And go."

"Do I dress quickly," asked Leonard jokingly, "or very, very slowly?"

He was almost finished dressing, when Sadie asked: "That day in the schoolyard—seventy-three dollars and change—what was that all about?" Leonard told her. About the lottery. At first hesitantly, uncertain of how she might react. Sadie was amused. And he was encouraged to elaborate on details, "A prize? I was gonna be a prize!" After a while she said, "Tell me, who won?"

"Ape," said Leonard.

"Ape?" she replied, "the Freedman kid—Michael—with black curly hair and long eyelashes?" Leonard nodded. "Him! And seventy-three dollars and eighty-five cents. Hey, maybe I made a mistake in turning it down!"

Sadie laughed loudly. Leonard's laugh was more uncertain.

"Instead you were the winner," continued Sadie, "you got me."

Having put on his shoes, he was sitting on the side of the bed once more. He leaned over, an arm either side of her. "Sadie, tell me. Are you what they say you are? Are you—y'know—do you do it for money?"

Sadie did not reply immediately. "What do you think?" she said finally.

"I don't know," answered Leonard, after a pause. "No. No. More than that. I don't care. I don't care."

Sadie smiled. "You're gonna be a good man, Leonard," said Sadie.

She stretched herself forward. Leonard kissed her. A mature kiss.

Leonard was at the bedroom door, almost out of the room, when he found enough courage to turn back to Sadie. "To say 'thank you' seems stupid. Not enough," said Leonard. "But I say it. Thank you, Sadie. And if there's ever anything that you want, that I can do, then just tell me and—"

"There is one thing," interrupted Sadie. "One last thing."

"Name it. Anything," said Leonard. "Anything."

"For me. Please. Don't ever talk about this afternoon. Not to no one. Your mother, your father, the gang, in years to come your girl friends, your wife. To no one. Promise. Don't ever talk about this. Ever."

Leonard never did.

COLOURS

The red of radishes. The green of Granny Smiths. The lime of limes. The orange of oranges. The yellow of squash. Pale cabbages. Dark aubergines. Purple marrows. Beet root reds. Violet plums. Peppers green. Peppers yellow. Peppers orange. Peppers. Peaches of many shades, including—when rotting—black.

No lawns on Baldwin Street. No pretty primroses. No titillating tulips. But still a street of colours.

On a bright summer day, the low early morning sun, rebounding off the colours. Stimuli. As each fruit stand pulled away the night-covering canvas to reveal the hidden colours. The colours of vegetables. And fruit.

Not to mention others. Materials. For the dressmaker, bolts of fabric. For the housekeeper, oil cloths, sold by the yard, for the table. And ready-made tablecloths. Piled high. Lino for the floor. Shirts white. Shirts green. Shirts blue. Ties. Ladies dresses. Ladies stockings. Ladies bloomers. Usually flannel grey. Ladies panties. Pink. Always pink. The beiges of earthenware bowls from black-brown to delicate cream. Pots. Pans. Aluminium or enamel. Cups. Saucers. Dishes. Porcelain or fine china. Glasses. Tumblers. Pitchers. Basins. Nuts. Beans. Barley. Chick peas. Combs. Brushes. Brooms. Mops. Undershirts. Undershorts. T-shirts. Trousers. Pants. Shorts. Jeans. If we ain't got it, lady, we get it for you, lady. What colour you want?

Baldwin Street was a mass of colours. Not organized. Not neatly planted arrays. Not row on row of pristine perfection. As with the front of other peoples' houses. Not here. But higgledy-piggledy. Random. Colours. Bombarding the eye. Colours.

SUGAR DOUGHNUTS &
SOUR PICKLES

"What's this? A sixpence?" The girl looked down at the coin in her palm.

"It's called a dime," said her father. "Ten cents."

"Looks like a sixpence," she persisted. And so it did. The profile of King George VI on the head. As on the coins she knew so well. But the back was foreign to her.

"Go outside," said the father, "look around. Be back in an hour."

Milly closed fingers round the coin. She led her younger sister, Gwen, away. "Yes, Daddy," she said.

Milly and Gwen were from England. Gwen was seven years old. Milly was twelve. It was their first night on Baldwin Street.

The two girls had travelled for weeks and weeks. In a convoy of ships. During the last year of the war.

"Gosh! What a big boat!" little Gwen had said when they first boarded. "Fun! This'll be fun, won't it?"

Milly had shook her head. "Boring. It'll be boring. Don't do this. Don't do that. Not at sea. No, you cannot. No. No. No. There's a war on. Always no. You'll see." She looked at her younger sister with a superiority she could never control. "And by the by it's a ship, not a boat. A boat is a small vessel that you row down a stream."

"Sorry." Gwen found herself often saying sorry to older sister Milly.

After landing in Halifax the family were pushed onto a train. Then another. Train after train. And more trains. Constantly unsettled. Constantly shifting. Sleeping whenever and wherever possible. Crammed onto seats, when lucky enough to find seats, between hordes of servicemen—sailors, soldiers, airmen—who were forever on transfer from one side of the continent to the other. Not that Milly ever complained. Complaining about the unchangeable was not in her nature.

"Twenty minutes from Toronto," said her father looking at a pocket watch, "twenty minutes." Many of the occupants of this final train got off at Kingston, affording the family some seats.

"Tonight you will sleep in a bed," her mother told Milly. "Though you may have to share it with Gwen," she nodded towards her youngest child, asleep, leaning, open-mouthed, on her sister's shoulder.

Milly nodded. Parental promises were not necessarily fulfilled in wartime, Milly knew. Still the thought of a bed brought an occasional smile to her face. A bed. A soft fluffy bed. Yummy. She looked forward to that. Meanwhile she stared out of the train window at the desolate darkness roaring past.

Her father, Harry Miller, had found a room at the Poronsky's. This was one of the few houses on Baldwin Street yet to be converted into a shop and consequently still retained an empty space out front that earlier in the century had been a lawn or garden of some sort. This front area was available for renting. Mr. Poronsky was keen on renting out what he could. He was a plumber. Eager for any extra income.

Harry and Beatrice Miller wanted time to sort out the room. To unpack the few remnants they struggled to bring with them. Change a chair here. Move a table there. So the two daughters were sent off on the exploratory trip.

The Millers were from a suburb near Manchester. They knew no one in Toronto. No one at all. Harry thought he had been clever to ask for the market area when he got off the train. He had been raised in similar markets. How different could it be? And at least he would be among his own people.

On the elevated front stoop of the house—it was hardly a porch—Milly stood wondering which way to turn. Gwen tugged at her older sister. And pointed. The brightest spot was on the corner. A bakery shop. Since it was not far away, Milly nodded agreement.

It was late summer. Darkness had come early. And it was Tuesday. Not the busiest of nights. Still the noise, the colours, the shouts, the people, were enough to arouse the senses of two girls from half a world away. Passing a fruit stand, Milly wanted to stop. Was that a pineapple? A real pineapple? She had only seen drawings of such exotica in books. But Gwen kept walking. Drawn to the dazzling lights.

"Please, Gwen, let me ask about—" pleaded Milly.

"No, no," said Gwen who, despite her size, succeeded in tugging the larger girl away from the fruit stand. She was about to step off the curb oblivious of an oncoming car.

"Hey! Watch it!" A boy's hand firmly pulled Gwen back onto the sidewalk. "Y'can get killed doing that!"

Leonard Abelson stood smiling at the two sisters.

"She—I—we, we forgot. Looking the wrong way. Forgot," said Milly. "You drive on the other side of the road. Forgot." She was quite shaken. "Thank you," she said to Leonard.

"Nothin'," said Leonard with a grand gesture. "Y're Ingell-lish, aintcha? My Maw told me. Greenies. Livin' with the Poronskys. Right?"

Milly stretched to her full height. "We are certainly not green," she said emphatically. "Sort of an indeterminate pink is how the biologist defines it, I believe."

"Love the way you talk," laughed Leonard. The sisters moved away. "My name is Leonard," he shouted after them. "See ya around!"

"Not if I see you first," replied Milly. But when she was certain he wasn't looking she sneaked a sidelong glance back at Leonard.

The girls reached the corner shop. Pearl's Bakery. The entrance stood between two large right-angled windows. Bread and Kaiser Rolls and bagels and such mundanity were restricted to the back of the shop behind a long practical counter. The windows displayed the stars of the show. The jewels. The sweet produce of a bakery. Each window was high and wide and filled with tiers of glass shelves suspended on brass wires. Each shelf crowded with goodies. And each goodie more tempting and more inviting than the delicacy next to it. Cakes. Round cakes. Square cakes. High cakes. Thin cakes. Chocolate. Coconut. Cinnamon. Coffee. Raspberry. Strawberry. Sponge. Cream. Cheese. And permutations thereof. Strawberry and cheese. Chocolate and coffee. Chocolate and cream. And more. Some of the cakes still bore the rectangular outline of the oven tins. Others lay in filigreed sugar elegance. Cakes. And pies. Open apple. Closed apple. Ditto cherry. Peach. Apricots. And muffins. Blueberry muffins. Pearl's bakery specialized in blueberry muffins. Mr. Pearl insisted on real blueberries. Not ersatz blueberry jam. After he died, the bakery would pass into more business-like hands and jam filler would replace fresh blueberries. Good economics. Bad muffins. Next to the muffins, tarts. And scones. And biscuits. A multitude of biscuits. The best seller of these was almond bread, *mandel broit*. "I had this in Italy, y'know," said a local soldier returning to Baldwin Strect. "It's called *biscotti* there. Not as good your *mandel broit*, Mr. Pearl."

Milly and Gwen stood staring at this array of wonders. First on the Baldwin Street window. Then rounded the corner to the window on Kensington Avenue. From the price tags Milly knew she could afford to buy something for herself and her sister. "Come along," said Milly heading for the door. Gwen did not reply. Shook her head. And backed away. "Oh for heaven's sake," said Milly. And manhandled her sister into the shop.

"What would you like, Gwen?" Milly asked her younger sister.

Gwen again did not reply. But stood staring up at the laden shelves surrounding her.

"What would you like? Tell me," insisted Milly.

Gwen was silent, her body still. Her head swivelled in one direction. Then the other. She looked at one cake. Then another. And another. Her breathing, through an open mouth, became shallow. "Tell me what you want, Gwennie," demanded Milly. Two lollipop-sized tears emerged from Gwen's eyes and began a slow route down the cheeks. "It's all right," said Milly. "Why are you crying? Daddy gave us money. What do you want?"

Still not getting a reply, an exasperated Milly started to pull her sister away. To get her out of the store. But this time there was no moving Gwen. She was a boulder. Weighted to the floor.

"What is the matter with you and why—" demanded Milly. Gwen was fixed to the floor. And as her sister began to shout, Gwen, eyes wet and wide and with a mouth to match, reacted. She urinated. On the floor.

Fortunately the store was relatively empty. The few customers present left, either oblivious of the goings-on, or because of a desire not to get involved. Milly, after a dumbfounded moment, ran from the store. To get her parents.

Mr. Pearl had been in a far corner of the shop. Talking to one of his bakers. Mrs. Pearl had gone off. Probably to make dinner. The Pearls were successful business people and, unlike most of the residents on Baldwin Street, did not live above the shop. A house a few doors away was home. And the rooms above the shop were a warehouse, filled with flour, sugar, tins, moulds, and other essentials of the baking trade. A startled Mr. Pearl now turned to the child standing in a small puddle in the middle of his shop.

"Vaht is the matter, vith you? Vhy you come in and—" Gwen did not move. But as Mr. Pearl advanced towards her she emitted an atavistic howl. It stopped Mr. Pearl. He raised hands in surrender. "It's a'right. Dear child. *Liebe kind*. I von't hurt you. No. It's a'right." He turned to a shop assistant. "Get a towel. Get some rags. Get—get—get Mrs. Pearl!"

By the time Milly and her father entered the shop, Mr. Pearl and a shop assistant were on their knees mopping up the mess. Gwen stood nailed to the spot. In contrast to her motionless feet, tiny waves shuddered up and down her small frame. The shakes. Her mouth still wide open, invited air to enter, rather than forcefully breathing. At the sight of her father, she broke. Disintegrating into his arms. With his free hand he brushed his youngest daughter's hair, continually calling her name. "Gwen. Gwen. Gwen. My Gwennie. Gwen."

Milly was battling with herself, determined not to cry. It was a battle she was losing. As her moist eyes revealed.

Harry Miller apologized at some length. "M'nime is 'Arry," he said, "'Arry Miller." Since he spoke with a definite North Country accent, Mr. Pearl had some difficulty in understanding him. "Par'm me," said Mr. Pearl, often. And Miller would start again, speaking more slowly and somewhat louder, as if to a deaf alien. Mr. Pearl turned for guidance to the half-dozen bakers clad in white—from shoes, to trousers, to undershirts, to hats—who had abandoned the ovens to witness the consternation in the shop and now crowded into the small doorway that separated the manufacturing area from the retail area. "Eh?" queried a still-puzzled Mr. Pearl. "What's he saying? *Vus zugt er? Kenst redin Mama Loshen?*" Miller shook his head. The Mother Tongue was beyond him.

Carrying Gwen, Miller took Milly's hand and shepherded his children back to the Poronsky house.

When Mrs. Pearl entered the store, her husband looked at her accusingly as if she had deliberately contrived to be absent leaving him to deal with this difficult situation. When told what she had missed, Mrs. Pearl said, "Why did it happen here? Why couldn't it have happened—?" she pointed to the bakery across the road—"to the Lottmans?"

The talking began. Mr. Pearl talked. Mrs. Pearl contradicted. The bakers talked. Mr. and Mrs. Pearl both contradicted. The shop assistants offered an opinion. The bakers, the Pearls, and a few customers who had joined in the conversation, disagreed. Finally it was decided that a family of Greenies, newcomers, such as the Millers, would be almost penniless and would need help and that at the very least the young daughter should be seen by a doctor.

Ah, yes, said Mr. Pearl. But which doctor? Therein began a survey of the medical assistance available to local residents. The general view was that "Dr. Levine had the biggest heart. No doubt about it. The nicest man. But he is getting old." The rumour was that when his old Model T Ford had broken down on Baldwin Street recently, Dr. Levine got out and administered an aspirin into the radiator. Dr. Rosen? "Good man. Yes, a good man. And younger. But always busy."

"And more expensive," Mr. Pearl pointed out. And since by unspoken consensus it was Mr. Pearl who would be paying, this factor had to be seriously considered. Dr. Woolfson? "He's close. Just here on Spadina Avenue. He's never busy. And he's the cheapest." Dr. Woolfson got the job.

Bedside charm was not one of Dr Woolfson's attributes. He was either abrasive because he was not successful or he was not successful because he was abrasive. Which came first? No one knew.

But even his coldness thawed at the sight of little Gwen in bed. The child shivered. A small shiver. Then a spasm. An uncontrollable spasm. Shivering and shaking repeatedly. Dr. Woolfson examined Gwen quickly, not wishing to prolong her discomfort. Lowered his voice to speak gently. And suggested, directly to Gwen not to her parents or her sister who were also in the room, that what Gwen needed most was sleep. When it became clear that what he was offering was an injection, Milly stepped forward protectively and with pleading eyes shook her head from side to side. Dr. Woolfson heeded her silent request. He turned to Beatrice Miller and told her to go down to the Poronsky kitchen and mix-up a tea-less tea. Sugar in hot water. Which he spooned out to Gwen after dissolving a tablet in the solution. He signalled to Milly to get into bed and comfort her younger sister. And all waited—father, mother, Milly, the doctor seated at the bedside—until Gwen fell into a deep sleep.

Dr. Woolfson, first-generation Canadian born in Toronto, had no trouble with Harry Miller's thick accent. But in the hallway outside the room, his usual impatience when dealing with the ill returned. He talked. The Millers listened. He laid down dictates as to how Gwen was to be treated. Rest. Plenty of it. Sleep. Plenty of it. He left behind a box of pills, samples from the drug company, to save the cost of a prescription. And when Harry Miller extended a handful of coins intermingled with a crumpled one-dollar bill, Dr. Woolfsoon brusquely shoved the hand away. And left. As the doctor descended the stairs, Miller shouted after him, "Thank you, doctor."

Dr. Woolfson did not turn. Did not pause. Kept his back to Miller. He raised one hand in a minimal gesture of acknowledgement.

Dr. Woolfson liked visiting Baldwin Street. Like all doctors of that era when making house calls he carried a small leather satchel. Filled with drugs. Twice this had led to trouble. The first time, behind the deserted playground on McCaul Street, he was surrounded by a gang of youths who pulled the bag from him. A few years later he entered a darkened house. He had no idea who assaulted him. He was knocked unconscious. After that, reluctantly deciding that in a changing world his profession no longer shielded him—as it had done for years—he was cautious about entering unknown territory. But the market was safe. Street life. People about. People who respected a medical man. People whose deference towards him was measurable. Of course, receiving proper payment from the poor of his patch happened infrequently, but that was another matter.

"Oh that's my favourite," said Dr. Woolfson. Mrs. Pearl was serving him. A sponge cake, still warm from the oven, was being partitioned by the long knife in her hand. The canary yellow of the cake contrasting with the luxurious brown of the cinnamon filling. Sponge and cinnamon. Delightful, thought Dr. Woolfson. He was smiling in anticipation of the pleasure the cake would bring him for the next few days. A good-sized tranche of cheese cake was next. Then six apple turnovers. A few custard tarts. Four chocolate éclairs. A dozen Kaiser Rolls. A black bread. A pumpernickel.

"Y'don't like coffee cake?" asked Mrs. Pearl. Her husband, who had been watching Dr. Woolfson so relentlessly enlarging his pirated proceeds, gave his wife a severe glance. She's gone crazy, *meshuga*, Mr. Pearl told himself.

"Well, if you insist," replied the doctor, as if it was necessary for him to be cajoled into accepting the succulent, round, cream-rich pastry. Mrs. Pearl's knife moved to allow for an above-average portion. Dr. Woolfson smiled. Mrs. Pearl defiantly cut. Mr. Pearl looked to heaven.

It was all a game. The doctor knew that the baker would be paying for this night call. The standard fee for a house visit by a member of the medical profession was one dollar. To some of the more prosperous clients a doctor might screw up his charge to two dollars. On the other hand a bit of judicious whimpering might get the fee as low as fifty cents.

Dr. Woolfson, called away from his dinner on this as on many other occasions, was not about to settle for a measly dollar. He would take his fee in goods. A barter. And a much better deal for him.

By the time the doctor reached the cash register, Mr. Pearl had made mental calculations. A total of $3.65. No, wait, I forgot the éclairs. Makes $3.85. He's walking out of here with $3.85 worth of stuff. Goods totalling $3.85 cost me $2.50—maybe more—to produce. And he doesn't have my troubles. No overheads. No police threats because of opening the store on Sundays. No arguments with Yitzik, the head baker, who is giving me ulcers. Come to think of it, I should ask him about my ulcers. But if I did he would walk out of here with the whole store. God, Mr. Pearl prayed, in my next life let me be a doctor. And I won't go stealing from hard-working people like me. That Dr. Woolfson, Mr. Pearl decided, is a devil, a *mamzer*. Why did we call him? Dr. Levine wouldn't have had this man's cheek. Audacity. *Chutzpah*. And Dr Rosen wouldn't have taken so much cheese cake. I hate you Dr. Woolfson. Wait till you go to pay. You're going to get from me such a mouthful, you won't forget. You just wait.

As he approached the cash register Dr. Woolfson made a show of reaching for a wallet. "Please, doctor," said Mr. Pearl immediately, with a broad sweep of his arm, "don't insult me."

The two men walked to the door. And discussed the young patient. Dr. Woolfson in his usual detached manner gave his diagnosis as to what ailed Gwen Miller. Mr. Pearl listened and did not interrupt. Mrs. Pearl longed to overhear the conversation. She contrived to work on the display near the door. But as if to spite her the shop began to fill with customers. And in a choice between earnings and gossip, earnings had to win. Besides, the two men spoke quietly. And she would not be able to eavesdrop without being obvious.

After a while Dr. Woolfson said, indicating the large paper brown paper bags he held, "Thank you for this."

"You mus' be good at pinochle," said Mr. Pearl.

"Poker. I play poker. And yes, I am thought to be good at it. How did you know?" asked the physician.

"Because you got some nice cake in that bag," said the baker.

———•••———

"So? Wha' did he say? Wha' did the doctor say?" demanded Mrs. Pearl as soon as the store was empty.

"There's no sugar over there," explained Mr. Pearl. "No sugar. No candy. No puddings. No cakes. Nothin'. For years those people have had nothin'."

"So?"

"So a child comes from over there. From over the seas. Comes to our store. Sees my chocolate doughnuts, my open cherry pie, my apple strudel, things like this she's never seen before. And then she's told, pick one. You can have one. What do you want?"

"So?"

"Nerves," said Mr. Pearl nodding his head sagely. And struggling to pronounce the words correctly. As Dr. Woolfson had done. "Nerves. A brr-reakdown. That's what the doctor said." Mr. Pearl sighed. Before saying, "Poor kid."

His wife was about to ask for more details when Milly came back into the shop.

"Please," said Milly, pointing at the tray of sugar doughnuts on a window shelf, "how much are these?"

"T'ree cents. Two for a nickel," said Mrs. Pearl.

"A nickel?"

"Five cents," said Mrs. Pearl.

"I just want one," said Milly proffering a dime.

"For you, no charge for one—" said Mrs. Pearl.

"Please. I was told I must pay," said Milly.

Rebuffed, Mrs. Pearl nevertheless selected the largest specimen she could find. Wrapped it in crackling tissue paper. Handed it over.

"Eat in good health," she said to Milly.

Milly turned. "Oh, it's not for me," she said. "It's for my baby sister. She made up her mind. Y'see, she remembered. What it tastes like. She had one once before. A long time ago. She remembers. Now she wants one. She's howling and screaming. Kicking her heels. She wants one. A sugar doughnut."

Mr. and Mrs. Pearl watched Milly sashay out of the shop.

The weeks went by. Blue plums—*vengerkes*—replaced yellow peaches on the fruit stalls. Watermelon was gone. Wine grapes appeared. The harbingers of autumn. On Baldwin Street the seasons were indicated by the produce on the stands.

As time passed, Milly, addressing others, no longer said "Good morning. Isn't it a lovely morning." or "Good afternoon. You're looking well" or "Good evening. Bit of a chill this evening, isn't there?" All were changed. "Hi ya," she now said. Other phrases left her vocabulary to be replaced by "Yeah" "No" "Okay" "Gimme five." Assimiliation.

Her father no longer dressed in over-worn suits. But instead outfitted himself in a cut more suitable to his adopted country. He even occasionally—Saturday nights and Sundays—went without a tie. Vests, waistcoats to him, were abandoned. And he bought his first sport shirt. A qualified bookkeeper, he soon moved up the ladder of a Bay Street firm where, with the manpower shortage, his abilities were welcomed. He went to night school. Determined to become a Chartered Accountant. Soon. 'Arry was Harry now.

Gwen would not go into Pearl's bakery. In fact she avoided bakery corner, Pearl's on one side, Lottman's on the other. If she had to pass by, she would do so quickly. Averting her eyes. It was not only the shame of that first night that inhibited her. But also knowing that the sight of all those cakes could still make her head spin. But sometimes, at night, like a moth to a flame of sugar, when the lights in the shop were out, unseen by others, she pressed against the window of Pearl's bakery, gazing intently at the nearly empty shelves. Forlorn stragglers of sweetness. Remnants were all that remained on the shelves at such times. Left behind. Waiting. In darkened windows. Waiting for morning when new supplies, fresh from the ovens, would be brought forward by flour-dusted bakers. And the windows once again sprang to life. Crowded. Packed. Pleasing. But Gwen never saw that. Never brought herself to witness the full displays. If she wanted something from Pearl's, she sent her sister.

One Friday night, as the girls ambled along, Gwen produced a nickel.

"The usual?" asked Milly. "A sugar doughnut?"

"Uh-huh," nodded Gwen.

"Wanna be brave tonight?" suggested Milly. "Wanna do something different?"

"Sure," shrugged Gwen.

"Meet me in front of Leibovitch's," said Milly.

Milly emerged moments later from Pearl's with two sugar doughnuts. She led her sister to the barrels that lined the front of Leibovitch's store. "Two small pickles," she demanded of the big man leaning lazily against the door jam. Joe Steinhardt worked for Mr. Leibovitch. He was German. Though no one bore him any ill for that. What Joe's thoughts were of what his countrymen, his Aryan brothers, were doing to people of the same faith as those around him in the market, he kept to himself. Wisely. Milly was of course unaware of such things. She was more aware of Joe's massive hand filtering through the brine. Two shining sour pickles appeared. To be wrapped in wax paper. Then newspaper. "Anyt'ing else, ladies" asked Joe.

On the porch of the Poronsky house Milly unwrapped the packages.

"Take a bite of the pickle," instructed Milly. "Sour. Right? Then bite the doughnut. Sweet. Right? First one. Then the other. Sour. Sweet. Sour. Sweet. Yummy."

Gwen nipped at the donut.

"Y're supposed to start with sour, the pickle."

Gwen munched. "I like sweet first," she said. Then, hesitating for a moment, she bit the pickle. Chewed. Milly waited. A pause.

"Well?" Milly could wait no longer.

After a while, Gwen said, "Yes." Then after another pause, repeated, "Yes." Finally adding, "Yes, yes. Good."

The two girls stood on the porch. Eating. Enjoying. Delighted with the contrasting tastes. Some of the juice from the pickle ran down Gwen's arm. She licked at it. This caused her to giggle. Milly, seeing her sister's antics, licking an arm, also began to giggle. Soon both were laughing.

Because it was Friday, the activities on the street were minimal. Most of the customers had long gone, hastening homewards to prepare the Sabbath dinner. The storekeepers, with the rush of the day's sales abated, braced themselves for the anticipated business of tomorrow. Saturday. The one day that could make or break the week's fortunes. Shops were being swept. Displays re-stocked. Fresh fish into tanks. Fresh oranges into pyramid piles. Squawking chickens from crated coops into windows.

"Gwennie, what do you want to do tonight?" asked Milly.

Gwen shrugged. "I dunno. Mebbe look at Katz's window?"

"Don't be dumb. Katz's window is always the same. Bubbling water. Filled with fish," said Milly. "Carp. Or pickerel. Once in a while, perch. Be great if one day he puts a shark in that window." She waited for her sister to laugh. "Want to take a walk? A long walk?"

"Where to?" asked Gwen.

It was, as Milly had promised, a long walk. More than two miles. But the euphoria of doing something different and seeing sights new to her made Gwen's little legs oblivious of the distance. Besides Milly's trilling conversation was more than enough to distract her younger sister. Conversation about school—at which both the girls excelled. About neighbours. Itzik Horowitz who rented the front of the Poronsky house. "He stinks," said Milly, "of drink. He's a drunkard." Conversation about Mrs. Bermant. About her moustache.

"Why doesn't she shave it off?"

"Silly, women don't shave."

"Won't her husband show her how?" Laughter.

"No children," said Milly. "That's why she's always giving us candy."

Spadina Avenue became Spadina Road. Up the hill. The steep hill that divides the north of the city from the south. The richer from the poorer. The girls walked past Casa Loma.

"Spooky, i'n't?" asked Milly.

Gwen looked up at the forbidding gothic stones of the dark castle. And agreed. "Dances here, though. Look," said Gwen. She pointed at a sign proclaiming Mart Kenney and His Western Gentlemen played every Saturday night.

"When we're older, we'll go," stated Milly. "I'll get Leonard Abelson to take me. One day."

"You like Leonard. You like Leonard," chanted Gwen.

In the intervening weeks since first arriving, Milly, much to the consternation of her sister, had become fast friends with Leonard. Leonard enjoyed observing the people on Baldwin Street, both shoppers and shopkeepers. As did Milly. Leonard had a quick mind. Milly's was quicker. Leonard could turn a phrase into a joke. Milly could turn it to sarcasm. Leonard was fun to be with. And even at that young age Milly knew she needed help being happy.

"An' you like his brother Benny." Milly sing-songed back, "Gwennie and Benny. Gwennie and Benny. . ."

Soon they reached the lower streets of Forest Hill Village. Large stone-fronted houses snuggled close to each other. Making a statement. Smug. Proud. Self-satisfied houses. Inviting comparison with each neighbouring house.

The lawns stretched down to the curbside. Pavements were rare. As were pedestrians. The girls walked in the middle of the road. Gwen's wide eyes swinging from one side of the street to the other. To her these houses, these streets, were the height of sophisticated urban living.

"Gosh," Gwen said after a while, "how did you find this place?"

Milly gave a little smile but said nothing. The two of them walked along in silence.

As they rounded a corner, noises from a party could be heard. At first the girls kept on walking. But then, after a moment's thought, Milly pulled at Gwen. "C'mon," said Milly. She led her younger sister to a hedge, perfect for concealment, which overlooked the partying house.

Milly pushed foliage to one side. And she and Gwen stared. The party was taking place in an elegant semi-basement, a lower level of a grand house. Through leaded windows, smartly dressed guests could be seen chatting or moving molasses-like from one cluster to another. A head would be thrown back. A burst of soprano laughter. Followed by the baritone notes of more steady conversation.

Trays of food weaved amid the partying people. And drinks. Canapés and champagne. Sandwiches and spirits. Petits fours and wine. Being handed round. By whom? Who was doing the serving? Who was being waited upon? Were these employees or guests, Milly wondered. So much easier to tell in England, where a worker looked like a worker.

Milly thought of her mother, who at this moment might be threading a needle. Or sewing. Shortly after her arrival Beatrice Miller let it be known that she was willing to take in jobs as a seamstress. Mending. Restoring garments. A valuable source of income. But leading to long hours. And her father, continually running from his desk at Baker and Baker and Winslow, the Bay Street firm, to night classes. Again, long hours. So much so that meals for Gwen and Milly were often hastily contrived snacks. With tired parents. Impatient elders. The household atmosphere constantly deteriorating into tensions and squabbles. No time for leisure. No time for pleasure. No time to party. Only to work.

On the plot of land next to the party, a new house was being built. Milly could see rubble. Just what she wanted. She pulled away from the hedge. Found a baseball-sized stone. And a fragment of brick.

"Y're crazy!" said Gwen when Milly returned to the hedge.

"One for you, if you want," said Milly offering up the brick.

"No. No. No," said Gwen.

"After I throw them, we run like hell," said Milly.

"I don't want you to," said Gwen. "I don't want you to." Gwen began to weep.

"What are you gonna do," demanded Milly, "pee in your pants again?"

"Please don't, Milly. Please. Please," beseeched Gwen.

Milly's lips tightened to a scowl. She threw the stone. A sound of smashing glass. A beat. Milly then threw the brick.

This time she did not wait for the sound but pulled at her sister and ran. The two girls were some distance away before some of the partygoers appeared at the front door. Looking for the attackers. Milly glanced back. Knew she was safe.

Gwen would not stop crying. When they reached Bathurst Street, she sat on the edge of the pavement. Refusing to go further. "I'm tired," said Gwen. Milly looked down the hill.

"We'll take a street car," said Milly.

"We have no money," Gwen managed to say between sobs.

"It'll be crowded," said Milly. "When it stops, the driver won't see if we jump on at the centre doors."

That made Gwen howl even more. But the thought of the long walk back to Baldwin Street troubled her. So that when a street car finally appeared she joined in, running to a nearby stop and allowing Milly to push her on board.

In bed, the two sisters lying side by side, for the first time did not chatter into the night. Gwen turned away. When Milly said "Good night" there was no reply from Gwen.

In less than a year the Miller family moved away from Baldwin Street.

Milly eventually graduated from Harbord Collegiate with honours, winning a scholarship to the University of Toronto. After a course in Commerce and Finance, she went to work in Bay Street with the same firm that had elevated her father to executive level. But Milly found this to be too small a pond. Went on to Wall Street. Where, as an investment broker, she amassed a fortune.

"Y'hoid what happened to that Greenie's goil?" Mrs. Poronsky asked Mrs. Abelson, Leonard's mother, one day.

"No, what?"

"A penthouse in New Yoik. Not only a penthouse but d'biggest penthouse in d'whole East Side," said Mrs. Poronsky. "Y'shoulda made a match, a *shidduch*, with your Leonard when y'had d'chance. Those Greenies know how to make money."

By the time the gossip completed the Baldwin Street rounds, Milly was reputed to own most of Long Island—where indeed she had an elegant summer home—and be the proprietor of half the arable land in Central America—in truth she owned a farmed estate in Mexico.

Gwen, on the other hand, wound up in Winnipeg. She was always interested in ballet. She tried to succeed as a dancer but soon realized it was beyond her capabilities. She deemed herself lucky to have joined the Winnipeg Ballet where she worked in costume and design. She married. A musician. Two children. She lived comfortably and quietly among many friends and neighbours.

When, years later, Leonard Abelson was assigned by *Liberty Magazine* to write an article on the hard life led by Prairie housewives, he went to Winnipeg. He looked up Gwen. They agreed to meet.

In an Italianate café Gwen's eyes raked the glass counter containing the usual breakfast offerings. Danish pastries, cinnamon rolls, bran muffins. Leonard was alongside her, pushing a tray with two cappuccinos.

"Do you have any sugar doughnuts?" Gwen asked the teenage server behind the counter.

"Umm. I dunno. Le's see. No," said the girl. "Got choccy doughnuts. And these. Sugar on the outside. Jam inside. Is that what you mean?"

"Not quite what I meant," said Gwen. "But I'll have one all the same."

At a table Leonard positioned the two coffees. "You still big on sugar doughnuts, eh?" he asked.

"Love 'em," said Gwen. "There's a place here in town, Albermarle Street, makes them the old fashioned way. Round. With a hole. Just like Mr. Pearl's. Not like this." She pointed to the round doughy object she had settled for. "Brings back all sorts of memories. Sugar doughnuts do. You'd think I'd hate them, wouldn't you? Difficult times. Not much money. Furnished rooms. Always cold. Always hungry. But I love 'em. Funny, isn't it?"

"When we were on Baldwin Street," Leonard replied, "and there was no other food in the house, my mother would make us onion sandwiches. A thick slice of raw onion between two pieces of bread. With or without salt. With or without butter. Depending on availability. And now whenever I feel down or depressed or droopy, I make myself one of Maw's onion sandwiches. Works wonders. Comfort food. My own comfort food." He stopped to think for a moment. "Of course," he added, "I then have to stay away from friends for a few hours."

They both laughed.

"How'd you know about me and sugar doughnuts?" asked Gwen. "Milly must've told you, eh? On one of your numerous dates."

"Not that many dates. Once or twice. As teenagers," said Leonard. "I really liked Milly." He shrugged. "But it was not to be. How is she? If you speak to her, please tell her—"

"Ugh," interrupted Gwen. She had bitten into the sugary pastry and jam had spurted over her lips. She napkined the jam away. "Mr. Pearl, rest in peace, you have nothing to fear from this concoction." She wiped sugar from her hands.

"Last I heard," continued Leonard, "she had married again and—"

"Was that marriage two or three?" asked Gwen. "There was a husband four. Yes, don't be so surprised. But he's long gone. Long divorced. Then I was told, about four years back, she was living with some guy. And as you'd expect, much younger than herself." Gwen put the napkin down. "I never speak to Milly."

"Never?" asked Leonard.

"I wouldn't know how to get hold of her," said Gwen. "Wouldn't know where to start. Don't know. Don't care. She's gone. Don't need to know. Don't want to know." She smiled.

"You two were so close," said Leonard.

"Yes, at one time. Not any more," said Gwen. "Sugar doughnuts and sour pickles," she added.

The two sat in silence sipping coffee.

178 BALDWIN STREET

My name is Leonard Abelson. I lived on Baldwin Street. 178 Baldwin Street. Our store was called Abelson's Hardware. Not a good name. A misnomer. Wrong. Because aside from pots and pans, glasses and dishes, we didn't sell much hardware. No screws. Or nails. No hammers. No wrenches. Light bulbs, yes. Electric plugs, yes. But not sockets or wiring or ladders or lawn mowers or the sophisticated stuff of hardware stores. We also sold lots of clothing. Soft ware. Panties and stockings for ladies. Shirts, ties, socks, jeans for men. My friend Stanley says his predominant memory of our shop is of a never-ending mound of women's cotton dresses on a corner of the front stand. With a sign. Scrawled by my father. Black crayon on a piece of brown cardboard torn from a box reading SPECIAL $2.98. Except the C in SPECIAL would be backwards. Paw could speak fourteen languages—yes, fourteen, from French, which he found simple, to Flemish, which few outsiders master—but writing in English was always difficult for him.

It's my fault, the "hardware" store idea, my fault. I was a teenager—well, almost—when we moved into 178. And I thought it sounded better. Classy. Smart. Abelson's Hardware. Better than Abelson's Dry Goods. Most of the stores on the street—we had a lot of competition—that sold clothes had the words Dry Goods writ large on the outside awnings. Not us. Abelson's Hardware.

Of course it's an indication of the insecurity of my parents with a foreign place that they would let their second son, third child, at such a precocious age, influence the name given to the store. But Paw liked the idea. His round face smiled when I first suggested it. "Sounds good," he nodded. My father's accent, which decreased with each passing year, was Russian. As was my mother's. From tonguing the various dialects of the Slavic continent. Neither of them spoke with the comedic rising inflections at the end of a sentence.

Abelson's was not known for either ladies' cotton dresses or pots and pans. Sugar bags. That was our leading seller. Bags once used to hold sugar were bleached. And in a cotton-deprived economy—because of the war—the bags, opened and stitched together, became bed sheets. Or dish towels. Pillow cases. Diapers. And much else. My mother's aprons, for example, were made from these bags. The cotton was thick. Sturdy. Functional. Long-lasting.

At first our customers insisted that the bags be whitened to perfection. So that the country of origin—usually in the Caribbean—and the manufacturing company, and the shipper, all of whose names had been stamped boldly on the bags, were bleached away. The bags became segments of cotton. Not revealing their lowly beginnings.

Then fashion changed. Lettering sometimes appeared faintly on bags that hadn't been bleached adequately. Usually these were rejected. But some customer somewhere along the way must have preferred it that way. Chic. To leave the names emblazoned faintly on the cotton. For all to see. Smart to have a sheet on the bed with faded lettering. Or so it was thought.

"Any sugar bags today?" was a common request. They were not always in stock.

"Yes, lady," was the reply, "you want 'em with letters or without letters?"

When we first sold sugar bags they were seven cents each, four for a quarter. Then ten cents or three for a quarter. Then 15 cents, two for a quarter. Then 25 cents. Then half a dollar. Finishing at a dollar a bag. Hard to believe. A bag that started as a simple container of sugar, once bleached, cost a dollar each. With or without lettering.

Our mark-up on these items as with most other goods, was

small. The Abelsons would never get rich from such sales. But sugar bags meant a number of customers regularly visiting our store. And that was good. Customers coming into the store for one item rarely left without buying something else. A butter dish, a Royal Doulton cup and saucer, a tie, or a scarf.

Hired help in the store did not exist. The family. No one else. From early morning until late at night. From the eldest to the youngest. A customer was once startled by my baby sister approaching her to ask, "Yes, lady, what would you like?" Sandra was barely three years old at the time. You grow up quickly on Baldwin Street.

MURRAY AND MOLLY

Murray and Molly Millstein huddled together. Always. No other word for it. Huddled. Other couples walked hand in hand. Or arm in arm. Or gripped each other. But not Murray and Molly. They enveloped each other. Crowded close. Overlapping. As if trying to reach into each other.

Walking down the street. Huddled. Holding tight. With the frightening February winds of Toronto bellowing at them, the two were as one. In dog-day August's clammy heat, still seamless, united, integrated. One. Plato's four-legged monster incarnate.

The Millsteins lived on Augusta Avenue. Round the corner from Baldwin Street. A step away from the market noises. In a two-storey house—like most houses in the area, narrow front area daring grass to grow, wooden verandah with fat pillars in each corner—where they rented rooms. A kitchen, complete with table, small, for dining. A bedroom, with settee, also small, for all else. The toilet-bathroom was along the hall, shared by the landlord and wife, Mr. and Mrs. Cohen and ten-year-old son, Lionel. Beyond the toilet was another tenant. A Mr. Krovich. A huge Pole. Who went about continually uttering anti-Semitic phrases, quietly, for he dared not say them aloud. He disliked the fact that life's circumstances had forced him to live in a Jewish area. And he seemed to take his revenge by occupying the bathroom, to which he had the closest proximity, for as long and as often as he could.

But such petty annoyances hardly dented the happiness of Molly and Murray. Giggling. Chirping. Talking. Complete within themselves. Needing little from the outside world. Chubby. Middle-aged. Cheerful. A happy couple.

Until Molly became ill.

The Millsteins were not seen much on the street after that. An occasional glimpse as Murray helped Molly into a taxi. For hospital visits. And Dr. Rosen became a frequent caller. The Cohens began to do most of the shopping for the Millsteins, with even Lionel proving useful. And Mr. Krovich started to limit his visits to the bathroom.

It was a long illness. More than a year.

Murray refused to send her away. Either to a hospital or a home. He stayed with her. To the end. Molly died in Murray's arms. Pressing herself hard against her husband. Huddled.

After the funeral, a glass of water was brought to Murray at the curbside in front of his home, which he poured over his hands in the traditional manner. Then weighted with woe, he went up to the sanctuary of his rooms. A believing man, Murray mourned his beloved. As decreed, he did not cook. Mrs. Cohen brought him meals. He sat on low stools. He slept on the floor. Mirrors were covered. For seven days.

When this period of honouring of the deceased, *shiva*, was over, Murray decided that his two-room apartment needed attention. Molly would not approve of the state it was in. For instance, in the sink a number of glasses with lemon slices and tea still apparent, waited for cleaning. Mrs. Cohen had done what she could. But she was not Molly. Molly did not leave dishes in the sink. Molly washed the linoleum floors at least once a week. Usually before the dusk of Sabbath. Then polished the lino. Then spread newspapers strategically to intercept walking feet. Molly dusted. Everywhere. Nooks and crannies. Objects and surfaces never escaped Molly's dusting. Molly polished. Molly punished carpets in the back yard, hanging from the clothes line, with a swinging stick worthy of Joe DiMaggio. If cleanliness is really next to godliness, Murray thought, then Molly must be standing somewhere alongside God at this moment. Probably saying His white locks needed a shampoo.

Murray once told Molly a joke. About two cockroaches. One returns to the nest and says to the other, "I've just been to this Jewish house. And everything is so clean. So clean. Clean! Clean!" To which the other cockroach replies, "Please, not while I'm eating."

Molly's apron hung from the hook on the back of the kitchen door. As Murray reached for it, he sighed, remembering the many times she wore it. Swallowing to suppress tears, Murray put the apron on. And began sweeping the floor.

When he returned the broom to its tiny cupboard, the array of Molly's cleaning utensils stood ranked in disciplined columns. New rags, in descending order of newness. Old rags, in descending order of age. Tins of polish. For the floors. For furniture. For brass. For silver. In the corner of the cupboard was a galvanized pail. Inside was an hour-glass scrubbing brush. And a brown brick-sized bar of soap.

Murray wanted to wash the floor. He found the kneeling-pad Molly had made and re-made through the years specifically for this task. But Murray decided that what he was wearing was wrong. If he sloshed the soapy water over the linoleum properly, as Molly had done, he was bound to get his trousers wet from the knees down. No. Trousers were a mistake. He took them off.

Later he went into the bedroom to wait for the kitchen floor to dry. Carefully removing his shoes, he stretched out on the bed top. The previous night, for the first time since Molly's death, he had actually slept in the bed. A disturbed sleep. Whiffs of Molly, the smell of her still clinging to the bed and its abundant mound of clothing, invaded his thoughts. He had rolled over to her side continually, hugging the sheets, hugging pillows, hoping to grasp the aura of his late wife. In the morning he had smoothed out the sheets, made the bed—hospital corners and all—as Molly would have done. Put on the bedspread. As Molly would have done. Now Murray lay there. He breathed deeply. Trying once again to recapture his Molly. His nostrils widened. Nothing. The bedspread further suppressed the scents of Molly. And he yearned for the smell of her. His senses cried out for the essence of her.

When they first moved into the flat, Murray—who was good at such things—had built into the bedroom a small closet. Hanging space. Drawers. Shoe rack. A wardrobe. But since Molly's death he had not dared open it. Not until now. He stood before its door. Hesitated. Then pulled at the door.

The perfume that was Molly reached his yearning nostrils. Not merely store-bought perfume. But her odour. Her smell. Her body. Mingled. To produce a uniqueness. Individual. To her. Only her. Molly.

He stared at her clothes. The blue suit. Bought on Bloor Street. Retail, not wholesale as his friends suggested, because Molly hated the supplicating, begging—*schnorring*— that went with visiting a manufacturer in order to buy direct. The blue suit. Worn only once. Put away for special occasions. Too good to wear. To keep. Special. He lifted a sleeve of the suit against his cheek. His other hand crinkled the complimentary yellow-beige cashmere sweater. Murray closed his eyes. Leaned into the wardrobe. Inhaled.

Murray was still not wearing any trousers. Shirt ends draped over his underpants. From the closet he removed a hanger. On it was only one item of clothing. Yellow with a soft-gold plaid. A skirt.

Murray was a cutter—in truth he was an assistant cutter—at the Society Shirt Company. He liked his job. And was respected for his abilities. On the way home, after getting off the streetcar on Spadina Avenue, he would shop on Baldwin Street. When Molly was still alive he would always go home first. Meet her. And they would shop together. But now it was easier for him to shop first. He was loyal to the stores he liked. So it was to Gelman's for groceries. Kruger's for fruit. Fish at Leibowitz. Meat at Skolnick's. The shopkeepers noted recently that while he could not be called happy, he seemed to have adjusted to life without Molly.

Mrs. Cohen, being a good landlady, invited Murray to dine with them. Often. But he refused. Always. After a while Mrs. Cohen became aware that once Murray entered his room in the evening, he never emerged again until morning.

One night Mrs. Cohen, bearing some cinnamon cake, knocked

on the door to Murray's rooms. She did not wait for an answer. The door did not have a lock. She entered.

The plate of cake fell from her hands.

"Murray! Murray! Dear God! Murray, what are you doing?" asked Mrs. Cohen.

Standing before her was Murray, dressed from head to toe, in Molly's clothes.

The landlady's eyes bulged. Murray looked at her blankly.

A more literate man perhaps would have said something. Perhaps would try to explain. Or chastise Mrs. Cohen for her unforced entry. But not Murray. He was not given to verbalizing. And his thoughts, whatever they were, he kept to himself. He simply retreated into the kitchen and emerged with a dustpan and brush. And began, kneeling as a woman does with knees together, to clear up the cake and plate mess.

Mrs. Cohen, gasping, backed out of the apartment. She was also wordless. For all her energy was devoted to breathing. Until she reached the top of the stairs. Then her heels rattled down the lino-lined steps to the safety of her own domain.

Mrs. Cohen did not tell many people. Her sister Rachel, of course, had to be told. And Mr. Cohen. And, after a while, her son, Lionel.

How Mr. Krovich found out is difficult to ascertain. But one night he marched into the Cohen kitchen and with many a gesture towards Murray's rooms, circled the table where the Cohens were dining and barked many a vehement curse about the ethnic group among whom he lived. All in Polish. And none of the Cohens understood the language.

"What's he saying?" asked Mrs. Cohen.

"He's drunk," shrugged Mr. Cohen. And returned to the more important task of eating his beef-bone-and-barley soup.

"He's always drunk," said Mrs. Cohen gently. She rose from the table to placate the giant Pole. "Yes, yes," she said raising her voice in the usual assumption that loudness leads to comprehension, "it was a surprise to us too. Now go have some sleep."

Mr. Krovich's eyes blinked at her. Repeatedly. He had little idea of what she was saying. But he felt better that finally, at full volume, he had managed to release the prejudices he had brought with him from his native Poland.

From that time on Mr. Krovich avoided Murray.

And access to the bathroom became easier. Mr. Krovich disliked using the toilet after one of Murray's visits. As if some sort of contagion would result if he followed-on too soon. One evening the bathroom reeked of a particularly pungent shampoo—feminine, Molly's brand—and Mr. Krovich found the bottle that had been left behind. He roared. Smashed the bottle into the wastebasket. Kicked at the bathtub. Punched the wall. And swore. His need to empty his bowels was severe. But he could not bring himself to use the toilet. He stormed out of the bathroom. Several times later, the cramp in his stomach increasing in severity, he found himself at the bathroom door. But he could not enter. The sweet smell drove him away. So he suffered for hour after hour. Until in the middle of the night, with the pain too much for him, he sneaked into the bathroom, still reeking from the shampoo. And sat on the toilet. Weeping. Cursing himself. And cursing God who had forced him to such an existence.

The word spread. Storekeepers soon heard the news. Don't you know? About Murray Millstein? At night he puts on women's clothes. But aside from gossip little was made of Murray's strange predilection. Conversation might come to a stop as he approached Gelman's to squeeze the oranges. Greetings of hello and good morning were replaced with nods. Silence. Stares. A whisper or two. A rare snigger. Behind the man's back. Not much more than that. The burghers of Baldwin Street were tolerant people.

Only Izzy Birnbaum, who had a fruit and vegetable stand, once planted himself in the middle of the sidewalk blocking Murray's path. Murray tended to walk with his eyes down, rarely looking ahead. When he came across Izzy's confrontational stance, Murray stopped. He raised his eyes, slowly, appraisingly, from Izzy's feet to the fruitman's agonizingly patronizing smile. The two men looked at each other. For a moment. Murray's face was expressionless. And Izzy Birnbaum, who measured other men purely by their physical strength, stepped to one side. There was some conjecture as to why. Some said it was because Murray was no slouch physically. A man who worked in a shirt factory all his life was not a muscle-less bookkeeper. And that Izzy was basically a coward. Or that even someone like Izzy needed a motive to fight. And nothing Murray had done could be said to provoke antagonism. But the most often agreed reason for accepting Murray as Murray was Murray himself. His deportment. He did not cower. Not in front of Izzy. Not in front of any storekeeper. Not in front of anyone. He simply went about his life. As he had always done. He was the same Murray.

The popularity among his peers of young Lionel Cohen rose as the notoriety of the tenant in his parents' house increased. Hidden by the doorway of the William Houston Public School, Lionel sat with two of his closest friends, Normie Katz and Leonard Abelson, telling tales about Murray and smoking punk. Punk was an aerated reed used to prevent breakage in the china and crockery shipped to the Abelson store. A cigarette substitute, tobacco-less, but— important to the boys—suitable for being inhaled and exhaled. Leonard Abelson was the local supplier.

The school grounds were deserted. Dusk was approaching.

"An' he shakes his shoulders," said Lionel spewing out the awful-tasting smoke, "like this! Jus' like a girrrl!" Lionel performed what he considered to be a feminine version of shoulder waggling.

Normie hooted with laughter.

Leonard Abelson did not laugh. "I don't believe you," said Leonard after a while. "You're making it up."

Normie stopped laughing. The smile left Lionel's face. Leonard Abelson was his friend. Not as close a friend as Normie Katz. No, no way as close. He could never like Leonard as much as Normie. Normie would never call him a liar. Normie liked to laugh at his stories. All the guys in the gang liked his stories. Except Leonard. Who commented on, or, worse still, questioned everything.

"It is so true," said Lionel. He wondered if his enactment of the strange man who boarded in his house had been embellished just a little bit too much.

Lionel looked for support at Normie. But Normie just looked

away, waiting for the problem to be resolved.

After thinking desperately for a moment, Lionel blurted, "I know what!"

"Well, what?" asked Leonard.

"Come and see, smart guy," said Lionel. "Come and see for yourself!"

Normie's eyes widened. "Can I come too?" he asked.

That Friday night, Lionel, forefinger to mouth forever requesting silence, snuck up the stairs with his two friends. Advancing towards a keyhole. To look. To see. A pin to see the peepshow. C'mon, guys, come and see. But no noise. Shh. Quiet. Stop sniggering, Normie. Look. Look. Eyes to keyhole. Normie Katz looked. Leonard Abelson looked. Lionel looked. Framed by the keyhole was the sight of Murray on his hands and knees. The pail to one side. The scrubbing brush. The soap. The kneeling pad. Making the apartment Sabbath clean. Wearing Molly's work clothes. Bandana on head. Worn sweater. Shapeless old skirt. Lisle, not silk, stockings. Flat shoes.

Normie just managed to withhold his hilarity until reaching Lionel's room downstairs. When, goaded by Lionel's screech, he whooped into uproarious laughter. Lionel, laughing loudly, then elbowed Norman's ribs. Screaming laughter resulted. Even Leonard, sceptical Leonard, could not suppress his mirth any longer. First he laughed at his two friends. Then with his two friends. Lionel pointed at laughing Leonard. And his own uncontrollable laughter this time led to tears pouring out of his eyes. Each time one of them caught sight of the other, the weeping, shouting, laughing, escalated towards hysteria.

Mrs. Cohen was in the kitchen. Boiling and boiling and boiling a chicken in order for the fowl to fulfil its dual functions as both soup and main course. The loud laughter of the lads disturbed her. She went to inquire as to the cause.

When told she was furious.

"Normie, go home," she said firmly.

"Yes, Mrs. Cohen. Sorry, Mrs. Cohen," said Normie. His laughter changed to hiccups. Which made him laugh again. "Sorry, Mrs.

Cohen," he said again. He could stop neither laughing nor hiccupping as he left the Cohen house.

"Leonard," Mrs. Cohen shook her head, "I'm surprised at you, Leonard. A boy like you. You better go home too."

"I wanna be a writer," said Leonard, "I have to see these things." A last involuntary giggle escaped from him. "Sorry, Mrs. Cohen."

"Lionel, go to your room," she had turned to her son.

"Ah, Ma!" protested Lionel. "There's nothing to do in my room."

"Bang your head against the wall. *Shlugsush kop in der vant,*" she suggested. "Knock some sense into it."

"Ah, Ma!"

"Y'don't come out 'til I call you to dinner," she said. "Y'hear me?"

Mrs. Cohen returned to the kitchen. To ready the gefilte fish. Thin slices of cooked golden carrot added much needed colour to the pale fish balls. She found it hard to concentrate. Above her head she could hear the sound of shower water drumming on the bathtub. Having cleaned his abode, Murray was now cleansing himself.

A stealthy approach to Murray's door was more difficult for her to achieve than her light-weighted son. But she managed it. The climb up the stairs made her breathe heavily. She had to put a restraining hand over her mouth to muffle the sound as she lowered herself to squint through the keyhole.

At first she could see nothing. But after a few flashes of adjustment an image filled the screen of her eye. The apartment was different from when she had seen it during the period of mourning. Spotless. Molly could not have cleaned it better. The table, polished, gleamed. A lace tablecloth in place. The floors, polished, gleamed. The newspapers in place. After a while Murray appeared from the kitchen. He was wearing Molly's make up. Full lips. Rouge. Mascara. And dressed in the best of Molly's clothes. The cashmere sweater. The complementary skirt. On his head was a delicate white shawl. He carried a candelabra. Placed it on the table. And began the ceremony of blessing candles, *benching lecht,* as the female of the household was required to do on the Sabbath eve. His lips moved rapidly through the ritual phrasing without emotion. But when he brought his hands to hide his eyes in silent prayer he paused. His lips faltered. Twisted. His body began to shake. With sobs.

Mrs. Cohen slipped away.

She did not tell Mr. Cohen of her plan until he sat down at the dinner table. Her husband was not a religious man, not a *frummer*. Went to the synagogue, *shul*, only on High Holidays in the autumn. If then. He did not cover his head at meal times. But one routine established in his childhood had impressed itself on Mr. Cohen. He dressed for the Friday night dinner. Home from work—he was chief buyer for Goodman's, the treble-fronted hardware store on Spadina Avenue—he would bathe. Find a laundered shirt. Best suit. Best tie. Sparkling shoes.

As he reached the dining table Mr. Cohen was uneasy. Lionel sat in his chair, looking reasonably scrubbed for a child of that age. Mrs. Cohen, made up, hair coiffed, elaborately but neatly clothed, sat opposite. Glistening plates were in place. Twinkling cutlery alongside. Tumblers. A pitcher of water with lemon slices sliding past ice cubes. The horse radish reddened by beetroot, *chrayne*, waited in its crystal container. Pickles—some half-sour, some full sour—sat gleaming in appetizing juices on a side plate. But the bowls for the fish were empty. His gefilte fish balls, like his family, were always in place by the time he sat down to Friday dinner. But not tonight.

"So? What is it?" asked Mr. Cohen.

"I'm going to ask—no, I'm going to make Murray come down to eat with us," said Mrs. Cohen.

"Leave 'im alone," said Mr. Cohen. "He won't thank you."

"This has got to stop," insisted Mrs. Cohen.

And so it began. An argument. In the classic sense of the word. A discussion. A debate. Between husband and wife. Calm. Rational. Mostly objective. Without, except for a lapse or two, raised voices. On the merits and demerits of having their tenant join them for dinner.

It was Mr. Cohen's view that as long as Murray harmed no one and did not break the law and continued to pay the rent, he should be left to live his life as he wanted.

His wife's opinion was that a normal man should not be allowed to behave in such an abnormal manner. And that such behaviour reflected badly on a man she considered to be loveable, kind, intelligent, and worthy of respect. "Better than some of the other devils—*mamzers*—around here," she said, fighting to control emotions. For she liked Murray, just as she had liked Molly, and felt she must do something to help him. She couldn't just stand aside and do nothing. "I'm going to get him," she said firmly.

This time she knocked on Murray's door. No answer. "I know you're in there," said Mrs. Cohen, "I want to speak to you." Still no answer. She twisted the handle. Pushed. A chain intervened. Allowing the door to open only a few inches. "Oh, Murray," she said, disappointed at these new precautions, "let me in." Then added. "Please."

Murray brought his face up to the narrow space between door and architrave. "Go away, Mrs. Cohen," he said.

"No," she said. "I want you to come downstairs. Now. To eat with us."

"I have my dinner here, thank you," said Murray.

"Murray," said Mrs. Cohen, "We—I, I want to help you. Please. You must let me help you." Then an afterthought. "Molly"—she emphasized—"would want us to help you."

Murray undid the chain. The door opened. The two faced each other. Mrs. Cohen's eyes were wet. Murray's eyes were blank as usual. He was in full Molly regalia, clothes and make up.

"I'll just get my purse," he said.

At the table it was only after repeated urging from Mrs. Cohen that Murray lifted his fork to try a fragment of her gefilte fish. He minced the morsel tentatively on front teeth as if hearty chewing might be a sign of disloyalty to the memory of his late wife's fish. "Very nice," he said. "I'm sorry, no offence, but I like Molly's better." Mrs. Cohen's back arched. Her gefilte fish was thought by many a *maven* to be the best in the neighbourhood. In fact she supplied Mrs. Herzel, two doors away, as well as Mr. Levy, across the road, with balls of the comforting food every Friday night. And on

Murray's plate she had surrounded the oval delicacy inside a wall of slim cucumber tranches holding back jellied sauce, salivating juices, opaque onion rings, and carrot slices topped with parsley. A dish fit for a king, she told herself, albeit a Jewish king. "Molly grinds an almond into the fish," said Murray, "makes it wonderful." Mrs. Cohen somehow managed to restrain from replying.

When Murray first came into the Cohen quarters that night, Mr. Cohen, extending his hand, ignored his tenant's costume and greeted him in matter-of-fact fashion. "Hello, Murray. Nice to see ya. Si'down," said Mr. Cohen gesturing to the extra chair. Young Lionel did not dare look at Murray. He wanted to. But did not dare. Only when he felt Murray would not return his gaze did Lionel attempt to lift his eyes. Sidelong glances. Fraction of a second peeps. Darting glimpses. Was all that Lionel allowed himself. His being in the same room with Murray removed all humour from the situation. And his two friends were not there to support him. Laughter was far from his inclinations now. Replaced by curiosity, wonder, and a tinge of fear.

Murray sat primly throughout the meal. The purse on his knees. Clasped firmly by both hands.

"You never have chicken soup?" Mrs. Cohen was aghast at the news Murray had just revealed. "Well, no," he replied, "Molly gets a lean chicken. Then she bakes it." To Mrs. Cohen part of the joy of Sabbath shopping was to find the right fowl. A plump bird. Held firmly by the chicken dealer while she squeezed the breast. And then the entire shop waited—including all the other matrons who were about to make a similar purchase—for the pronouncement. A "no." And it would be thrown back into the slatted crate. A "yes." Meant it was fat enough for the needs of her table. For a substantial soup. For the hearty boiled dinner that followed. Anything else was heresy.

The gold-on-gold ringlets within the soup made it look especially appetizing this evening. A sliver of carrot cut length-wise floated on the surface. As did a lightly greened celery stalk. And in the middle of the bowl, in a proud place, the yolk of an unborn egg.

Murray was badgered. Cajoled. Pleaded with. Begged. Still he sat stiffly. Finally he yielded. And tried less than half a spoonful of the soup. He took a dainty handkerchief out of his handbag. Dabbed at his mouth. "Very nice," he said again.

Mrs. Cohen knew then that her attempt to make him part of the Sabbath household, hoping that this might be his salvation, had failed. She did not press him to eat again.

"You can go out and play now, Lionel," she told her son as she cleared the table.

"No. Don't want to," said Lionel. He wanted to stay to the end of this extraordinary evening.

"Do as your mother says," ordered Mr. Cohen.

Lionel reluctantly rose from the table. Went around the back of the chairs first to peck at his father's cheek. When he was behind his mother he looked at Murray fully for the first time. Murray proffered a forced half-smile. The boy quickly looked away. Kissed his mother. And ran out.

A silence followed. Murray had no need to speak. Mr. Cohen was certainly not going to be first. It was up to Mrs. Cohen. Both men stared at her.

"Murray," she said gently, "it has got to stop. You can't go on. Not like this. Dressed like that. Wearing Molly's clothes." By the time she finished, Mrs. Cohen was breathing heavily again.

Murray appeared to be thinking over what she had said. He nodded. An almost imperceptible nod but a nod nevertheless. Mrs. Cohen was encouraged by this. "Go upstairs," she said. "Be a man. Be yourself. Wash. Take off the make-up. The lipstick. The rouge. Take off the clothes."

"No," said Murray simply. "At first I wanted it to be like Molly was still here. I did what she did. Cleaned. Shopped. Washed the dishes. Washed the clothes. Made the beds. Cooked. Pickled. Made jams. Paid the bills. Put savings in the cocoa tin. All that. Wasn't enough. It wasn't enough." He looked from Mrs. Cohen to Mr. Cohen then back again. "You mean well, I know. But no. No. I won't stop wearing Molly's clothes. I won't. I can't. If I stop then Molly dies." He stood up to leave. "I can't let Molly die."

At the doorway Murray turned. "Thank you," he said.

Mrs. Cohen could not reply. "For what?" Mr. Cohen intervened. "For the dinner? You being smart-aleck? You ate nothin' and—"

"Not for just the dinner," said Murray. "You see me as I am. Like this. Like Molly. From now on more people are going to see me. I'm going shopping tomorrow. On the street. Like this."

And he did.

The gaping mouths, the stares, the sniggers, the pointed fingers made no attempt to hide or be concealed in polite discretion when he appeared this time. The storekeepers gawped. Shoppers stopped shopping. Looked. Usually in bemusement. Sometimes with a giggle. As he walked along the sidewalk people stepped to one side. As he appeared before a reduced-price bushel of apples, crowded with customers, space was made for him.

Even Izzy Birnbaum, who was willing to face Murray dressed as a man, turned away in dismay when he saw Murray dressed as Molly. And shuddered.

Murray took his familiar route in the market. Mr. Kruger, stuffing a pound of apricots into a brown paper bag, looked embarrassed. And was obviously relieved the strangely clothed man was making only one transaction that day. Mr. Simon had an expression of pain frozen onto his face as he served Murray.

No one knew how to treat Murray. How to approach him. What to say to him. And since Murray was his usual taciturn self, his wordlessness did not help matters.

It was Mr. Gelman who, with the insight with which simple people are sometimes blessed, solved the problem. As Murray approached, Mr. Gelman did not look away or find a pretext to be busy as most of the others had done. He addressed Murray. "Yes, Molly," said Mr. Gelman to him, "what can I do for you?"

As easy as that. In Molly's clothes he wasn't Murray; he was Molly.

From that day on when Murray shopped wearing women's clothes, he was called Molly. At other times, to and from work, at work, in his usual clothes, he was Murray. By day, Murray. By night, Molly.

Only on Sundays when the street was closed was Molly not to be seen. Otherwise she appeared every night. To shop. Following an oft-repeated route from Kruger's to Bermant's to Skolnick's to Gelman's. Every night. In summer in gaily patterned cotton dresses. In winter under a thick brown-black overcoat. Clutching a straw shopping bag and a purse in one hand. Leaving the other hand free to examine the merchandise. Little boys did not chase after her. Adults did not stop and stare.

Soon it was accepted that Molly was just another shopper on Baldwin Street.

POTATO POTS

On Saturday nights the day's intake was heaped on the kitchen table. The last customer gone. The store door locked. Paw emptied his pockets. Maw emptied her apron. Paw would sit, light his pipe, start to stack the bills. Like to like. In ones, twos, fives, and tens. The youngest children, Lorraine and Sandra, piled the coins.

A fifty dollar bill was extremely rare. And twenties were scarce. But purple tens, blue fives, brown twos—considered by some to be unlucky—"I should be unlucky enough to have a million of 'em," said Maw—and green one dollar notes were to be seen. A colourful harvest. Reaped from the day's hard labours of all the family.

Quarters were stacked one on top of the other as high as possible. Dimes were trickier. Nickels were okay. And one cent coins were boring, piled like bronze soldiers, in groups of ten.

Paw would count the money. Jot the amount down. I would be asked to confirm. Sometimes there was a discrepancy. A dollar or two. Or as small as fifteen cents. A solemn recount. Until the difference was settled.

The dollar bills were then rolled together, an elastic band around the rim, and given to my mother. She returned them to the safety of an inside apron pocket. To which no mortal other than herself had access.

One Saturday night my father appeared to stumble in his count. He took his pipe out of his mouth.

"You better do it," he said to me.

I could see why he had faltered. The takings, for the first time, were going to amount to over $1000. A momentous day.

I had visions not of sugar-plum fairies or cakes or cars or jewellery but of my parents being able to repay some debts. The store was always in debt. To suppliers, to wholesalers, to the gas company, the electric company, the phone company. And in debt to neighbours. One storekeeper often borrowing from another storekeeper to pay off a persistent creditor. Ask Mr. Bermant, the grocer, to loan us twenty dollars. Pay him back. In a day or two. A week or two. Next month. Whenever. Don't worry, said Mr. Bermant, pay me when you can. Ken McDougall, the manager of the bank at College and Spadina, said it was little wonder the people of the market didn't have bank accounts. Or use bank facilities. No need. They wanted money, they borrowed from one another. And no interest paid.

A thousand dollars. In cash. On the kitchen table. A big day.

My mother decided that amount of money was too much for an apron pocket. Hide it. But where? In a potato pot.

The cellar of the store was always filled with butter dishes and graters, plates and mixing bowls, cups and saucers, and many, many pots and pans, the most prevalent of which were potato pots. My father had been offered a special deal of several dozen such pots. Reduced price. A bargain. Cheap. He couldn't resist. He bought the lot. The problem was potato pots were not a hot selling item. A rounded pot with an open spout capped with a lid was not in great demand. Perhaps two or three were sold in a year. A good year. We had more potato pots than space to put them in.

From among the many facing her, Maw selected a remote pot. Put the money inside.

On Monday morning, having spent most of the previous day deciding in which order to repay a number of creditors, she went down to the cellar. She looked at the potato pots. Blankly. She could not remember which pot had the bundle of money. Panic.

No one is to sell a potato pot until we find the money, was the decree. My sisters were told to take care of the store. The rest of us descended. My brothers Syd and Sol and Ben and I began the search. Finding enough room in the crammed cellar to open each pot was difficult. It took hours. Paw was furious. Maw was impatient, kept pulling the pots out of her sons' hands. We kept bumping into each other. I started to giggle. Paw shouted. Which made Maw giggle. Soon we were all laughing. Searching. Looking. Laughing. Crying. Eventually the thousand dollars was found.

Maw jammed the bundle into the secret apron pocket.

"See, being rich is also a problem," said Maw. Even Paw laughed at that.

BLEACHED BAGS

Martin Danzicker always waited until late in the evening before entering the Abelson store. Some time after ten thirty. On Saturdays. When the hubbub of the day had settled. And the store was quieter. He would appear. To be paid in cash. Always in cash. Every Saturday.

He was the supplier of bleached bags to the Abelsons. His company manufactured bags. Burlap for potatoes and other root vegetables. Canvas for coal. String for citrus fruits. The company also collected for resale used bags of flour and sugar. It was Sam Abelson who suggested bleaching the bags. Bags made to hold flour did not bleach well. Too thin. But bleached sugar bags were an instant success.

Of course Danzicker could have had his pick of any dry goods store in the market as an outlet for his well-selling bleached bags. But he was loyal to Sam Abelson. Despite being waylaid many a time with tempting offers from rival retailers. He also enjoyed his Saturday night visits to the Abelson store. For social reasons as well as business. Danzicker was a man weighted with the world's woes—which, mindful of what was being revealed in Europe, were many—who smiled infrequently. After being paid, conversation with Sam Abelson inevitably followed. These talks, mostly intelligent but sometimes light, mostly profound but at times superficial, were therapeutic to Danzicker. And if Sam's wife, Pearl, joined in,

Danzicker was doubly pleased for he admired this woman who had so ably raised seven children.

One Saturday as Danzicker entered the store, Sam Abelson was talking to a young Negro woman, Effie Jones. The only other person present was Leonard Abelson.

Sam turned to Danzicker and said loudly in Jewish, shrugging his shoulders towards Effie, "*Dos iz mein geleibte.*" This is my beloved.

Danzicker, employing the language always used when outsiders were not meant to understand, replied also in Jewish, looking at the Negro woman, "*Dos is dos beste vos du kenst tiyan?*" Is this the best you can do?

Danzicker was not to know that Effie, abandoned at an early age, had been raised by Sam Abelson's sister-in-law Baila and although negroid in every respect, Effie could speak Jewish. "You don't like it?" said Effie in fluent Yiddish, "then you can take your . . ." She made the usual anatomically impossible suggestion, embellishing it with details. The words echoed round the store. Bombarding the recipient's ear. Poor Danzicker. Shock. Shock. And more shock. And horror. The words in his beloved language emanating from this black face stunned him. And the viciousness of her words made his own face turn tomato red. His eyes popped. He gasped. He gawked. He struggled to speak. Nothing. Sounds he managed. But not sentences.

He indicated he wanted to sit. Leonard thought he was about to have a heart attack and, alarmed, steered him towards a tea chest.

Effie meanwhile gathered her belongings and stormed towards the front door of the store. And would have been gone had Danzicker not managed to call out after her.

"Wait," he said, "please wait."

He struggled to his feet. Advanced towards her. Danzicker was always neatly dressed. Unlike the storekeepers of Baldwin Street who wore odd trousers—and some were odd indeed—and windbreakers, Danzicker dressed in immaculate suits, a navy wool overcoat, yellow scarf, gloves. As he approached Effie he removed his fedora.

"I am sorry," he said. "I am most truly sorry. Please, you must forgive me." He was obviously wondering in which language to continue. He switched to the Mother Tongue, *Mama Loshen*. "I insulted you. My reply earlier was meant to be a joke. Not funny, I know. Please forgive me."

Effie, nostrils flaring, was not certain she had such Christian forgiveness in her. "Your people," continued Mr. Danzicker, "are bound together by your skin. Your colour." He gestured towards the Abelsons. "We—my people—are bound by our language." He went on to explain. From every shtetl in Europe emigrants came to this area in this city in this country. Sharing only one thing. A language. Yiddish. To hear that language spoken so vividly by a Negro had shaken him. "I am sorry," he apologized again. Effie thawed slightly.

"No reason a black person shouldn't speak another language," she said.

"No," he said hastily, "no reason at all."

"Lots of blacks speak Jewish," she said.

"So I've been told," he was eager to agree. "A word here and there. But not like you. Not with your facility."

Effie warmed to him. She smiled. His conversation was not patronizing in any way. And flattering to her personally. She switched to speaking in English.

She told him about the woman who had raised her, Baila Quitt. How she almost never saw her parents, and consequently had not spent much of her life in the black community. A fact she regretted. "I am a Negro. I should be with my own kind. Maybe my parents couldn't afford to keep me." She waited. "Your people were slaves in Egypt. And escaped. Thousands of years ago. My people were slaves in America. And escaped. Not that long ago. To here. To Toronto." She smiled again. "No one parted the Red Sea for us. Or even parted Lake Ontario. Just a sneak across the border. From the States. To the Promised Land. And that's all it's been giving us. Promises. Not much more. Promises. No rich coloured folk in these parts. Doorkeepers. Maids. Factory workers. Porters on trains. Not much more."

"And what do you do? Where do you work?" asked Danzicker.

"The Eagle Laundry," said Effie.

"In the office?" assumed Danzicker, "I know the owner, Mr. Girst—"

"Not in the office," said Effie. "At the tubs. On the floor."

Mr. Danzicker paused. Looking at her. From his breast pocket he produced a large leather wallet. For a moment it appeared he was about to proffer money. But he produced his card.

"Call me on Monday," he said.

Effie read the card. Nodded a small nod.

From that night on, the Saturday visits with Mr. Danzicker became progress reports on Effie. At first he put her to work ironing bleached bags, stacking burlaps, servicing machinery, checking supplies, that sort of thing. Menial. Not much better than the job she had at the laundry. But he paid her more. And since he employed fewer than a dozen people in all he was always aware of where she was. He watched her. Discreetly. But definitely. Keeping an eye on her. Seeing how she related to other workers.

After three months he moved her into the office. Where she learned the names of customers. The names of suppliers. What an invoice looked like. What a receipt was. What ledger books were for. When he thought she was ready Danzicker instructed Lou Axler, his bookkeeper, to show her the accounts. And teach her accountancy.

Lou Axler was a wizened little Dickensian man. He did not sit on a stool as the Victorians did but came close to that image. A narrowly mean desk in the darkest corner of the office was his domain. Which he rarely left. Even at lunch. When he would unclasp his black tin lunchbox, remove the small thermos, munch at two thin Kraft cheese sandwiches, swallow his sugarless tea. He arrived each day precisely at 8:30 and left each day precisely at 5 o'clock. He almost never spoke. To his fellow employees he grunted when passing. To Danzicker, on entry and departure from the office, he jerked his head in a gesture that was a mixture of obsequiousness and politeness but managed to be neither. He was, not surprisingly, a bachelor.

If Axler needed to communicate on vital matters such as a late payment, he would bring the invoice to his boss's desk, point at the date and at the offender's name and bark out as few words as possible. "Eli Coal Company. Late." "Simon Mossop. Late. Again." It was Danzicker who picked up the phone to speak to the client. Just as it was Danzicker who signed the cheques when presented with the bills. And it was Danzicker who handed out the little brown pay packets to each employee on Friday nights.

The company's finance books were only ever viewed by the bookkeeper and his employer. For Axler to show the accounts to Effie was a shattering experience. But he did not conceive of arguing with Danzicker. He knew his place. He also knew that his retirement was approaching. He had hoped his replacement would be someone he would recommend. Like his nephew Morri. Such a good boy. Such a good student. First in his class. At the high school called Commerce and Finance. Or his niece Malky had a friend Lucy who was suited for the job. But not this girl. Not Effie. A black, a *schvarze*. What was Mr. Danzicker thinking? To employ such a woman. Feh!

In less than a year Danzicker retired Axler. He gave him a watch, inscribed, thanking him for his years of service. He would also have given him a dinner or a party but was afraid that none of his other employees would attend such a function. Instead Danzicker added extra funds to his bookkeeper's final wages.

Effie took over the company accounts. And she was better at it than Axler had ever been. She lessened Danzicker's work. She spoke to suppliers. She chased late payers. She knew the foibles of the workers on the floor. Who was likely to slump off to watch the Leafs plays baseball. Who was likely to cheat, to make a deal with customers for unlisted goods, and pocket the money.

She became indispensable to Danzicker. As he became indispensable to her.

Encouraged by him, financed by him, she enrolled in a course in chartered accountancy at the University. Then another course. Social Studies. The economic and social development of the society she lived in fascinated Effie. Especially as to how it related to her own race. The descendants of slaves, of which she was one, who followed the stars—"follow the Drinking Gourd"—to freedom north of the border. And a yearning to know more about recent immigrants from the islands of the Caribbean seeking a change. As well as the flamboyant émigrés from Harlem, Chicago, Washington, Los Angeles, and such like. Settling in Canada just for the hell of it. Or perhaps fleeing. From a wife, a policeman, a debt. But all of them—slave's offspring, islanders, Yankees—as with immigrants everywhere, escapees from a world they wanted to leave behiind.

Danzicker was not in any sense a frivolous man. He did not bother with movies. Too childish. Except for the occasional foreign film, Italian or French. He liked the ballet, the opera, recitals and concerts. And the greatest of these was a concert. His escape. His joy. His love. Nothing stirred Danzicker more than the sweeping sounds of a symphony orchestra.

Rose Danzicker, his wife of many decades, accompanied him on trips once a fortnight to Massey Hall. The two great pleasures in Rose's life were, firstly, her black Persian lamb coat which covered her ample frame at the first hint of a chilling breeze, and secondly, her husband. She was of Polish stock. She and her family left the Warsaw ghetto shortly after the First World War. Her husband's antecedents on the other hand were German, who arrived in Canada before the turn of the century and had assimilated with such amazing success, they looked down on the waves of fellow Jewish immigrants who followed. Few of the Germans married what to them was "the great unwashed." But Rose managed to snare young Marty Danzicker. In the years of marriage—she kept a kosher home, produced an acceptable amount of children, two sons—only one difference had ever come between husband and wife. Rose wanted to change the name. To find an Anglicized version of Danzicker. After all, most German Jews had reformed their names. Much as they had reformed the Jewish religion, insisting that women be allowed to sit in the main congregation with men, that sermons and the service be held in English, and much more. To Rose's chagrin, even before the wedding, Marty was adamant. Danzicker was his name. Danzicker would remain his name. And hers. She tried every trick. And a child of the ghetto knew a trick or two. She tried logic. After all, she argued, Danzicker couldn't have been his family name in the Holy Land all those thousands of years ago, now could it? He agreed. Probably sometime in the last millennium, or perhaps even more recently, yes, say, as recent as the 12th or 13th century, his forebears had taken on the name of Danzicker. That still made it a family name older than any president of the United States or any lord in England.

That argument having failed, she tried a more gut-wrenching approach. Three weeks after the ceremony, while the relationship was still in the full blush of marital happiness, she let a flood of tears cascade from her eyes—surprisingly easy, she realized—and announced she was going to the bedroom. She would not come out again until he complied with her wish. He watched her run to the bedroom. Fling herself on the counterpane. Weep and wail. She had contrived, of course, to leave the bedroom door open. She heard him approach. Hesitate. He did not enter. He closed the door. Leaving her all alone.

Danzicker waited six hours. He knew that by then his wife—a healthy girl with a healthy appetite—would be starving. He knew also that her pride would not let her emerge.

He tapped on the bedroom door. A too-weak voice said, "Come in." He pulled up a chair alongside the bed. Water still hosed out of her eyes. Her tiny handkerchief was drenched. Through sobs, prolonged and overdone, she said he was forcing her to do this and that if he loved her, he would change the name of—

Danzicker cut her off. He said he was willing to leave the room. Now. This instant. To pack his bags. To leave. He would arrange for a rabbinical divorce, a geht. Rose's eyes widened. The tears stopped. Danzicker continued. She was not to mention the subject of name changing. Never again. Ever. Not in a whimper. Nor a whisper. Not a sigh. Not a joke. Not a nudge to friends. Not a look. Nothing. And if she ever lapsed from this absolute decree, the marriage was over.

He put the chair back to its position. "You have five minutes," he said from the doorway. "Get up. Make me dinner." Then he added, "Please." And left.

Rose Danzicker did not test her husband's resolve ever again. It was said to be a happy marriage.

Unlike her husband, Rose had a tolerance for music rather than a love. A tolerance bred from wanting to share experiences with Danzicker. Not from personal needs. Or her own wishes. Not that she objected to the visits to Massey Hall or Varsity Arena. A chance to get out. To put on the lamb coat. To leave the house on Palmerston Boulevard behind. To get into the DeSoto. To drive downtown. Some performances were more enjoyable than others. The night Paul Robeson sang. That was good, she told Danzicker. I liked that. Usually she was bored. Usually she could think of things she would rather do than sit in drafty concert halls. I could have done with going to bed early, she told herself. More and more often.

One night as they were preparing to leave for a "Pops" concert, Danzicker suggested that Effie might like to join them. Rose thought for a moment. And agreed. Good idea, she told her husband. And so it began. An ageing white couple accompanying a young Negro woman to places of culture. An eye-catching trio.

That soon became an eye-catching couple. Rose started to drop out. Less and less became her compunction to join her husband. He would not be alone, she reasoned. Why should she suffer while sitting alongside the enthusiastically applauding Danzicker. She had had her fill of concerts and plays and operas. Besides, she was always given a full report by Danzicker or by Effie or both—filled with humour and incident—when they returned to the house for the compulsory post-concert tea and cookies at the end of the evening.

In the lobby of the Royal Alexandra theatre, Danzicker and Effie, a curious and contrasting couple, often aroused interest.

"Look at the way she looks at me," Effie said to Danzicker in Yiddish. "The lady in the silver fox collar. Can't take her eyes off us." The fact that they were speaking in a foreign language made them the subject for even more speculation.

That summer when the muggy blasts of humid heat hit the city, Danzicker invited Effie to join them at the cottage. Belle Ewart. The timber-framed bungalow in row after row after row of other timber-framed cottages on the shores of Lake Simcoe was indeed cool. Danzicker also found it restful. Away from the turmoil of the town. Quiet. In the country. Peaceful. He had a radio on the screened porch, which worked, sometimes. And he had his books. The Torah, in Hebrew. The stories of Sholem Aleichem, in Yiddish. And in English he struggled through many a volume not only for enjoyment but also in an attempt to improve his knowledge of the language. Shakespeare, Milton, Wordsworth, and other such classics—in paperback of course—all were at hand. As were more popular novels by Ernest Hemingway and John Steinbeck.

Late at night, when the noise from the other cottages—the children playing, the adults arguing—had died down, and Rose had taken her aching body to an early bed, and the most dominant sound was of crickets calling, and the most prevalent smell was fresh from the lake, he would sit and talk to Effie. For hours. She was a good listener. He liked to talk. About what he read in the books. What he heard on the radio. What was in the newspapers. Not only the *Toronto Daily Star* but—more important, more to be trusted—the *Forward*, the Yiddish newspaper from New York that somehow the local drugstore managed to obtain for customers. Effie, fluent though she was in speaking Yiddish, was illiterate. Danzicker would read aloud. Paragraphs from the paper, the *Forward*, pages from the books of Sholem Aleichem. Or he would translate from the Bible. Or in English. Why was Hamlet so weak? Why did Lear's daughters treat him so badly? Danzicker talked. Effie listened. For hours.

When they returned to the city Effie moved into the house on Palmerston Boulevard. She was given one of the bedrooms formerly occupied by one of the Danzicker sons. It made sense. She drove him to work. She drove him to warehouses. To customers. It was another chore he was glad to give up. Traffic in the city was getting worse, he thought. The road outside his factory used to be empty. Plenty of room to park. Not any more. Now another car, sometimes two, took his favourite spot by the front door.

On Saturday nights when Danzicker appeared on Baldwin Street he was no longer on his own. Effie was always with him.

Warm greetings heralded their entrance into the Abelson store.

Parking as close as she could, Effie would commandeer one of the Abelson sons to carry in the stacks of bleached bags, carefully ironed and wrapped, waiting in pristine parcels at the back of the car. Sam Abelson would hand over payment. Then Effie would bring Pearl Abelson up to date on recent events. How she was getting on at the Danzicker works. How she progressed in her studies. And such like. She would ask after the Abelson children. "Look at Sydney, he's getting so tall," she said. "Hey, good lookin', soon be time for you and me to cut a rug. Have us a time somewhere. Eh?" She would ask about Baila. And Baila's children. Pearl Abelson always finished such conversations with the same question, "How about you, Effie? A beautiful girl like you. When are you gonna get married? And have children?" Effie's white teeth gleamed against her dark skin in a smile, "When you find me a nice Jewish boy," was always Effie's reply.

No one knows how Axler, the former bookkeeper, found out. Someone working at the bank must have phoned him. A relative. Or maybe a clerk he had bribed. Someone. At the Canadian Bank of Commerce, College and Spadina branch, told Axler. And Axler told Mr. Danzicker.

Something unheard of, unprecedented, was about to happen. The Danzicker account was about to be marked NSF. Not sufficient funds. Overdrawn.

At first Danzicker dismissed the idea. A mistake. Nothing more. Or an oversight on Effie's part. Nothing more. Soon to be corrected.

It was not until he spoke to the bank manager, Ken McDougall, that Danzicker became alarmed. The bank manager confirmed that the company chequing account had been hovering near the overdrawn mark for several days. That cannot be, Danzicker stated on the phone. Which soon changed to a question. How can that be? Until he found the answer Danzicker asked that all cheques be honoured. The bank manager readily agreed for he had no intention of losing Danzicker's valuable custom. To cover any possible overdraft on the company account Danzicker sanctioned the immediate transfer of $5,000 from his personal savings account. Too much, said McDougall, it needn't be that much. Danzicker insisted. He did not want to be obliged to the bank while he sorted out the problem. And he knew the sorting would take time.

Axler could hardly contain himself. Waiting outside the Danzicker business premises for his former employer to arrive, he shifted from one foot to the other as much in a dance of glee as a means of keeping warm. His face came as close to a smile as his embittered nature would allow.

It was a Sunday. Danzicker made sure that Effie would be away. Seeing her family. Or friends. Using his pass keys he unlocked the many doors protecting his factory. "Leave the lights off," he told Axler. Behind panels of frosted glass was the office area. A desk lamp was switched on as the only source of light. The books, the company's financial records, were in the usual place. "This may take some time," said Axler. Danzicker nodded. He had no intention of doing anything else but wait. And watch. Axler, rubbing his hands, sat down at Effie's desk. And opened the accounts.

The accounts for the previous month revealed nothing. And the month before that. And the month before that. Nothing. Though Axler pawed his way through every page of the books in painstaking detail.

He went back as far as last year. Nothing. First he checked the outgoing funds. That would be the easiest way, Axler had decided. Create a fictitious supplier. Siphon off a parcel of money to a phoney account. Easy. But every cheque issued, signed by Danzicker, was to the correct recipient. The receipts, properly validated from the company beneficiaries, were all in order. He turned his attention to incoming monies. A cheque or two, thought Axler, slipped under the old man's nose, deposited elsewhere. But all cheques received from customers, endorsed by Danzicker, were deposited by Effie. Invoices balanced receipts. The bank statements confirmed that nothing was amiss. Axler, aware that Danzicker had not taken his eyes off him since the moment he began to scour the books, said "For a *shvarze* she's got a good head."

"Check the cash," said Mr. Danzicker.

And that's when the discrepancies were found.

Sunday night dinners in the Danzicker home were comparatively frugal. A milk meal as opposed to meat. A beet borscht starter was usual. Followed by cheese. Bagels. Smoked fish. Carp. Salmon. Bucklings. With apple strudel and coffee to finish. A minimal meal.

Both Rose and Effie noted how quiet Danzicker was that evening. "*Er darft pishen*," laughed his wife. He has to urinate. "Dr Bardenstein says it's the—what's it called? Marty? You know, what the doctor says you have?" Her husband put down his knife and fork, "The prostate," he said. "Last night," said Rose, "was bad, really bad, so many times in and out of bed. He used to keep me awake at night for other reasons. Now it's to go to the toilet!" The two women laughed conspiratorially at this male affliction. Danzicker looked sternly at his wife. But said nothing. He was waiting.

A loud banging on the door startled both women. "It's for me," said Danzicker rising. "Effie could you come with me please."

"What's this? What's going on?" asked Rose.

"Business," said Mr. Danzicker. "Not for you."

After ushering in Lou Axler and firmly shutting the living room doors, Danzicker sat to one side. It had been agreed that Axler would conduct the inquisition. Effie sat facing him.

As the questioning proceeded it seemed to Danzicker that Effie's face became more implacable, more remote, darker.

"You were seen," said Axler, "going into another bank. The Royal Bank. Opposite our bank. Is that where the account is?"

"Yes."

"In what name is the account?" asked Axler.

"Effie Danzicker."

Danzicker started at this. But Axler smiled. "An easy name to remember, I presume?" said Axler. Effie did not reply.

"How much is in the account?" asked Axler.

"The exact amount? I don't know the exact amount," said Effie.

"Of course," said Axler, "you spent some. How much have you spent?"

"Whoever has the bank book knows the exact amount in the account," said Effie.

"And who is that? A friend? A colleague? Someone in this with you?"

"Yes," said Effie.

"Who?" demanded Axler.

For the first time since the interview began Effie looked at Danzicker. "Your wife," she told him.

Rose Danzicker did not like being disturbed on Sunday evenings. It upset her routine. After ablutions she would retire to bed early. With her magazines—*Life, Look, Ladies' Home Journal*—spread before her, she would switch on the bedside radio. And listen to Jack Benny. Followed immediately by Fred Allen. For years she vacillated as to which of these two men was the better comedian. Jack Benny she knew to be Jewish. About Fred Allen she had doubts. And this influenced her opinion. Also, because it was transmitted by a Buffalo station, the Fred Allen programme was often difficult to obtain clearly. She was struggling to find the right frequency, the sound wowing in and out, when Marty came into the room.

"Yes, I have the bank book. Here." Rose produced the maroon booklet from her purse. Having slipped into a dressing gown, she was now in the living room, on the Chesterfield, instinctively placing herself closer to Effie than to the two men. As drily as she could, suppressing emotions, which was difficult for her, she talked about the mystery bank account.

Effie had warned her from the beginning that all cash the Danzicker business received was vital to keep the company's bank account in credit. The amounts secreted away would therefore have to be limited. She wanted her, Rose, to make the deposits. But Rose insisted that she was useless in such matters. Effie agreed to open the account. To make the deposits. But all withdrawals were under Rose's control. No one else.

"But why did you want a hidden account? Why?" asked Danzicker.

Rose faltered. Looked at Effie before she spoke. Then turned back to her husband. "For you," she said.

"For me? What do you mean?" asked Danzicker.

"Tell him, Effie," said Rose.

Effie shook her head. Refusing to speak. She stared down at the floor.

The two women had decided, Rose said, that what Danzicker needed was a proper holiday. Not a week or two in Belle Ewart. For his sixty-fifth birthday, an escape from the Toronto winter to some tropical paradise. Somewhere special, something different, somewhere exotic. Miami, Florida. And to get there, a new car. Maybe a Buick. Or a Studebaker. That new Frazer looked nice. Effie was looking into it. Effie was taking care of it all.

"I would trust Effie with my life," said Rose. "Why shouldn't I?" She started to cry.

The room was silent. Except for Rose's sniffles. Danzicker could think of nothing to say. Axler grimaced. Effie said nothing. She kept staring at the floor.

Danzicker rose. To stand by Effie's chair.

"Effie, I'm sorry," said Danzicker, "I should have known."

From her purse Effie took various bunches of keys. They clattered onto the coffee table. "For the factory, the offices, the car, this house," she said. "I need about ten minutes to pack." She started to leave.

"Effie, please. I'm sorry. Forgive me," said Danzicker.

She turned. "As far as I can remember those are the same words you used when we first met. In the Abelson store. On Baldwin Street. 'Sorry. Forgive me.' That's what you said then." She stepped closer to Danzicker. "To you I'm still that same girl. That same *shvarze*. Not to be trusted. Not completely, anyway. You would take the word of this weasel—" she glared at Axler, "—a white weasel, a bleached weasel—rather than me." She closed in on Danzicker. So close she could hear his breathing rate increase. "I could never cheat you. Never," said Effie. "You were my father. No. More. More than my father. My mother. My brother. My sister. My teacher. My friend. All those you were." She paused. "I loved you," she said.

Danzicker collapsed into a chair. He wanted to chase after Effie. But didn't. Knowing it to be of no use. Effie was soon to be gone. From this room. From this house. From his life.

In time Lou Axler did achieve his dearest wish. His nephew Morri took over the company accounts. And after a while fulfilled many of the functions that Effie had performed. Though never as well.

Two years after Effie's departure, Danzicker died. He was an old man, it was said at his funeral, who cared too much for the world to live in it long. But Rose knew better. He died of regret. Remorse. Chagrin. Guilt. He died of guilt.

Danzicker never made it to Miami. Rose did. Her two sons, one a technical consultant to an international company based in Georgia, the other a doctor in Oshawa, were not interested in the bag business. Morri, the accountant, tried to raise a syndicate to buy the company. Tried hard. But failed. The business was sold for not quite its true value. Rose was not too concerned. She took her share of the money. And headed south. To Miami.

A few years later Leonard Abelson saw Effie. At a University dance.

An unusual place to find her, he thought. She was sitting at a table to one side of the orchestra, drinking coffee, her crossed top leg rocking to the music's rhythm.

"Do you remember me?" asked Leonard.

She looked the young man up and down. A severe check. "No, honey," she said eventually. "Who are you?" He told her. "Hey, baby, how the hell are you?" she exclaimed. "And how's them nice people, your Mama, your Papa?"

"You don't come round to Baldwin Street much these days," said Leonard.

"No. Not since your Auntie Baila died. Not since then." She pointed towards the band's drummer, a moustached handsome mulatto. "I'm with him now. Roy. Roy Clarkson. You heard o' him?"

"Good," said Leonard, "you going to get married?"

Her head tilted back as she laughed. "People like us don't worry about marriage much," she said, swallowed some coffee and then changed the subject again. "I offered my body, once, y'know. To the old man. To Danzicker. Turned me down, of course. If he had said yes, he'd have to *doven* for a year after. Hey, that's the first word of Yiddish I've used in years. *Doven*. Pray. Don't use that lingo much anymore. Mainly black-speak nowadays." She looked at Leonard. "I loved that man, y'know. Danzicker, loved him."

"I know," said Leonard.

"He was good to me. I loved him," she said.

"I know," repeated Leonard.

"Hey, baby, how much you sell sugar bags for now, eh? Seven cents when I first came along. Four for a quarter. Then a dime each. How much they now?" asked Effie.

"Guess," said Leonard.

"Le'see now," she said. "Fifty-nine each. Two for a dollar."

"A dollar each," said Leonard. "And we don't sell that many any more."

"A dollar? For a bag?" said Effie, "My, my. A dollar for a bleached bag. A dollar." She thought about this for some time and eventually said, "Things sure change. Time sure changes things. Ain't it the truth?"

Leonard agreed.

MAW

"Which one of us do you love most?"

Was a question none of her seven children needed to ask my mother. We knew the answer. Me. She loves me most of all. Me.

Each one of her children was convinced absolutely that he or she was the favourite child. Maw loves me best. Of course she loves the others as well. But not as much as me.

Each of us believed that to be true. Knew it to be true. Would secretly confess it to our inner souls. A secret not to be shared with the other brothers and sisters.

The greatest tribute to my mother was that she made each of us feel that we were the child she loved most.

"What does 'seven the hard way' mean?" she once asked me.

"It's an expression in craps. Dice. Not a four and a three. Or even a five and a two. But a six and a one. Seven the hard way," I explained. "Why?"

"One day I'm gonna write a book. About bringing you guys up. Guess what I call it? Seven the Hard Way. Good, eh?"

A fantasy. There was little danger of Maw writing a book. Ever. I can remember as a tot my mother signing her name with an X. Truck drivers delivering goods to the store would shove a receipt at her. Sign here, please. An X would be scrawled. The driver would shrug—the inability to sign was common among storekeepers—and print out the name underneath the marking. Ashamed of this failing, Maw subsequently learned, painstakingly, letter by letter, at a night school, to write her name. Mrs. P Abelson.

Of course she could write in Jewish. But not English. All store accounts and notes were written in Jewish. Which none of her children could read. Neither could my father. Despite his mastery of many other languages, he came to Yiddish last, and not only was he illiterate in the language, his vocabulary and grammar were limited.

My parents met at a function organized for Russian émigrés. It would be wonderful to know what her thoughts were when she first saw this handsome, suave man—fifteen years her senior—who seemed in command of himself and in control of the world. Ironic. It was not a marriage made in heaven. When poverty comes in the window love walks out the door, the saying goes. Maw later confirmed an early childhood memory of mine. Onion sandwiches. For six weeks we ate nothing but a slice of onion between two slabs of bread. A dab of chicken fat on the bread was an occasional addition. On good nights. On bad nights we went to bed with nothing in our bellies. Not an onion. Or bread. Nothing.

One night—I was five years old, probably less—Maw sat crying. She needed fourteen cents for half a pound of butter. She had eleven cents.

No one on Baldwin Street was on Relief—state benefits—of any kind. You were poor, you suffered. You were poor, you closed the door so the outside world would not know of your suffering. No handouts. Except for shoe vouchers. Some charity provided vouchers enabling the poor to either buy shoes at a large discount or, if the shoes were cheap enough, get them free. Running shoes were free. Not trainers, running shoes. Cotton topped, rubber soled. Thin. Not much warmth against February's ice. The free shoes, running or otherwise, were obtainable from any shop. But the family would head into town, Eaton's or Simpson's, to get the annual supply. Pride. A local shoe store dealer might know who we were. In the shoe department of a large store we could remain anonymous. Pride.

Even then my sister Ruth, the eldest child, would pretend she wasn't with us. She would get to the shoe department half an hour before the rest of the family, select a pair, try them on to make sure of the fit, take them to the counter, grandly tell the salesperson to put them aside for her, then wait to meet us outside the department store. My mother, using the voucher, collected Ruth's shoes. The rest of us, fitted and measured in the usual way, were not permitted the luxury of pride. "You can't have those! Those are not charity shoes!" a haughty saleslady would loudly—too loudly—declare. Red-faced, embarrassed, cringing, we would pick a different shoe. No matter what the Bible says "the greatest of these" is not charity. Not when dealing with saleswomen in the shoe department who delighted in our discomfort. It was a great day for each child when we finally had enough money to pay for shoes like everyone else.

Toilet paper was another joy that arrived later in life. Newspaper was the usual substitute. On a nail on a wall next to the seat. But Baldwin Street also provided another replacement. Orange wrappers. Oranges came wrapped individually in a waxy but soft tissue-like paper. To be collected from the fruit stores, or the pavement, or the gutters, straightened, then spiked onto the nail. Luxurious compared to newspaper.

In the worst of times we did not have a store. Paw would be looking to find a new shop. Waiting for someone to extend him credit. Waiting. Meanwhile he worked as a labourer. Breaking tarmac. Maw made toffee apples. To sell for pennies. Or she worked for Mrs. Skolnick, the butcher's wife. Maw was a good cook. "When Lennie wants a great meal, he eats at home," my friend Stanley used to say. My mother's mother ran a bakery in Russia. Continental style. A minimal amount of bread and cakes were baked but a handful of tables were also provided for diners. Maw was the chef. One of her specialties was peppers stuffed with a sort of coleslaw. Then pickled. Years later, when Mrs. Skolnick, who was from the same shtetl, heard of my mother's abilities, she hired her to make such delicacies. Stuffed peppers. Dill pickles. Sour tomatoes.

During the First World War army officers came to my mother's village and demanded that teenage girls be used to collect the dead soldiers at the front. To be loaded onto wagons. Carted away. My mother was forced to agree. Her younger sister, Leya, had a rheumatic heart. My mother pleaded with the authorities that such physical work was impossible for Leya. No use. Both girls were to report for duty. My mother had no alternative. She would sign on as herself to work. Then do another stint pretending to be her sister. For as many as twenty hours a day she suffered the grisly work.

It was one of the many reasons she left the Ukraine behind. Her father had died when she was a child. She was seventeen years old. Travel was not permitted. She led her sister, Leya, her mother, and her sister-in-law past border guards one night. To freedom. To a new life. In Toronto. Where her brother was waiting.

Pogroms in her shtetl of Rovna, near Lutsk, were common. She had been told of rampaging Cossacks using swords to pierce infants from cradling maternal guardians. Rape and murder, pillage and looting soon followed. The spoils of war.

One pogrom she did witness. Cossacks stormed into the community. Most of the inhabitants were barricaded in one particularly strong house. The Cossacks used sabres and bayonets to pry at the door. If no sound was heard, the Cossacks were known not to bother to go further. But at the slightest sound they would break in. A mother and new-born babe were on the other side of the door. Inches away from the marauder. The baby started to whimper. The fearful eyes of the refuge seekers looked on in horror. A wordless plea. Many wordless pleas. The mother placed her hand over the baby's mouth. Firm. In place. Over the mouth. Over the nose. When several minutes later the Cossacks finally departed, the mother removed her hand. The baby was dead.

Toronto, for all its hardships, must have been as nothing compared to what was left behind.

Maw ran our store. Paw did the buying. Maw worked the store. Opening it early, closing it late. When the last customer left, whenever that was, often after midnight. She paid the bills. When possible. We were always in debt. To a supplier, a wholesaler, a neighbouring storekeeper, a friend. Maw kept the accounts. Some on paper. Mostly in her head. She cooked. Breakfast, lunch and dinner. Fresh food. Daily. Opening a tin, except for an occasional Campbell's Soup, was heresy. All the children came home from school for lunch. Hot. Dinner was expected to be ready for a family of nine. Daily. Maw mended. Sewed. Repaired. Cleaned. For years she insisted on baking her own bread. "I don't know what Mr. Pearl and Mr. Lottman put into their bread. I know what's in mine," she said. "But Maw, you haven't got the time," I appealed to her, aged nine. She blinked. She could see the sense in that. From then on she yielded to store-bought bread.

The stove fuel was coal. The hot-air furnace in the cellar was also coal-fuelled. Coal up and down steps. Ashes up and down steps. Liver was cooked as a chunk wrapped in several layers of wet newspaper, thrown into the coal. When the paper burned away the liver was edible, suitable for being chopped. Maw kept the house kosher—sort of—and observed the major religious holidays. Never knew a day off. Holidays centred on eating. Candies at Purim. Walnuts in honeyed-toffee. Poppy seed in honeyed toffee. Thin, thin, thin eggy pancakes. Called handkerchiefs. So thin ambient light shone through. No thicker than the finest handkerchiefs sold in our shop. The pancakes were usually wrapped around cheese and cinnamon. For the eight days of Passover different plates, cutlery, utensils were used. The other kitchenware stored away. And although it was one of the busiest times of the year for the store—shoppers wanting new pots, pans and dishes—she found time to prepare special meals. And to bake. Cakes. Sponge cake streaked with cinnamon was the family favourite. Each child rivalled the other to lick the mixing spoon when Maw had finished preparing one of her cakes. At her funeral the rabbi pointed out at Passover my mother collected money for the Jewish poor. And at Christmas she collected money for the Christian poor.

She went to hospital only twice. To have a goiter operation. And a few weeks after that operation—she was still recovering—for the delivery of the youngest boy in the family, Ben. The other six children were born on her bed. Wherever that bed was. The first three without much help. My grandmother was present. But no anaesthetic. No midwife. From time to time a harassed doctor appeared.

When she was pregnant with her first child, the family physician tried to frighten her into giving birth in a hospital. He told her of possible complications. "If I'm going to die, I'll die at home," was Maw's reply. She was twenty-two years old.

After her seventh child, Sandra, was born fourteen years later, she tried to learn about contraception. She and a few other Baldwin Street wives heard of a state nurse giving talks on the subject. Privately. In some urban house. The premises were raided by the police. The women fled. The nurse was arrested. As were a few others. My mother escaped by jumping a garden fence.

Maw was an emotional tower against whom all her children leaned. For help. For support. For love.

Whom did she love most? Ask any one of her seven children and the same answer comes forth. Me. Maw loved me most of all.

KURTZ'S HORSE

His eyes were black marbles. Rolling marbles. Pivoting up and down and from side to side as he contemplated the request. Then, after many moments, he bellowed out a laugh. Or a sound close to a laugh. Mr. Kurtz was not a laughing man.

"Well?" asked Leonard Abelson, facing the old man, impatiently shifting from foot to foot, but fearful of pushing too soon for an answer.

Mr. Kurtz's head rocked up and down vigorously in small shakes. The nod became bigger.

"Okay?" asked Leonard eagerly.

"Hokay!" replied Mr. Kurtz.

"Oh, thank you! Thank you," said Leonard. He extended his hand. Mr. Kurtz was bemused by this, to him, alien gesture but after a few moments clamped his two hands around the young man's. He emitted another of his unique laughs.

Leonard left him and ran into the Abelson store. Up eight steps into the kitchen at the rear. Pulled the hanging receiver from the wall phone. Waited for the numbers to twirl round. And when connected couldn't conceal his excitement.

"We're on!" shouted Leonard. "The horse is ours! Wednesday morning!"

Mr. Kurtz lived next door to the Abelsons. A fruit and vegetable dealer. Leonard had asked if he could borrow Kurtz's horse and wagon. For just a few hours. To take to the University of Toronto.

Every day students arrived on campus by various means. Most would walk. From nearby housing and homes. Others came by bus. Others by streetcar. One or two or three at most—eccentric to near madness or truly poor—travelled on bicycles.

But many undergraduates arrived in cars. All Papa-bought, of course. Donations from Daddy. Status symbols. Cadillacs with charisma, Buicks black and beautiful, Chryslers curvaceous, Mercurys, Lincolns. The appearance of a lowly Pontiac was a rarity.

Stan, Harvey, Syd, and Leonard would watch enviously as girls, whose attractiveness seemed to increase with the monetary value of each car, were deposited at the bottom steps leading up to the entrance archways of these buildings of higher learning. Then the cars would be driven off. Parked. On the road ringing the campus. By sweatered young men—usually with an unlit pipe clenched between radiant teeth—who emerged from cars to be greeted warmly with shouts and gestures from other passing students before rejoining their female passengers. A ritual. The morning arrival of the students for the first lecture of the day. Performed each day from Monday to Friday by appealing young ladies and striving young men.

"Good looking girls," said Stan one day.

"Good looking cars," said Harvey.

"Not good looking guys," said Syd.

Leonard said nothing. Leonard was thinking.

"We're the good looking guys," said Stan.

"We got no cars," said Harvey.

Stan's father, in fact, had generously lent the boys his car on some Saturday nights for dating ventures. But an old Chev was hardly likely to make an impact in this situation.

"Something must be done," said Stan. The rest agreed. But what?

Stan later said it was Leonard's idea. Leonard attributed this to Stan's innate modesty. He believed it was Stan's idea. At any rate, sitting on the steps of University College watching the girls and guys and cars arrive, it was decided. There was only one answer. Kurtz's horse.

The horse was called The Fairdel. Through the years a succession of horses, each one appearing wilder than his predecessor, bore the same name. The Fairdel. The Horse. Appellations were a simple matter to Mr. Kurtz.

Wednesay morning arrived in clear, crisp, sunny autumnal fashion. "I vill help," volunteered Mr. Kurtz. He spread car oil the length of his right arm. Then selected a large onion from a display of bushels that stood on the pavement outlining the front of his stand. Peeling away the brown top skin brought tears to his black eyes. But he ignored that. He rolled the now-naked onion in his hand. Satisfied, he moved to the rear of his horse, lifted the animal's tail, and rammed the onion into the anus as far as he could. His arm, beyond the elbow, disappeared up the creature's behind. The horse, after a momentary surprise, began to roll his eyes as if in envious imitation of his owner's eye-rolling ability.

Leonard set off. Mr. Kurtz, knowing Leonard to be a lad from the street, showed little reluctance in handing over the reins. Leonard sat on the wagon's seat, to one side, in the approved manner. With the well-worn leather strips in his hands, he felt in control. No reason not to. It was simple. Pull left to go left. Pull right to go right. Pull straight to slow down. Pull harder to stop. Snap. And the beast goes faster. No brakes. Of course not. A lead weight could be attached to the bridle once the horse was stationary to keep it from roaming. Simple.

Harvey, Stan, and Syd were waiting on the corner of Spadina and College. Harvey smiled, raised a fist above his head in silent approval. He was more overt than the other two. Who looked about to see who was watching.

Kurtz's wagon was a flat cart about two feet deep. Used mainly for portering boxes and bushels of fruit and vegetables. It was well worn. And despite the hosing Leonard had given it early that morning, bore stains of the produce it carried. A bordering ledge ran down both sides of the wagon. The back flap lowered for easier accessibility. But the usual way to get on board was to use the centre spoke of a back wheel as the first step, then onto the outer rim of the wheel, before jumping on. The three friends bravely but self-consciously went through this boarding procedure.

The wagon clip-clopped along College Street towards the campus. Syd sat down beside Leonard. The others clustered behind.

"Why are we doing this?" asked Syd. "I think it's childish."

"Of course it's childish," said Harvey, "that's why we're doing it."

"I thought we wanted to make a statement," Leonard said.

"Remind me, what was the statement?" asked Syd..

"That there's more to life—and to education—than arriving at college in a Cadillac," said Stan.

Syd nodded. "What will it achieve?" he asked.

"Maybe notice will be taken of our protest," said Stan.

"Maybe notice will be taken of our existence," said Harvey. "By those gorgeous girls in beanie caps and angora sweaters. Just a few dozen girls, okay? No? Half a dozen? Two girls? One girl?"

"Listen, Syd," Leonard said, "if you to want hop off, you can."

"Don't be silly," said Syd.

At the corner of King's College Road stood the Mining Building. A forbidding, squat-looking structure, brown-bricked dark. Unlike the grey gothic stone of most buildings at the university. And a building where Stan, Harvey, and Leonard tried desperately to stay awake—Stan sometimes succeeded—during lectures about stones. Geology. Ugh.. Leonard turned The Fairdel north, towards the main campus. Perhaps it was the ugliness of the Mining Building that created the mood. But the four young men on the wagon became sheepish. Quiet. Worried.

The first fellow students to see them laughed gently. And made a gesture towards the wagon. A head nod. A pointed finger. But soon, from others, the pointing became more pointed. And jeering began. One undergraduate—must be an Engineer, thought Leonard, an Arts student would never be so insensitive—took up a position as close to the passing wagon as he dared and then, arms akimbo, put his head back to roar as loudly as possible.

Syd looked at Leonard for support. Leonard smiled back. A weak smile.

"They're supposed to be laughing with us," said Syd, "not at us."

Leonard shrugged.

"Let's stop. Let's stop it now!" said Syd. "Go back!"

"No!' said Leonard.

Harvey stood up and bowed exaggeratedly towards the jeering onlookers like an actor to a receptive audience. "To our College, James," he shouted, "and don't spare the horses. Umm. Sorry. Don't spare the horse!"

"Yes, sir. No, sir. I won't, sir," Leonard replied. "But please don't report me to the chauffeur's union. I promise to wear the peak cap next time."

"Mater wants this means of ambulating next, old boy," continued Harvey. "Shopping on Bloor Street."

The few others who could bother to hear this dialogue chuckled appreciatively. But mocking and scoffing guffaws from students were more dominant. Suddenly Stan tried to hide. Which in an open wagon is difficult. He made himself as small as he could behind Syd. "It's her," he explained. "Look! Look! No! Don't look! Don't look! It's her. Dusty McAllister."

A young co-ed named Dusty McAllister was staring at the passing wagon.

"Dusty McAllister is the most desirable lass at this University," Stan had declared on first seeing her some weeks earlier.

"Dusty McCallister is the most desirable *ass* at this University," Harvey had countered.

At tea dances and basketball games, Stan had manoeuvred and wangled his way to try and meet her. But failed. And here she was. Watching the foursome on the wagon. Smiling. Albeit a patronizing smile.

"O Gawd," said Stan, "she didn't see me, did she? Say she didn't see me."

"She saw you," said Syd and Leonard in unison.

"What a stupid idea," Stan said in anguish. "Whose stupid idea was this?"

"Yours," Leonard said.

The Fairdel's shoulders, as always, drooped as he towed the carriage along. The shoulders of the four occupants also began to droop. Wagon wheels squeaked. The procession was becoming a weird cortège. Accompanied not by funereal noises but by sounds of laughter. Sneering, ridiculing, derisive laughter.

Dr. J. J. Ketchum, lecturer in social psychology, heard the noise of the approaching procession. He turned. And stood on a small mound for a better vantage point as the wagon paraded past him. Like the undergraduates around him, Ketchum also had a pipe in his mouth. With a difference. Smoke chimneyed out from the bowl. His pipe was lit.

"Well done, gentlemen," said Dr. Ketchum. "Well done," this second time was said more loudly. He smacked his hands together. Applauding. "Well done! Yes! Well done!"

As a result of this comment a lot of the insulting laughter dwindled to a stop. One or two of the other Cadillac-withouts joined in light applause. The shudder-making embarrassment was metamorphosing into something different. Pride. Not much. A small tinge. But nevertheless pride is what it was. Harvey looked at Leonard for confirmation. Leonard smiled. No longer a weak smile.

And so The Fairdel, the wagon, and quartet of passengers arrived at last at the front of University College.

"Aw'right, aw'right! Get that contraption outa here," said a burly security guard coming straight towards the vehicle. "Look at the traffic you're holding up."

Impatient horns tooted from the line of Cadillacs and convertibles stretched out behind the wagon.

Syd looked at the approaching guard. "Leonard, you speak to him," said Syd.

"Yeah, Leonard, you speak to him," said Harvey.

"I guess I'll speak to him," said Leonard. He jumped off the wagon. Placed the restraining lead weight on the pavement. "I have as much right," said Leonard, "to convey my friends to the lecture hall—Psychology 2a—as anyone else."

The guard picked up the weight. Put it back on the wagon. Brought his face close to Leonard's. "Another word," he said, "Jus' one more word. And it's no psychology lecture you'll be going to. But the hoosegow. Then the disciplinary committee. And the President of the University. And then expelled. Got that? Okay?"

Leonard looked up at his three friends in the wagon. Stan, Syd, and Harvey said nothing. Leonard sighed. Also said nothing. Got back on the wagon. Cowed. The threat of expulsion was too much. It would be impossible to explain to hard-working parents how this act of protest had led to him not getting his degree.

"Good!" said the guard smugly. "Now get this thing outa here!"

With that he slapped the horse on the rump. Mistake. Whether the slap was too high and hit the lower abdomen or his large palm hurt the animal more than he intended or it simply was time for Mr. Kurtz's onion-suppository to do its work, whatever the reason, the eruption out of the horse's ass was phenomenal.

The lower half of the guard's trousers was instantly covered. His shoes soon stood dripping. The open red convertible stationed alongside the horse became a car of a different colour. Dashboard, leather seats, upholstery had not escaped the barrage. The occupants of the car—one smug Cadillac-owning type and her handsome companion—fortunately were protected by the windshield. And escaped with small but malodorous splashes.

At that moment of the exotic expulsion from The Fairdel, a howl went up from surrounding bystanders. A sound that was both a yelp of shock tied together with a whoop of laughter. Whether it was this noise that provoked a reaction or simply the surprise of what his body had committed, The Fairdel took off. Bolted.

Leonard pulled on the reins as hard as he could. Nothing. When the horse hurtled into action the threesome behind him were flattened on the wagon's floor. Harvey was the first to force his way to the front. He pulled on the reins with Leonard. Then Syd joined in. Then Stan. Nothing.

The Fairdel careened his way round the ring of the campus. Cars screeched to a stop. Or collided. Or played at dodgems trying to avoid a horse and wagon hurtling towards them.

Facing a phalanx of cars, The Fairdel left the road and mounted the grass centre ring of the campus. Where softness of the turf seemed to calm his hooves. And slowed the wheels of the wagon down. Horse and cart came to a stop.

Leonard jumped out. He had seen enough John Wayne movies to know that the thing to do was cradle the horse's head. And speak gently into his ear. To his surprise it worked. The wild Kurtz-like look left The Fairdel's eyes.

He led her—or rather, The Fairdel allowed him to lead her and the wagon—back to the front steps. The Security Guard was bearing down on him with a face the colour of a Mountie's jacket.

"You— you—" was all the Security Guard managed to get out before a voice interrupted.

"Just a minute." It was Dr. Ketchum.

He took the still-growling guard to one side. Out of earshot.

The other three members of the wagon quartet dismounted. And shuffled towards Leonard. The ride had shaken but not injured any of them. They waited to learn what retribution was to befall them. In the meantime other students from other faculties and other colleges, having seen the morning's activities, formed a ring around the foursome.

Eventually Dr. Ketchum returned. The guard followed.

"You are in my class, aren't you?" was the first thing Dr. Ketchum said to Leonard.

"Yes, sir. All of us, sir."

He smiled. But the smile was brief. "You will make good any damage you have done," he said emphatically.

"Yes, sir. Of course, sir. Yes, sir," the quartet agreed.

"Insurance, I imagine, will take care of the cars," he said. "But the campus lawn will need work. And there's going to be a few cleaning bills." The four boys nodded. "You will take care of it all," he added.

"And you— you—" demanded the guard, "You will never bring that animal back here again."

That was easy. "I promise," said Leonard.

The guard jutted his chin down affirmatively before marching off. Grunting. Looking back at the boys. Often.

Dr. Ketchum also turned away. But only went a few feet before he came back. "In many ways you are to be congratulated," he said. "No one was hurt. And you have made a comment. On behaviour. Not an easy thing to do. As a teacher of social psychology, an instructor on mores and ritualistic patterns, I can hope for nothing better than attentive students. You have noted that our society, particularly your contemporaries, place too much value on external appearances. The look, shape—but most of all the cost—of the vehicles driven here daily is prized too highly. You have obviously been thinking. And listening. To my lectures. I appreciate that. Let me assure you that I truly do. Thank you, gentlemen." And he left.

The crowd broke up.

"I'll take the horse back," said Leonard quietly. "I'll come with you," said Stan. "Hell, we'll all come with you," said Harvey.

Leonard flapped the reins lightly. A bit apprehensive as to how The Fairdel might react. But the horse simply lowered his head and tugged the wagon away. The nearest exit off campus was behind them. Getting a horse and wagon to manoeuvre round to face the opposite direction in a small space is no simple task. And Leonard wasn't brave enough to try. There was only one way out. Forward. The long way round the campus ring. Slowly. Inviting the jeerers to jeer once again.

Down the narrow opening left by parked cars, the wagon started to chug along.

"Can I have a lift?"

It was the girl of a thousand fantasies who spoke. Dusty McAllister.

"Sure," said Leonard. "Hop on."

Stan offered an eager hand.

Leonard looked at Harvey. What about that, eh? Leonard's face beamed. We got the pride of the campus on board. Brave girl that she is. Lovely lady. Not bad, eh? As if reading Leonard's thoughts, Harvey winked. And stood up.

"Anyone else?" Harvey shouted, "Anyone else for a romantic tour? An exotic trip around our beloved seat of higher learning?" A second campus cutie extended her hand. "The ride of a lifetime!" Syd picked up the spiel, "and it's absolutely free. No charge!" Another girl clambered aboard. "Ride with us or regret it the rest of your days," continued Harvey. Another girl joined. Then another. And another.

"Better than any damm convertible," shouted a male student who strode alongside the wagon.

"Yeah, more airy," said another catching up.

"Cheap on fuel too. Just oats."

"How many oats to the mile?"

"I'm going to tell Daddy I want one of these for Christmas!"

"Jingle bells, jingle bells. Farting all the way."

"I'm with you guys!"

"Yeah. What a great idea!"

By the time the campus circuit was completed the wagon was so full, new arrivals both female and male had to be stopped from boarding. A horde of students herded alongside. More filed in behind the wagon.

A marching cavalcade of high-spirited youngsters. Bantering. Joking. Laughing. Singing. Rejoicing in a mini-rebellion against the Cadillac culture.

The Fairdel, the wagon, its many passengers, eventually made a triumphant exit from the campus. The crowd waved farewell. The last sounds in Leonard's ears were applause. And cheers.

Stan and Dusty McAllister became quite serious. It was thought they would marry. But parents intervened. It was deemed their backgrounds were too dissimilar. And the two of them, with much reluctance and a lot of tears, eventually agreed.

Harvey, Syd, and Leonard made a number of new friends. Many of them, pretty girls. The story of the ride spread throughout the University. And the four lads enjoyed it while it lasted. Celebrities. Flavours of the month.

There was talk that the voyage of Kurtz's horse was to be remembered as an annual event. On October 18th. Every year.

And six years later a group of students did repeat the trip. With a much more docile horse. And that wagon was gaily bedecked in all sorts of colours. Not quite the same.

Will it ever happen again? Probably not. Where would one get a horse and wagon? Not from Kensington Market. The last horse and wagon clip-clopped out of Baldwin Street a long time ago.

PAW

When he was fifteen, Paw found his father binding phylacteries around his arm in a small room—a cupboard, really—in a small house deep in Russia. Until that moment Paw did not know he was Jewish. My grandfather was in the army. What rank is a bit uncertain. Some—cousins—say he was a corporal. Some—other cousins—say he was a lieutenant. Or maybe even a captain. Since he was a bookkeeper in the Imperial Army, it's more likely he was a corporal. I am inclined towards believing he was a corporal.

The family, because grandfather was in the army, was allowed to live in Veronezh. On the banks of the Volga. Where no Jews could live. Jews in Russia could only live in designated towns and villages. Shtetls. Confined to themselves. Or in the ghettoes of some bigger cities. Still confined. Restricted. Limited to a life among one's own kind. One of the conditions for allowing Grandpaw and family to live in Veronezh was that he did not practice Judaism. He agreed. Maybe he tried to stick to that agreement—he seems to have been a most honourable man—and maybe he didn't. Again, on this matter, the family lore is not clear. But of course he could not escape his own heritage, his own indoctrination, and did uphold the religion. Secretly. Without involving his children.

My father's coming across his father at prayer with these strange black ribbons on his arm, a black box on his forehead, an

Arabic shawl on his shoulders, and a skull cap on his head, had a profound effect. As one would expect.

Paw became a communist. He often quoted a line, originally Bernard Shaw's, he thought, "Any man who is not a Communist before he is twenty-five has no heart. Any man who stays a communist after twenty-five has no head." At the age of sixteen he was caught distributing communist literature on the streets of the city. The old boy network didn't want the son of an army man—corporal or otherwise—to get into trouble. The night before his arrest he was smuggled down to Odessa. And put on the only ship in the harbour. A merchant ship. British.

For the next two years he sailed around the world. Twice. And discovered his ability with languages. He also discovered he had an ability with currencies. Sailors would want money changed before the next port of call. Roubles to sterling to marks to francs. He obliged. And charged a small percentage. Had he kept it up American Express might today be known as Abelson Express. "Jews are good with money," he would say to me. "Ask any anti-Semite." Then he would roar at this joke. "Remember it isn't true. There are more poor Jews than rich Jews in the world." The exchange business went kaput after two of his fellow sailors, masked, came into his cabin one night, beat him, and took his money. All the currencies.

Paw was a big man. Taller, before age shrinkage began, than I would ever be. And twice as broad across the shoulder. But he didn't pursue his two robbers. Just shrugged. And moved on.

His career as a sailor came to an end with a shipwreck. Off the coast of Malta. The ship ran aground. A crew of thirty-seven on board. Only fourteen survived. Most of the crew couldn't swim. My father could swim. Paw was in cold waters throughout a long winter night. Only one other crew member was Jewish. He was awakened in hospital by Herschel, the other Jew, in the next bed, "Wake up, Sam. Wake up. Yawa doesn't want us yet."

It seems incredible to me that a man with such luck, such fortitude, such a good head for business, did not achieve much success in life. In the late twenties, for example, he opened a record shop. A huge store. Stacks of records from floor to ceiling. He was the original Sam the Record Man. But then he was told that radio—all the best songs played free—was certain to kill the record business. He panicked. Sold out for a pittance. Went into ladies dresses. Then a delicatessen-café. Then a candy store. So it went on. And on. When I learned that George Gershwin's family, when he was a child, also moved from store to store, I was much consoled. Not that there was a George or an Ira in our family. But like the Gershwins we did not live long in one place.

A few months here above one shop. A few months above another shop. Move in. Go broke. But look here's another store. Good location. The store has been empty a long time and the landlord is keen for it to be occupied. First month's rent free. Wait, no. He wants a deposit. Ten dollars. Devil, *mamzer*. Raise ten dollars. How? By going to the Society Shirt Company. Two dozen shirts. One dozen white. One dozen blue. All sizes. Pay you next week, Mr. Schwartz, okay? Thank you, you're a good man. I thank you. My family thanks you. Then Paw stands outside the gates of General Steel works. Or Frigidaire. Waiting for the factory workers to leave. The shirts sold at half the price of Eaton's. Here's your ten dollars. Given credit. Opening another store. Always a store or a stall or a stand to be let on Baldwin Street. And so Paw lurched from one bankruptcy to another. Sometimes bringing it on himself by mismanagement. Sometimes bringing it on himself as a form of self-punishment. But usually by becoming bored. And careless. And lazy. And unlucky.

When he was in the merchant navy he was encouraged by the captain of the ship to box. A sport he did not enjoy much. His physical aggressiveness was minimal. Boxing one day, he clinched, and noted there was something familiar about the smell of his opponent. He remembered. It was the odour of one of the men who had robbed him of his money. The captain, who always appointed himself as referee, for the first time had to intervene in a fight involving my father. The fight was stopped. The opponent had taken too much punishment.

Paw always enjoyed telling me that postscript to his naval experiences.

MISMATCH

It was no match. They were going to fight and it was no match.

"Here, hold my jacket," said the bigger boy. He was tall, well over six feet; his hair was dusty blonde, a thickly built lad with the sort of good looks approved of in Coca-Cola ads. One of his friends eagerly pushed forward to take the jacket.

The boy he was to fight was smaller, a head or more shorter. Round shouldered. A weasel. Skinny. With black hair. A dark topping to a dark complexion. With a sickly aura underneath his pallor so that he managed to appear at the same time both musty and pale. No advertisement for any Cola company was he.

The bigger boy rolled his sleeves up slowly, slowly, smiling with confidence. The smaller boy shuffled out of his top coat. He had no friends to take it from him. He was alone. And as he pulled his shirt sleeves up beyond his elbows a shiver rattled his lean frame. The fair haired boy saw the shiver. And smiled more.

Mismatch. Uneven. Not a fair fight. Uneven. Stop them.

———

Leonard Abelson was ten years old. A day in early spring. The street was closed. No shoppers. No shopkeepers. No aproned man or woman standing before stalls and stores urging passers-by to buy their goods. No shouts from the tomato seller:

> Taste 'em and try 'em,
> Before you buy 'em.

Nor the appeal of:

> A nickel a pickle,
> A nickel a *shtickle*.

From the dill man. Or:

> Sugar bags, y' wan' 'em
> With letters or without letters, lady?
> Sugar bags for the sweet.

No noise of cars hooting. No noise of trucks delivering. No voices raised in anger, no voices raised in laughter. Silenced. Gone away. Not here. Not today. Here the day was still. A holiday. Passover. Fruit stands jutting onto pavement were covered with heavy tarpaulins held in place by nailed wooden struts. Outside other stores—dry goods, chicken dealers, spice and beans merchants, fish shops, chicken dealers, grocers—empty wooden stalls stood barren, lining the sidewalk, waiting for the holiday to end. No customers on the street. Shops closed. A rare day.

Passover is a joyous holiday. Like Christmas. A joyful holiday. A holiday that celebrates something. Not perhaps the birth of a child and new beginnings. But joyful because it honours an escape. From tyranny. To freedom. A joyous time. It does not commemorate a death. Or ask for an atonement of sins. Or the relinquishing of pleasures. Or self-inflicted suffering. No. A joyous time. And the joy conveys itself. Especially to children. Even though Leonard Abelson's father had communicated none of the holiday's religious significance to his children. What happened in North Africa four thousand years ago was of little significance to a supposedly free-thinking man like Sam Abelson. Just another day, he insisted. Best ignored. And he did. Except for the joke. Sam Abelson told a joke. The same joke. Every year. Moses has just parted the Red Sea so that the multitude of thousands could pass through the stormy waters harmlessly to freedom. But one Israelite looks down at his shoes and says to Moses, "Bit muddy, isn't it?"

Games with marbles and alleys were favoured by children in those days. But marbles had the taint of the rest of the year on them. And were forbidden during Passover. Not allowed into the house. Put aside until after the eight days of holiday. Something new was demanded, something fresh, something clean. Hazel nuts made a splendid substitute.

Norman and Izzie Katz, whose father was a fishmonger— Leonard was always intrigued that Katz sold fish—were playing nearest-the-wall with Leonard. Five go's each. Nearest wins. But you could knock the other guy's nut aside or hit your own farther forward. A simplified form of bowls or curling. There were other more complicated games involving holes in the ground, but Izzie wasn't old enough for such sophistry. Norman was losing. When Mrs. Katz appeared to call her sons in. "Aw, Maw—" protested Norman, "can't I just—" "No," said Mrs. Katz firmly. Arguing with parents was not practised on Baldwin Street at that time. Her two sons followed Mrs. Katz indoors.

Leonard was jamming his nut-winnings into bulging pockets when he first heard the youths approach.

Strolling. Sauntering. Parading holiday clothes. Laughing loudly and talking loudly and swarming loudly as teenagers do. To Leonard they appeared the height of sophistication. They were five to six years older. The leader of the gang was the tall blonde boy. Brown shoes gleaming with newness, fawn slacks, beige sweater, a tasteful suggestion of plaid in a contrasting jacket, his clothes reflected his handsomeness.

On the same side of the road as Leonard, opposite the gang, was the dark little fighter. He had apparently been following the roisterers for some time. Wanting to join them. Be a part of them. He seemed to know a number of them by name. But the gang declined.

They wanted nothing to do with him. So the small dark boy taunted, jeered, and pestered the gang.

The blonde leader appeared determined not to let the dark weasel join his select group. He told the small boy to go away or he would make him go away. "Then make me go away," the dark boy had said. And that was when they squared up to fight.

A flutter of fists as they charged at each other.

When they separated the dark boy's nose gushed torrents of blood. Knuckle marks were imprinted on his cheeks. The tall boy's gang cheered. It was what they expected. And so they cheered. They had not seen in the exchange that the small boy had jammed clenched fists up to the top of his tall opponent's rib cage. No. That went unseen. But then none of the members of the gang lived on Baldwin Street. Leonard did. This fight would end differently than any of those strangers—strangers who lived as much as two or three blocks away, strangers to fighting, strangers to blood—could predict. What did they know about fighting? Leonard knew. Leonard knew about fighting.

It was no match. Leonard wasn't yet ten years old and could see it wasn't to be a fair fight. Leonard knew who was going to win.

⁕

On Baldwin Street one became expert on violence at an early age. Trucks blocking other trucks as deliveries were made to the street often led to words and words all too frequently escalated to brawls. Also such sights as Izzie Brodsky's crowbar swiping at a bullying truck driver's head, for making a racist remark, were fairly frequent. Or watching Mr. Glicksman—old and wizened and small— the chicken dealer, flatten a thieving customer without disturbing the yarmulke on his head or a hair of his chunky white beard. Leonard had also seen his father fight.

About five years earlier a man, somewhat drunk, had stopped in front of the Abelson store and fondled the cheek of Leonard's sister Ruth too much and too long. Sam Abelson told the man to stop. The man protested his innocence. And kept fondling Ruth. Refusing to stop. Leonard's father swung a massive blow. The man struck back. When a child sees his father hurt and hurting another, bleeding and causing bleeding, his seemingly massive frame so capable of love and laughter now lashing out in vicious hatred, the child screams. Leonard screamed.

That fight was no mismatch. The two protagonists, Leonard's father and the drunk, were about the same height and weight. And kept inflicting pain on each other. And could have done so for some time. Then Sam Abelson backed away and charged at his opponent, head lowered, like a bull—a tactic he had brought with him from Russia—and by jerking his head up at just the right moment, the full impact of his considerable weight caught the man under the chin. Leonard watched the drunkard's body arch backwards through the air until it landed smack on the pavement. And lay there. That fight was over. Leonard screamed and screamed and screamed.

So Leonard had no wish to see any more of this fight between the tall blonde boy and his ferrety dark opponent. Some fights are good. Some fights see fairness restored. Two slobs on Baldwin Street once confronted a devout man walking from prayers. Taunts. Insults. Gestures. Changed to pulling on the religious man's beard. Until Harvey Simon intervened. One massive blow and a lout fell down. The other ran away. Street justice. Quick. Fast. Orderly. The punishment fitting the crime. Good will prevails. All is well. Isn't that what happened when Hitler's fighter made those terrible slurs about Negroes? Didn't the Brown Bomber Joe Louis knock out Max Schmeling within seconds of the first round? Right will triumph. In the world as on Baldwin Street. Bet on it. But some fights, Leonard believed, are too upsetting to watch. This, between the dark runt and the lofty blonde, was sure to be one.

And Leonard knew who would win. He had to tell someone. An adult. But who?

Leonard went through the family shop, up the small run of steps to open the door that separated living quarters from business, into the kitchen. His mother was gossiping with her sister-in-law, Chana. Leonard tried to interrupt, to tell his mother about the fight outside. He was waved to stillness. Leonard's mother, Pearl Abelson, and his Auntie Chana, had a running war. Started when Pearl led her own mother and her sister Leya and her new sister-in-law Chana, out of Ukraine, illegally, over the border. With only packs on their backs, one night the four women were to steal through the woods to freedom. All but necessities were to be left behind. But Auntie Chana had a tin kettle. Shiny. Modern. New. Not a samovar. Old-fashioned things samovars. The kettle was life ahead. The samovar was life past. She refused to abandon the kettle. Carried separately. The lid rattled. The noise was heard by border guards. Shots. Running military feet. More shots. My mother— she was 17 at the time—flung the kettle into the air. The women watched as the metallic pot reflected searching lights. And a split-second later rifle bullets ponged holes into the kettle. And then ran. Free. To the next country. To the new world.

So it was not surprising the two women continued a war-like relationship. War. Armistice. Peace. War. Often Pearl and Chana did not speak to each other for days or weeks or months and it occasionally stretched into years. Silence was the weapon. Silence. Then, for no reason, armistice. War over. Words flowed again. When they did see each other there was a lot of catching up to do.

"Maw," Leonard tried again.

"Why don't you go outside and play?" she asked.

Leonard went upstairs. The living room was above the store. A large piece of free-standing polished brown furniture had pride of place. The radio. Leonard elbow-polished away a slight smudge on the glass above the name Marconi. Leonard loved that radio. The glittering wood. The dial under smoked glass. The source of so much pleasure. But now as he scoured the dial he could find nothing. Well, concert music, of course. Fiddles. Saccharine scrapings. Ugh. Or soaps. Oxydol presents. Or talk. Polysyllabic incomprehensible talk. Nothing. No Bing Crosby. No Benny Goodman.

Nothing. No Mozart, Tchaikovsky, Greig. No opera. Paw loved opera. No Caruso singing *Pagliacci*. Paw's favourite. Nothing. He picked up the *Daily Star*. The front page was worth only a glance. Killings and mayhem in Europe. Foreign. Adult. A world away. Nothing to do with Leonard and Leonard's world. He turned to the comics. And re-read *Li'l Abner* and *Katzenjammer Kids* and *Steve Canyon*. He searched for a book. In desperation settled for a school text. History. The story of Charles II. The divine right of kings. Anything was better than thinking of the fight outside. But escape was not possible.

When he came out into the street the leader, the tall good look-ing blonde boy was lying on his back in the gutter. He would never be a good looking boy again. His face was being kicked repeatedly into the curb. By his dark smaller opponent. A kick. Blood squelched. Another kick. Toe against cheek. Shoe against skin. Making the head impact into the concrete gutter wall. Squelch. Blood. Cheek hitting curb. Squelch. Skin breaking. More blood. Kick. Kick. Kick.

All the time the dark boy was kicking, he was crying. He seemed unable to stop kicking. Unable to stop crying. Tears and toe in constant motion.

"I'm not good enough for you," said the dark boy. Kick. "Eh? Eh?" Another kick. "Think yer smarter than me." Kick. "I hate you. I hate you." Kick. Kick.

Leonard looked around to see if he could see the tall boy's gang of friends. Scattered. Down the street. Round the corner. Running. Hiding. Glancing back. Whispering. Pointing. A distance away. Hiding again. Occasionally from a store front recess a head appears. Somebody must do something, one of them says, some-body must stop him. Yes, we must, we must. After a while one lad musters enough courage to hesitantly approach. A ferocious glare from the small dark boy is enough to convince this last of the brave to be off again.

The street became empty except for the boy being kicked. The boy kicking. And Leonard.

Leonard moved towards the two fighters. Slowly. His Adam's apple bobbed up and down rippling the skin on his neck. He swallowed repeatedly.

"Please," said Leonard. It was the only word he could get past a blocked throat. "Please." He came a little closer.

The dark boy looked at Leonard. Leonard did not move. A long moment. Frozen. The dark boy looking. Leonard being looked at. For a long time. Then the dark boy looked down. Weeping. Always weeping. He had stopped kicking.

Leonard ran into Bermant's Grocery & Fruit store and came out a few moments later with Mr. Bermant. With what little help Leonard could give, Mr. Bermant bundled the tall boy into the back of his delivery truck. And drove off towards Western Hospital. On Baldwin Street only outsiders called the police for help.

The dark small boy stood watching, waiting, until the panelled truck left. Then clumped weary feet, following the same direction. Stopped. Came back, picked up his jacket lying on the road, and was pushing an arm through a sleeve when he saw the jacket of his tall opponent abandoned on the sidewalk a short distance away. He moved to the jacket, hesitated, stood looking down at it for some time before he picked it up. After a while he brushed the jacket with vague strokes, fingers plucked at debris, until he painstakingly folded the garment over his arm. Then walked off again. Weeping. Still weeping. Always weeping.

Later that night there was a lot of talk about this strange fight. When Leonard's mother asked if he knew anything about it, he shrugged innocence. He was learning. Some people like fighting. Some people like watching a fight. Almost everybody enjoys talking about a fight.

Leonard felt he owed some sort of loyalty to the dark boy. Who had stopped kicking at his pleas. Leonard did not join the talk.

By the time Leonard saw either of the two fighters again Bermant's Grocery & Fruit store had sold more chickpeas than Mr. Glicksman had hairs in his beard. The Abelson family had left Baldwin Street. Leonard grew up, managed to get to university and somehow get a degree, went to live in New York and Los Angeles and a few places in between. But almost every time he went home, he visited Baldwin Street. Mr. Bermant was dead. Mrs. Bermant— a lady who had fascinated him as a toddler, because of the dark hairs on her upper lip, and was not of a generation to do anything about it—ran the store.

Leonard dropped in to say hello to her. A tall man was leaning against the counter. Talking volumes. Mrs. Bermant was behind the counter, listening carefully. Nodding. Agreeing. Or shaking her head. Disagreeing. But listening. Bermant's was a dark store. The main source of light was the large front window. Leonard couldn't see the man's face until he turned. Scar tissue puffed his face, particularly around the eyes, but he was still recognizable. The tall blond fighter.

A noise came from the shadows of the far corner of the store. Amid the rich, lusty, dusty, musty smells of bags of peppers and paprika, of dried mushrooms and dried maize, of lima beans and lentils, of barley and peas, was the other man. The dark fighter.

"I'll take these as well," said the little fighter coming out of the darkness to put down several packages on the counter. "How much do I owe you?"

Mrs. Bermant began to list figures on the back of a small brown bag.

"Let me pay," said the tall one.

"No. No. It's me. I pay," said the little one. "You paid last time."

"No, it's my turn," said the tall one, pulling dollars from his wallet.

"No. It's me. It's me." The little one restrained the dollars from emerging.

"Are you sure?"

"Yeah, I'm sure."

The tall one picked up the cardboard box filled with the groceries.

"Let me carry it," said the short one.

"No."

They headed for the door. And with a quick look and a nod back at Mrs. Bermant, left.

Mrs. Bermant looked at Leonard. And smiled. She was obviously unaware of the details of the Passover fight. Leonard saw no reason to tell her. He simply asked if she knew those two men.

"Been coming in here for the last few years," she said. "Don't know the names. Always together. Always arguing." Mrs. Bermant laughed. "Must be friends. Really good friends. They argue so much. Always arguing. But always together. Together. Always." A pause. "Funny about friends, isn't it?" said Mrs. Bermant.

LIVING ROOM

Yosef went to see the rabbi. "My wife's mother has moved in with us. And you know how small our cottage is. There's no room," said Yosef.

"You have a brother Meyer?" asked the rabbi, "and his wife and three children are homeless. Ask them to move in with you."

"Are you mad?" asked Yosef.

"Do as I say," ordered the rabbi.

A week later a complaining Yosef went again to see the rabbi. "Ask your Uncle Chiam and his wife to move in," commanded the rabbi. A week after that the rabbi told him, "Your sister Rachel, the widow, her father, her two sons, invite them to live in your house."

The following week, in tears, Yosef pleaded with the rabbi. So many people. So many families. Such chaos in the house. "Tell your brother Meyer and his family to leave," said the rabbi. Two days later the rabbi said, "Chiam and his wife are to go." Two days after that the rabbi said, "Say goodbye to Rachel and her family."

Yosef went to see the rabbi. "O rabbi, it's wonderful," said Yosef, "there's just my family and my wife's mother in the cottage now. And there's so much room!"

In our house at 178 Baldwin Street the conditions were not quite as crowded as Yosef's. But almost.

Store and kitchen were on the ground floor. Three rooms above. The largest of these, the living room, doubled as a bedroom.

In this room Paw and Maw slept on a pull-out sofa. Lorraine slept on two armchairs shoved together. Sandra, the youngest, slept either with Paw and Maw or on a rug on the floor. In the back bedroom, three beds were jammed. For Syd, Sol, and me. Ben slept either with one of us or else in the front room. On the floor. He was lucky. He got to choose.

What about the third bedroom? Surprise. The third bedroom had one bed and only one occupant. Who? My eldest sister, Ruth. Why? Why did my parents not take this room? Why give it to their eldest child? Why?

I don't know why.

A concession to the first born. A consideration for womanhood approaching. Perhaps. For whatever reason Ruth had a room of her own. Fortunately she was good looking. And married young. Bequeathing her bedroom to my parents. The additional space was a blessing.

Otherwise we would have to ask for advice from a rabbi.

THE VERYS

"She's small," he said. "Down there. She's small." He paused expecting sympathy or understanding or both. "And I'm big. Down there. I'm big."

He leaned across the corner of the kitchen table to get closer to Leonard. Under an ill-tended pencil moustache was a mouth with teeth both blackened and missing from which came a sweet-foul odour. Leonard felt fortunate he had finished his dinner.

Leonard was lingering over coffee, reading the *Star*, when he heard the tread of feet up the eight steps leading from the store. The uninvited guest plonked himself down on the chair nearest to Leonard. Sighed. Sighed again. Then started to tell Leonard in sincerest man to man fashion his problems.

He was very short, very thin and very ugly. His wife of two months was very tall, very fat, and also very ugly. Leonard had dubbed them, only to himself of course, as The Verys.

"A match made in heaven," Leonard's mother once said. Certainly they were a startling sight as they walked down Baldwin Street arm in arm. Arm in armpit would be more accurate, for in order to be linked to him, that is where her arm rested. She was almost twice as tall and certainly twice as wide as her man. "They'll be all right," added Pearl Abelson. "God loves lovers." She smiled. Looked at the twosome again. "Just shows, though, even God has a sense of humour."

Leonard did not like the role this little man was forcing him into that night. He did not want to be this man's confidante. Or medical advisor.

"Melvyn," Leonard put down the newspaper to address him directly, "there's not much I can do. Have you seen a doctor?"

The moustached face nodded. And added, "Sent us to a gyna—what's it called—gyna somethin'." Melvyn's diction was never clear. Nasal phunph sounds obliterated most of his vowels.

"Gynecologist," Leonard said. "And—"

"Nothin' wrong with her," he said. "That's all the man said. Nothin' wrong with her. That's no help. There is somethin' wrong." His face was pinched with misery. "So I come to you. Y'r from the street. Y'r a doctor . . ."

Leonard gestured a protest. "Well okay," he said, "a medical student." Another gesture from Leonard. "Well y'r an educated boy . . . man." His eyes pleaded. "Can y' help?"

Leonard had long ago given up trying to explain to neighbours that he was an arts student. Anyone going on to higher education, about to enter the grey forbidding buildings of the University of Toronto, had to be a fledgling doctor. Nothing else was comprehensible.

"There's a book called *Ideal Marriage*." Leonard wrote the title on a scrap of the newspaper. "Pricey. So go to the Reference Library on College Street. Read it first. Try that."

Melvyn stood up. His hunched shoulders slumped towards the door. "Thanks," he said. "I hurt her. Y'know, when we do it, did it. It hurts her. I don' wanna hurt her. So we don' do it anymore. Just two, three times. No more." He looked down at the bit of paper in his hand. "I hate her. I hate her for bein' small. But I don' wanna hurt her." He opened the door. "She's too small." He left.

In early autumn two years later Leonard was helping to unload a truck full of glass preserving jars—embossed glass, rubber rings, screw tin tops—when his mother, after chatting with neighbours, returned to the store with luminous eyes. Pearl Abelson rejoiced in life. And loved any and all talk of life which others belittle by calling gossip. When, as in this instance, she had news to convey, the excitement bubbled over into dark flashing eyes.

"Have you heard," she said to Leonard. "Goldie Rabinowitz is goin' to have a baby."

"What?" Goldie was Mrs. Very.

"Yes. Melvyn and Goldie are going to have a baby." Mrs. Abelson laughed. "I told you it would be okay."

A few days later Leonard was passing the Crescent Grill on Spadina Avenue. Through the glass-fronted window Melvyn could be seen sitting on a stool at the counter. What was said could not be heard but gestures showed he was declaiming grandly to those around him. And, surprisingly, the others appeared to be listening.

"Mazel tov." The seat alongside Melvyn was vacated for Leonard.

"Hey, doc!" said Melvyn. "How 'r ya? Whad'll y'have?"

Salami and eggs. A dish fit for kings. Others may yearn for steak en croute from Tour D'Argent in Paris. Close. But definitely second, in Leonard's opinion, to salami and eggs made by the Crescent Grill. Beef garlic salami, not too thick, not too thin, fried to light gold on one side, turned, goldened again, over which milky eggs were poured. The mixture of milk and meat—forbidden at home, not kosher—only adding to its zestfulness. Salami and eggs. While waiting for a plateful to arrive, Leonard glanced at the man beside him.

He appeared taller. And not nearly so thin. But certainly as ugly as ever.

"What happened? Did you read that book?" Leonard asked.

"Me? Read a book?" His laugh revealed more blackened teeth. "Y'gotta be kiddin'."

Leonard waited.

"C'mon, let's get a booth," said Melvyn.

They headed towards the supposed privacy of an open booth.

"Hey Moishe, how's Bella? That's good. Hey Georgie, I like the suit. Where'd'ya get it? Tip Top Tailors? Only kiddin', Georgie, only kiddin'." Melvyn spoke to other diners like royalty dispensing comments.

The two of them slid into plastic seats. Melvyn immediately started playing with the salt shaker, the pepper shaker, the mustard dispenser, the ketchup bottle, and the metal stand holding paper napkins.

"Started at the Bellevue. Y'know, the moo'm pictcher place on College Street. Nice pictcher. With that Gregory Peck. Is he Jewish? I think he's Jewish. And Katharine Hepburn. Takes place in Rome. Looks nice. Rome, I mean. No, not Katharine Hepburn. Audrey Hepburn. Nice filim. You seen it? Sad ending though. They split. Sad. So my Goldie starts to cry. I don' like to see her cry. I'm laughin' at her. Then it changes. Before y'know it, I start to cry. We leave the Bellevue cryin'. Both o' us.

"I need a hankie. An' all she's got is this itty-bitty square. Purple edges, flowers in the middle, but small. One good honk and it's gone. But I use it. She needs it. Pulls it out o' my hand. I pull it back. Can y'believe this? We stand there, by the door, under the lights of the movie house, pullin' on a hankie. And then we start. Shoutin'. Screamin' at each other. I was gonna hit her. I raised my hand like this to hit her. Know what she said? 'You hit me you little pisspot and I'll fart and blow you away'." He paused. The pepper banged against the salt. "That killed me. That killed me. Callin' me that. Imagine callin' me that!"

He waited for Leonard to speak.

"Well, yes," said Leonard, "it's not nice being called pissp—"

"Who cares about that?" he shouted. "Little. She called me little." His eyes widened. "I am not little!"

"Of course not," said Leonard.

"Just below average height," he said. "Y'can checks the records." He stopped fidgeting the condiments about the table.

"Of course," Leonard agreed.

"Statistics prove it. I'm not short." Salt, pepper, mustard, ketchup, napkins, were returned to their places. "And I can take care of myself. I can. Not afraid of any man. No matter who."

"Of course."

Leonard's food arrived. Fortunately for him the French fries were separate. Melvyn leaned over to take two hot fries which he juggled from hand to hand. Then reached for the ketchup bottle. Leonard watched.

"Y'like ketchup?" Melvyn asked.

"No," said Leonard.

"Sorry."

It was too late. The fries were covered with large dollops. "Sorry," he said again as his fingers began to probe for unreddened specimens at the bottom of the bowl.

"Forget it," Leonard said, "you have the fries."

"Sure?"

"Yes. Sure. What happened then?"

"I went home. Got my case from the clothes closet. Started to pack. Pack? Well, y'know, throw things in. Socks, underwear, shirts, ties, sweaters, y'know, all them things. When she comes in. I'm mad. An' when I get mad I'm mad. Mad. Don' wanna see her. Don' wanna talk to her. Don' wan nothin' from her. 'Watcha doin'?' she says. I say nothin'. Just keep puttin' clothes in. I go for another load. She grabs my arm. 'Please, Mel' she says, 'Don' go. Don' go. Please.' I throws the clothes down. 'Should'a done this long ago,' I says, 'Y'r not for me. Look at ya. A big, fat, lump.' Tears in her eyes. Humendous tears. 'That's what y'are,' I says. 'How'd I get stuck with you? Ya big fat lump.' She collapses on the bed. 'I'm not big. Fat, maybe. Some. Not much. But I'm not big.'"

"'You called me little,' I says. 'Y'r my wife and ya called me little. If I'm little to my wife than I'm nothin' out there.'"

"'You called me big,' she says. 'Big and fat is what you called me.'"

"'You started it,' I says, 'you said it first.'"

"She bites her lip. 'I know. I'm sorry,' she says."

"I'm un'ner the bed. Lookin' for shoes."

"'Mel, why am I so big? People laugh at me. 'Cause I'm so big. People laugh at me. They do. An' they laugh at us.'"

"'I don' care about people,' I says. 'I care about us. What matters is that we don' laugh at us.'

"She un'erstan's. She shakes her head. An then says, 'I don' laugh at you, Mel'.

"'An' I don' laugh at you, Goldie'.

"She falls back on the bed. Bawlin' her eyes out. Lookin' soft. Lookin' sad. Lookin' afraid. An' meanwhile her dress is ridin' up. Above her knees. Crumpled dress. An' I can see the top o' her stockin's. Skin. White skin. An'—An' I'm thinkin'—well, I'm a man, an'—well, ya know what I was thinkin." His voice clogged.

"I then sits on 'a bed. What a situation, eh? She's bawlin'. Here's this woman. My wife. I can't do it with her. I can't touch her. I hate her. At least I think I hate her. Do I? I dunno what I know. How did this happen to me?

"Then she says, 'Mel, am I big to you?'

"'No,' I says.

"'But I am big,' she says.

"Now I say nothin'. She's lyin' there, cryin'. I'm sittin' there, thinkin'. Not speakin'. Just thinkin'. Finally, she speaks.

"'Mel, I wish I weren't so big,' she says.

"'An' I wish I weren't so little.'

"A flood comes out of her eyes. I can't take any more. I go out. Slam the door. I can hear her scream 'Mel, Mellie, don' leave me.' She thinks that's it, I'm leavin'. But I'm not.

"I'm back in five minutes. Only went round the corner. To Halperns. As I come up the stairs, I can hear the bed shakin' from her cryin'.

"'Here,' I says to her. She looks up. I shove a box of Kleenex at her. She's fightin' for breath. Sobbin'. An' between sobs breaks open the box. Honks away.

"An' me, well, maybe the walk to Halperns did me good. An' the walk back. 'While I was at the drugstore I got ya this too,' I says to her. Her mouth widens. Her jaw drops. 'A box o' chocolates!' she says. 'For me? Oh Mel.' I sit down beside her, on the bed. 'I won't eat them,' she says, 'make me fat. I won't eat 'em. Not even the hard ones. But I'll keep that box. Forever. Forever an' ever.' That's what she said. I lay down next to her.

"Well, what can I tell ya? No. Not that night. We cuddled that night. That's all. Cuddled. An' talked. Cried some more. An' laughed. That's all. That night.

"The next night. Cuddlin' again. Then the cuddlin' turned to playin'. An' the playin' turned to— The next night we did it." He wiped ketchup from his mouth. "I didn't hurt her."

He stopped. Leonard signalled to the waitress behind the bar for two coffees.

"After, I'm in the karzee, lookin' in the mirror, combin' my hair, when she comes up behind me. Puts her arms round me, starts kissin' the back o' my neck. 'Y'r my Mel,' she says. 'Y'r my big man.' I turns to her. 'An' y're my baby,' I says. 'Am I? Am I, Mel?' she says. I says, 'Sure. My baby. I love ya. Y'r my little girl.'"

The coffees arrived.

"That's what she is, y'know. She's jus' a little girl." He measured three over-flowing spoons of sugar into his coffee. "Ever since, doin' it, don't hurt."

As he drank his coffee, he looked up over Leonard's head. His eyes widened in pleasant anticipation.

"Hey, honey, what ya doin' here?" he asked. "Said I'd meet ya on the corner."

Leonard became aware of a mountain of femininity nearby. Goldie was at his elbow.

"Mrs.. Rabinowitz," said Leonard. "Congratulations. The baby. Congratulations."

Her face was a traffic light changing from yellow to red. "Thank you," she said coyly lowering her flushed face. "Thank you very much."

"Y'know the doc, don't ya?" Melvyn nodded towards Leonard.

"Sure," she said. "Hiya." Her smile and attention quickly returned to her husband. "Looked in. Saw you guys talking. Why don't we eat here?"

She was about to slide into the seat beside Leonard. A line from "filims" came into Leonard's head. This booth ain't big enough for both of us.

"No," said Melvyn firmly. "I told ya, the Mars okay, the Homestead okay, but not here, not the Crescent Grill. It's not for girls."

The clientele was, as usual, predominantly men.

Their exit towards the front door was noted by most of the other patrons. Melvyn again exchanged banter with almost every-one. "Hey, Lou, how goes it? She let ya out, did she? Marvin, fried chicken? With your stomach? Stick to noodle soup." Goldie said nothing. But held him so tightly he was in danger of being lifted off his feet.

At the door Melvyn loosened himself from her grip. Came back to Leonard, feeling the need for a final comment, slapped Leonard's shoulder. "One day soon, doc," said Melvyn, "you gotta find yourself some little woman."

HUNGER

Hunger is a monster. The head is in the centre. A round, fierce, angry, and bearded head. Lion-like and humanoid at the same time. Demented. A warlock. Snarling. The head is always snarling. Teeth snapping. Always snapping. Biting. Long teeth in a large jaw set below eyes glowing with hate.

From the head four arms extend. Nothing more. No body. Just four outstretched arms. At the end of each arm is a hand, a claw, with ten fingers, digits with curled razor-nails.

When the monster is roused the teeth bite and the nails pierce the inside of your stomach. Hurting. Hurting. Hurting.

I know. I know the monster. Rejoice if you do not.

THE BANANA MAN

Mike Manzi sold bananas. That's all. Nothing else. Bananas.

On the window was written MANZI BANANAS WHOLESALE & RETAIL. And inside the window hung three bunches of the fruit. Always. A store filled with bananas. Always. Some green. Some golden. Flecked fruit was always sold first. Or garbaged. The store was meticulously clean. Never a fruit fly in sight. No mean achievement with bananas.

Nobody else sold bananas. Only Manzi. In the entire market he was the only one to sell bananas. Considering the cut-throat nature of fruit and vegetable dealers—a wily customer could move from one stall to another, pitching prices ever downwards until he got a remarkably low price—it was amazing that no one else competed with Manzi. A sort of unwritten gentleman's code. Bananas meant Manzi. No one else. He and his quiet wife and an indeterminate number of children, mostly girls, were allowed to live and work in peace. Selling bananas.

Another unusual thing about Mike Manzi was that he was a Catholic. Every other storekeeper in the market was Jewish. Or some degree thereof. But not Mike. His religious difference never showed. Except on Sundays.

Other storekeepers slept late on Sunday. Or went to steam baths. Or sat on tarpaulin-covered stands playing pinochle. Or, in good weather, picnicked in High Park. But not Mike. Mike went to church.

Returning from church he would shake his head, weary with worldliness, as he passed Lottman's Imperial Bakery. Contingents of police cars would arrive at the bakery's corner shop to collect petty bribes. Cake. Cookies. Bread. For allowing the bakery to sell its wares on a Sunday. The Lord's Day Act. Contravened. With the inhabitants of Baldwin Street and the uniformed men in blue all turning a blind eye.

Mike's thoughts on religion were none too clear. He had left the village of Vettica just south of Positano just south of Naples in Italy in the 1920s with his wife, Rafaela, and his first child Angelina. And prayed. For a new beginning. For a new life. In his adopted country. His prayers were heard. And answered.

Mike had learned, vowel by vowel, three words in English. Yes. No. Okay. And, less than twenty-four hours after his arrival in Toronto, he was pronouncing the words out loud as he walked on Yonge Street, when two large men in dark suits passed him by. Talking Italian. The language of the angels! The answer to his prayers! Being a shy man he dared not approach the strangers directly. He followed them. For block after block. Hovering behind as they waited for lights to change from red to green. Pretending to look in shop windows when the two looked back at traffic. Eventually the two strangers became aware of his presence. Turned to confront him. Angrily. Menacingly. Who was this young man skulking behind them? They glared at him. Closed in. One on either side of him. "What do you want?" said one of the twosome. Mike thought for a moment. "Yes. No. Okay," he volunteered. The two men frowned. Puzzled. "*Patso*," agreed the men. Crazy. And started to turn away. "*Si. Es possible io sono patso*," said Mike, "*mas io sono anche Italiano.*" It is possible that I am crazy, but I am also Italian.

Finding a coffee shop in Toronto at that time was difficult. A café called the Honey Dew was the compromise. Gallons of the brown liquid which bore no resemblance to what the trio considered to be coffee were swilled. Mike told his story. Of how he had emigrated in search of a new life. The two men listened. We, said the two men, are in business. Importers. Of goods from the Caribbean. Bananas.

The Manzi banana store was created that afternoon. Mike, whose father farmed tomatoes and so was well aware of the quick-spoiling nature of fruit, insisted that the store have a retail sales ability as well as wholesale, an outlet for the small proportion of bananas that would ripen sooner than anticipated. A shop, in a street market, like we have at home, like in Europe, that's what I would want, said Mike. That kind of street market is rare in North America, said the two men. But there is one. Kensington Market. Close to Baldwin Street. *Ebreos*, said the two men, Jews.

Mike knew little about Jews. Followers of that faith were not common in Vettica. He had no personal knowledge. Never seen one, he told himself. The opinions of the Popes, he knew, varied from approbation to condemnation. And he himself found it hard to understand a sect who did not believe Jesus Christ to be the son of God.

But he settled quietly into a store in the market. Got on with his neighbours. A smile. A nod. Wordless. If a need arose to communicate more subtly than facial expressions allowed, French was soon discovered to be known to a select few. And he and his neighbours shared a common goal. To learn the new language. English. The fact that he intended to sell only bananas, made him eccentric. And different. And likeable. Especially to those who feared he would be yet another competitor in fruit. It was doubted by many that a living could be made by selling bananas exclusively. But not by Mike. And he was right. The business flourished.

Years on the farm had conditioned Mike to awaken as the first slants of daylight patterned themselves on the bedroom ceiling. As he did one day after living in the market a few months. He dressed, trying not to wake his wife who was pregnant with a second child. Downstairs he was preparing a bowl of *cafe con leche*, when he felt the strangeness of the day. He stopped. To listen. Quiet. It was too quiet. Usually by this time in the morning, particularly a sunny morning as this, isolated noises of the market day's beginning were to be heard. A fruit stand's tarpaulin being hauled back. A hammer straightening nails. Mothers from the shops' families rushing to Perlmutter's bakery for fresh Kaiser Rolls. To feed children before the start of school. To feed fathers before the arrival of the first customers. Banter. Talk. Voices. Always heard at this hour. But not this day.

Mike went outside. Mr. Kurtz's horse, The Fairdel, always in position ready to be loaded with the day's deliveries, was nowhere to be seen. In fact, not one horse was on the street. Nor a wagon. Nor a truck. Not even a car. The street was empty. Deserted. The canvass-covered fruit stalls were firmly closed by slats of nailed wood. The dry goods stores' fronts were bare. Each stout store door was firmly shut. Like a Sunday. But stiller than Sundays. Because the bakers were not working. The bakeries, including Lottman's, had no lights on. No delicate displays of cookies and cakes in the window to lure passing customers. The suspended glass shelves in the window were bare. The street was clean. Each storekeeper had gone to some trouble to clean the area in front of his premises. Pavements had been swept. Even the curbs were free of debris. The flimsy papers that individually wrapped Florida oranges were not fluttering about. Broken bushels, broken baskets, made of skimpy wood, did not litter the street. Empty. Barren. Clean. And no one in sight.

Cleats clopped on the pavement. Round the corner came the man Mike knew to be the ritual slaughterer of chickens. He was called the *shoykhet*. A rotund little man. On his head, a continual fixture was a skull cap, a rising bump in his hairline. Thick eyeglasses sat on his nose. The *shoykhet* started each working day with a full length white apron. The few mornings Mike had previously seen the slaughterer—white clothing, thick lenses, skull cap—he appeared to Mike to be some squashed version of Pope Pius XII. Of course as his day's occupational activities increased, the slaughterer's apron became redder and redder. But not today. Today he wore no apron. His suit was pressed, neat, immaculate. On his head a black fedora replaced the skull cap.

"*Scusati.* Excuse me," Mike had to face the little man to halt his rapid walking. "Where is people? Where is customers?"

The *shoykhet*'s manner was abrupt. "It is Yom Kippur," he said and tried to move on.

"What?" asked Mike, stopping him again.

The little man raised his spectacles to peer at Mike. "You're not Jewish."

"No," said Mike, "Italiano."

"Yom Kippur. The Day of Atonement. For our sins. A day of fasting. No eating. No drinking. Today we ask Him to forgive us. The holiest day of the year," said the slaughterer. He replaced his glasses. Began scratching a thick white beard. "Of course, strictly speaking that's not true. At least it could be argued it's not true. The holiest day is the Sabbath. Saturday. Holier than any holiday. In the twelfth-century Rabbi Moshe ben Maimonides said that the Sabbath— Aach! Why am I wasting time talking to you. I'll be late. The *shammes* (verger/sexton) is waiting for me. At the synagogue." He hurried away.

"But the stores," Mike shouted after him.

"No stores will be open today," the *shoykhet* shouted back. "It's Yom Kippur." With that the *shoykhet* was gone.

And so it came to pass. Not one shop in the market opened that September morning. Out of deference to his new neighbours, Mike kept the banana store closed that day.

But he marvelled at what he saw. These people, who to Mike were nothing more than acceptable infidels, but infidels nevertheless, showed enough religious fervour to observe a holy day. Surprising, thought Mike. Most of his fellow shopkeepers were not temple-goers, he knew, and paid a minimal secular lip-service to God. Most of them were also impoverished and could ill-afford to lose a day's profits. But still the shops stayed shut.

In the many years that followed, in the many subsequent autumns, Mike never lost his amazement at how faithfully Yom Kippur was observed. All the more surprising since he also witnessed the erosion of Saturday's religiosity. When he first arrived on Baldwin Street none of the stores opened until dusk on Saturday. The Sabbath day. The fourth commandment. Keep it holy. Violation would have led to condemnation by older shoppers. Simple enough in winter when short days still meant a full evening's trade. But in spring, the longer days, shortened nights, were too tempting. And the elders, the head-scarved ladies and white-bearded men, were diminishing. A shop or two opened an hour or two before sunset one Saturday. Then mid-afternoon. Then lunchtime. Within twenty years, Saturday became as else-where the busiest shopping day of the week with stores opening at dawn. The streets crowded with customers. Just another day. A business day.

But not Yom Kippur.

Mike Manzi's hair turned from blackest black to speckled grey to white to whitest white. He was a father, a grandfather a great-grandfather when he became ill.

"Tell your papa I want to see him," Mike told Leonard Abelson who had come into the store for a few breakfast bananas.

"Paw's away, in New York," said Leonard. It was a rare occasion. Sam Abelson had taken a few days off to see other members of his family.

"No rush," said Mike, "but tell him to come. Soon."

His father had been back in the house a matter of minutes when Leonard told him. "Mr. Manzi wants to see you," said Leonard, "and Paw, he doesn't look so good," said Leonard. Sam Abelson nodded. "Mike doesn't ask many favours. Something's up," said Sam, "C'mon Lennie, let's see what it is."

In the crowded main Manzi bedroom, Mike waved a greeting.

"Si' down, Sam," said Mike, "wanna talk to you." A chair was vacated. Leonard stood in the background.

The two men, Sam Abelson and Mike Manzi, had had many a conversation in the past. Now, amid the forced raised voices and forced bonhomie of deathbed chatter, surrounded by relatives and friends, Mike spoke softly. The room quietened. Abelson put his ear closer to Mike.

"Yom Kippur," said Mike Manzi hoarsely.

"Yes," said Abelson. "I have always wanted—we, other store-keepers and I—always wanted to thank you for Yom Kippur. You are not one of us. But you always closed your banana store as if you were. On Yom Kippur. You were like us. Thank you, Mike. I've been told to say thank you."

Mike was pleased. Smiled.

"Is there anything I can do for you, Mike?" asked Abelson.

Mike nodded.

Abelson was surprised. "What?" he said. "Name it. You got it. What?"

Mike waved Abelson's ear closer still. And whispered his request.

Sam Abelson stared at his dying friend. "Mike, I don't know if I can, it might be impossible," said Abelson.

"Try. Please," said Mike hoarsely, "for me."

"Impossible," Sam repeated quietly to himself. But to the dying man he smiled. And nodded.

Walking from the banana store to the Abelson store, Leonard asked his father, "Paw, what did he want?" Sam Abelson shook his head. "What he wants is impossible. Impossible. Impossible," Sam kept repeating. "But I gotta try." Father and son walked side by side silently.

Ten days later the funeral of Mike Manzi took place. The final request that he made on his deathbed to Sam Abelson had been organized and granted. It took some doing. A protest or two, considering the nature of his request, was expected. But in fact the number of protests was overwhelming. Almost every storekeeper objected. You crazy? Why should we do that? No. Not me. I'm not gonna. Dying man's request? So what. Who cares? I won't. Who does he think he is asking a thing like that? A goy! Why should a goy want that? No No. No. And that's final. But Sam Abelson persevered. Patiently. Quietly. Spoke to each storekeeper. Called meetings. Until it was agreed.

It was on a Tuesday when a hearse arrived to take the mortal remains of Mike Manzi from the living quarters above the banana store and drive through the surrounding streets.

Storekeepers stood on the pavements edge and watched the hearse pass by.

Every shop on Baldwin Street, every shop on Kensington Avenue, every shop in the entire market area, was closed. Shut. Stalls empty. Fruit displays covered. Doors locked. As if it was Yom

Kippur. As Mike Manzi had asked. His dying wish. Granted. By the storekeepers. A tribute. To Mike Manzi. To the banana man.

"It could have been worse," said Mr. Kurtz, the fruit man, watching the funeral procession.

"It' bad enough now," said Mr. Gelman, also a fruiterer, "how could it be worse?"

"The funeral could've been on a Saturday—" the truly busy day of the week "—that would be much worse," said Mr. Kurtz.

Mr. Gelman thought about this for a moment. "Shows you," he said, "what a nice man he was."

NAMES

Lottman and Liebermann. Gotlieb and Groskop. Shenderovich and
Menderovich. Rosenberg and Bloomberg. Pearl and Perlmutter.
Litovitz and Yackubowitz. What names. What names to be found
on Baldwin Street!

On awnings that capped the front of shop windows. Or emblazoned boldly on the window itself. Proudly proclaiming in large
gold letters what the store stood for. Daiter's Creamery. Never again
was the world to know such cream cheese as was prepared each
Thursday at Daiter's Creamery. Now, of course, a Toronto institu-
tion. But then only one small shop. Katz's sign was more artistic. A
drawing of a fish—carp, of course—leaping out of the water. And
the words KATZ'S FISH MARKET. WHOLESALE & RETAIL. Mr.
Jackson also sold fish. But his were smoked, soused, shmaltzed. Not
wet fish. And he sold pickles. Cucumbers. Sour and Half-Sour.
Large and deep-green, small and yellow-green. A nickel a pickle.
Only a nickel. For each and every pickle. A nickel. Five cents. And
he sold pickled tomatoes. And pickled peppers. And pickled watermelon. Yes, pickled watermelon.

Jackson. What's that? Is that his name? Jackson? Can't be.
Must've been somethin' else. He changed it. What's his real name?

Jackson. Jackson is his real name.

Really? And he seems like such a nice man. Like one of us.

The window of Glicksman the chicken dealer did not bear his name.

He was a religious man who believed God frowned on immodesty, so only the three Hebrew letters for Kosher were painted on the glass. Nothing else. Kosher. Clean, prepared according to dietary law, fit to be consumed. Kosher. Hence entering the English language as a synonym for right and proper and authentic.

Mr. Kurtz sold fruit and vegetables. He had no store front. But a stall in front of a verandah leading to his house. It was a throwback. A pre-historic relic of what all the buildings on the street must have been like before plate-glass shop fronts were added. But stall and verandah and every room in the Kurtz household including the bathroom were jammed with produce. While Mr. Kurtz's name did not appear in front of his business address, it did appear, as required by law, on the side of his wagon. In small print. Yes, he had a wagon, pulled by The Fairdel, one of two or three still be found on the street in those days. And it was not discretion that led Mr. Kurtz to give himself tiny billing. But commonsense. For he had assured himself that all traffic regulations in the middle of the twentieth century in the middle of Toronto could not be applied to a horse. For example, lights. How was a horse to know the colour red? Traffic laws were for multi-horsepower motors. Not for one horsepower carts. So he and his wagon would mount pavements at will. Park wherever he pleased. Drive the wrong direction down one-way streets. And was not often accosted by irate motorists. For the rotund little man that he was, when seen up close, Mr. Kurtz had a wild look in his eyes that was fearsome to behold. Only one thing more fearsome. The look in The Fairdel's eyes. No one ventured close enough to the wagon to read his name and send follow-up complaints.

Goodbaum and Mandelbaum and Birnbaum and Applebaum. The names of Baldwin Street. What names! Name to rejoice in. Names to celebrate. Goldberg and Hershberg and Bloomberg and Rosenberg. And just plain Berg. Altman, Lieberman, Grossman, Goldman; and a Goodman nowadays is hard to find.

Gelman, Simon, Levinson, Liebovitz, Brodsky, Sroka,

Starkman, Salem, Seiden. And more. Mel Lastman became Mayor of Toronto. Joe Berman founded Cadillac Fairview. Arthur Kruger was Dean of Arts and Sciences at the University of Toronto. Frank Gehry, architect, renowned worldwide. Baldwin Street boys. Alumni of the ghetto. As were countless other doctors, lawyers, accountants, film directors, television producers, writers, artists, artistes, boxers, business executives. And more.

First names were not far behind. The occasional Stanley or Alan were to be found. More often it was Yankel and Itzik. Shloymie and Mo. Voomie and Munis.

Names that rolled more readily off the Anglo-Saxon tongue came later. At school. Teachers. Miss Salter. Mr. Barton. Hollingsworth. Davidson. Alien names. Outsider names. Then in high school. Carlisle. Baker. Girdler. Hislop. Griffin. At work. O'Leary. Ryan. Macfarlane. Weatherup. Then socially. Meet Malcolm MacDonald. Do you know Sally Hughes? Have you met Ken Taylor?

And time brought changes. The Ostroffs became the Owens. Givertz became Givens. Shadlesky became Shadwell. Except for one of the Shadlesky brothers who steadfastly stuck to his name. Price had been Prutzky. Ralston was formerly Raffelovitch.

Since the names were themselves translations—from Russian, Polish, Ukrainian, Yiddish—there was no great loyalty to the original word. If life became easier, especially for the children, to be called Pollard rather than Polonski, then so be it.

Sometimes a considerate immigration officer effected the change before allowing entry into the new country. "Mr. Chackelenovsky from now on your name is changed." The newly named Mr. Shack would nod. Since he could not speak a word of English it made little difference.

Others made the changes willingly. Avrum Kissinger took legal steps to become Alan Kitson and as he left the courtroom is reputed to have said, I wonder who's Kissinger now?

Today the pendulum is swinging back. Ironic. People born Jones or Smith want, especially in the arts, a more exotic label. A man whose name ends in 'ov' or 'off' or 'ski', often has a birth certificate that reads something like Johnson. And the children of the offs and the skis and the Johnsons now spend hours on the web, checking family histories, deciphering, finding truths, about names.

Long names. Foreign names. Difficult names. In fashion one day, out the next. Change the name. Change it back. *Plus ça change*, so to speak.

Even Shakespeare, when introducing two characters in *Hamlet*, in order to make them noteworthy bestowed on them the out-landish names of Rosencrantz and Guildenstern.

And Shakespeare also wrote:

> What's in a name? That which we call a rose
> By any other name would smell as sweet.

But would a Rosencrantz by any other name be as memorable?

THE PERFECT LOVE

Six people sat in the darkened room. Silent. A courtroom. Without a judge. Without a jury. Without officials of any kind. But a courtroom nevertheless. Above Kleber's Dry Goods. Shoes & Slippers a Speciality.

Slits of sunlight from the curtained window were the only source of illumination.

In two kitchen chairs sat Rose's parents. Stiff, formal, bewildered by events. Her father wore his best suit. And tie. As if dressing for the occasion might soften any pain the day might bring. His wife matched him by wearing a party gown, complete with round blue-black straw hat. She clutched her purse fiercely with both hands. Rose sat in what passed for an easy chair.

Opposite, in an adversarial position, was the other family. Michael sat on an orange crate. From somewhere in the shoe shop below he had managed to find two more chairs for his parents. Who had also dressed as if for a formal arraignment, hoping at the very least to create a favourable impression on the couple facing them.

It had been decided not to have rabbinical intervention. The two lovers. The parents. No one else.

"Where do we start?" asked Michael.

If looks could kill. An expression. If looks could kill, then at that moment Rose's look would have killed Michael in the most tortuous fashion. Skinned. Castrated. Disembowelled. And forced him to eat the contents of his own stomach. Again. And again. And again. But Rose sat and said nothing.

"What happened? Micky, we don't know what happened?" said Rose's father.

Michael and Rose had met in his last year at Harbord Collegiate. A fellow member of the basketball squad, Donny Rosenberg, had introduced them after a game. A good game. For Harbord. They had won easily. Michael himself had scored three baskets. Elated, the team was whooping with excitement and just leaving the school gym when they ran into a gaggle of girls, supporters, who happened, by careful contrivance, to be passing at that moment.

Coffee and doughnuts were suggested by the guys. And accepted by the girls. "The Mars Bar on College Street, okay?" asked Donny. Okay. Okay. A celebration. With the rest of the gang. Nothing more. A few jokes. A few laughs. And goodbye. "Goodnight Rose. Nice to meet you." "Goodnight Michael. Likewise." A wave of hands. Goodnight. Nothing more. Not even a peck on the cheek.

That summer found them both at Camp Tamakwa as counsellors. The magic of the wilds. In July and August. By day, teaching children. By night, teaching each other. About each other. Learners. Apprentices in the art of love. Moonlight. Lakes. Canoeing. Canoodling. Petting. But not heavy petting, unlike some. Days off in Huntsville. To see a movie. To a restaurant. A summer romance. But this one not destined to fade in the fall. "I will love you forever," said Michael. Rose matched his pledge. "Likewise," she said. It was on an overnight trip to Little Bear Lake, sleeping bags side by side on ground sheets side by side on a mattress made of evergreen branches, that Rose and Michael vowed eternal love. And said they would marry. Not now. Soon. When Michael was a qualified lawyer. Not before. Rose invited him into her sleeping bag. The near-naked bodies brushed each other through the night. Kissing. Touching. Nothing more. In fact, in the subsequent seven years of intimacy shared by Rose and Michael, they never completed the sex act.

Once he touched her pubic hair. Once, in a moment of wild passion, she kissed his penis. But both agreed that consummation could wait. Until marriage. Better that way, said Rose. Better that way, agreed Michael.

Rose was from out-of-town. Guelph. As was Michael. Winnipeg. Without completing high school, Rose left Guelph to be nearer Michael. And found the cheapest possible accommodation with the Kurtz family. The room supposedly came with use of the kitchen. But since Mrs. Kurtz was ultra orthodox, Rose could not be in the kitchen without her landlady's hovering presence. Mrs. Kurtz hardly ever spoke. A silent presence. Frowning. Shaking her head from side to side. Condemning with continual tsk-tsking as Rose cooked. When a cloth went down on the table, Mrs. Kurtz would pick it up; put it back in its designated place. A knife on the sideboard would be whisked away. And rinsed. And heaven help Rose if she even glanced at the milk drawers when preparing a meat dish. Or vice versa. Rose was meticulous about leaving the kitchen pristine clean. But Mrs. Kurtz still spent ten minutes after each of Rose's departures cleaning what was already clean. Rose refused to be put down by this. She was cooking for her betrothed. For her love. For Michael.

At first Michael lived with his aunt on Brunswick Avenue. His father had died during one frozen Winnipeg winter, leaving three young children. To help her widowed sister, his aunt had agreed to house the eldest child, Michael, in Toronto for his last two years at high school. But when Michael talked of continuing his education, of going to University, of becoming a lawyer, the arrangement was obliged to end. His aunt needed the extra income she could get from renting his room. Besides she was not that fond of her nephew. His independent mind, freely expressed—"hanging a man who is a murderer makes us a murderer too," he once said at dinner—upset her husband. And her. She also felt him to be potentially a bad influence on her two much younger daughters. Michael left the house on Brunswick Avenue.

To Rose he said, we cannot live together, not now, not until we can live as one. I will find a place near you, said Michael. Rose agreed. It would be too tempting for their bodies to live under the same roof. Too tempting for tongues to tarnish reputations. Rose was determined to stand under the *chuppa*, the wedding canopy, unsullied in body and in name.

One day walking through the market Michael noted a store, one of the few, where the living quarters above the shop were not occupied. KLEBER'S DRY GOODS, said the window sign, SHOES & SLIPPERS A SPECIALTY. Mr. Kleber, a bachelor, lived with his sister on Dennison Avenue, but was initially reluctant to let the premises. It's cold, said Mr. Kleber, not much heat in winter, heat is bad for shoes. Michael pleaded. No kitchen, said Mr. Kleber, I ripped out the old kitchen, it's my storeroom now. Michael pleaded more. Kleber relented. He liked this clean-cut young man, whose openness towered above his own muddled life as his height did above his own short physique. And, Mr. Kleber reasoned, to have someone guarding the stock at night was not such a bad idea. Michael was allowed to move into the small back bedroom. For a nonsensically low fee. But of course to Michael it was a vast amount. His marks at school were not good enough to obtain a scholarship. Or even a bursary. He was only an average student. Not academically gifted. He earned a dollar when he could. Working at the Abelson store on Saturdays. Helping Mr. Kurtz with deliveries. With his first earnings Michael bought a two-ring electric burner. To make tea. To boil an egg. To heat a tin of Campbell's Soup. And on really cold nights to thaw Michael's hands, to unfreeze the ice on his ridiculously inadequate woollen gloves.

Michael went to university and got his degree. After three years. Then to Osgoode Hall to study law. Another three years. Then a year articling with a legal firm. After seven years he was finally in a position to earn minor amounts of money.

In all that time Rose prepared meals for Michael. Every night. She carried the precooked meals through the market streets, round the corner, to her man. Every night. In winter the plates—Rose's own plates, Mrs. Kurtz wouldn't allow dishes out of the house— were wrapped in an old sweater. To keep the potatoes warm. To keep the chops hot. On milder days Michael's minimal kitchen sufficed. A salad. A can of salmon. Bread. That's fine, sweetheart, that's plenty, said Michael. I'm glad, said Rose.

Shortly after arriving in Toronto, Rose got a job at Eaton's department store. Ladies underwear. To avoid the possibility of a problem, Rose lied. She hated doing it but felt she had little alternative. Church of England. Is what she wrote on the application form. A white lie. Why not? She asked herself. Makes life easier. The wage was not lavish. But enough. And on some days, by limiting herself to an apple for lunch, she could save enough to buy Michael a packet of Craven A cigarettes. On those afternoons she would be hungry. Worth it. To watch Michael that night blow smoke rings towards her. While he laughed. Talked. Laughed some more. She loved Michael so. "More than salt," she once said to him. "Likewise," he laughed, echoing the word she had so often used when they first met.

She gave Michael money. For books. For sweaters. For socks. For street-car fares. For himself. A grown man can't go out on the street without some coins in his pocket, she declared. She would have given him every penny of her earnings. But he refused. He was in no position to decline all her gifts. But accepted only that which he felt to be absolutely necessary. Except for the occasional pack of Craven A, of course. He would repay her. Every cent. Every nickel. Every dime. After they married.

"I love you," said Michael.

"I love you even more," said Rose.

The dimly lit room, the room that Mr. Kleber loaned to the two families for the courtroom adjudication, was, in most of the dwellings in the market the living room. When the houses in the area were originally built in the early 1900s this large room on the second storey was the front bedroom. When ground floor living rooms were converted into shops, the main bedrooms upstairs became sitting rooms. Mr. Kleber, however, used it only to keep a few unused shoe boxes. Rolls of string. A sheet or two of brown wrapping paper. Dust gatherers. Abandoned. Laced with spider webs. In a corner. An otherwise empty room. For Mr. Kleber did not like trudging up the stairs to get stock. It was therefore an ideal room for this confrontation.

"So?" It was Michael's father's turn to question. "So? You were going to get married. What happened?"

Michael looked at Rose. The slits of sunlight were enough to reveal the undiminished hatred in Rose's eyes. He stared at the floor.

"Well?" demanded Rose, "answer your father, Michael. Why don't you?"

Michael said nothing.

"I cooked for you," said Rose.

"Yes," said Michael.

"I sewed for you."

"Yes."

"I cleaned for you."

"Yes."

"Remember that night, just before the Purim holiday, the night of the storm? My skirt was wet from sleeting ice. Carrying your dinner here. I took the skirt off. It was so cold. We put on your electric cooker. We tried to get warm but couldn't. We got into bed," said Rose.

The orange crate Michael sat on began to creak. He was shifting about. Discussing sex in front of his parents was not comfortable.

"You began to rub me," said Rose. "To warm me up. You massaged me. I had my back to you and you massaged up and down. Fast at first. Then slower and slower. Then it wasn't a massage any more. You were touching me. Gently. Moving your hands from my neck to my waist to lower. Then you stopped. I told you not to stop. Do you remember what I said? I said, 'You're a man, you want to go all the way.' And you said, 'No. No. It's better that we wait.' I thought you said that out of consideration for me. But that wasn't the reason. You didn't want to have sex with me that night because you didn't love me. Isn't that the truth?"

Michael hesitated. "Yes," he said finally.

"You didn't love me that night and you don't love me now," said Rose.

Michael paused again. "No. I'm sorry Rose," he said. "I can't say I love you now. I'm sorry."

"Now?" demanded Rose, "what about at the start? You said you loved me. You didn't mean it?"

"No. I mean, yes. I loved you," said Michael.

"Then?" she said.

"Yes," he said.

"And since then. You've said you loved me lots of times." she said.

"And it was true," said Michael, "I did love you."

"But not anymore?" she asked.

"No," he replied.

"When did you stop? When did you no longer love me?" she asked.

"There was no specific moment," said Michael. "It just sort of happened."

"You started sending me notes," said Rose. "With the Abelson boy. Leonard. He said he saw you on campus. He would bring me your notes. You were going to be late. You had work to do. You were at the library. You were talking to a client. To another lawyer. To a professor. To someone. Notes. Lots of notes."

"There's no phone here," said Michael, "no phone at the Kurtz's. I didn't want you to worry."

"That's when it started," said Rose.

"Probably," said Michael.

"That's when it started," repeated Rose.

"Yes," said Michael.

"Notes. 'Not tonight, dear Rose.' 'Don't wait for me.' 'See you tomorrow, dearest mine.' After a while the Abelson boy began to look at me queerly. He became embarrassed. He'd hand me the note. And leave. Fast. As if he knew something I didn't. Do you think that's fair? Him knowing and me not knowing?"

"Leonard didn't know anything," said Michael. "I guess he guessed."

"The notes became less and less. Then stopped," said Rose.

"He wouldn't do it anymore, Leonard wouldn't" said Michael, "he refused."

"But notes or no notes, you still saw me?" she asked.

"Yes."

"Every day?"

"Yes," he replied.

"Sometimes more than once?" she said.

"Yes," he said.

"Why did you let me go on thinking that things were still the same? That you still loved me?" asked Rose.

"I didn't know how to tell you," said Michael. "I tried."

"Did you?" she asked.

"That Saturday morning, when I woke you, so early, remember, you were mad, remember?" asked Michael. "I said I couldn't sleep. Wasn't true. I'd been up all night, working out how to tell you. But I couldn't. I didn't want to hurt you. I don't want to hurt you. I couldn't tell you."

"Not until now?" said Rose.

"Not until now," agreed Michael.

She stopped questioning to reflect for a moment.

"I did everything for you," said Rose.

Michael looked her full in the face. "Yes, everything," he said.

"Wasn't it enough?" asked Rose.

"Too much. It was too much," said Michael.

Rose glared at him.

"Love has to be between two partners. Equals. As we once were," said Michael. "But now your love is so much bigger than mine. I can't match you. You are too good for me. Too perfect." He swallowed. "Rose, I owe you so much. Too much. You showed me love. Perfect love. I can't match that. Ever. In any way. You are too good. The perfect woman. You deserve the perfect man. Not me. I can't marry anyone who loves me so much. To whom I owe so much. With you I feel guilt. For the money. For the work. For the time. For the love. Most of all for the love you gave me." He was tempted to rise, to go to Rose, but he restrained himself. "I am sorry. Sorry. Try to understand. One day you will understand. I can't match you. I don't have that kind of love. I am not perfect. I'm not you. You love so much. So much. I'm not as good as you. I can't love as you do." He looked first at his own parents. Then at hers.

"We can never marry," concluded Michael. "It has to end. It has to stop. Our love. Has to end now." He sighed. Returned his gaze to the floor.

Earlier that day Rose had been to the Boy Scout section of Eaton's Department Store. As an employee she received a discount for all goods bought within the store. She smiled at that thought as she opened her purse. Her purchase lay snuggled at the bottom of the black bag. Gleaming. An eight-inch dagger. She smiled even more. In one deft movement she removed the knife.

And lunged at Michael.

STREET SMART

Guns were not seen on Baldwin Street.

Bricks. Sticks. Branches. Axe handles. Bats. Bottles. Hammers. Crowbars. And parts of the body; fists, heads, knees, feet. These were the weapons of violence.

Not guns. Nor even knives.

Armed robbery was almost unheard of. Burglaries were rare. The living quarters behind the stores were filled with families—a father, a mother and a cluster of children—and it would be foolhardy to attempt a break-in. Even in the middle of the night. The number of people on the street and the number in the dwellings must have been a deterrent against armed robbers. Certainly the market was crowded during summer months. In the depths of winter, however, the stores were more isolated and more vulnerable.

Mrs. Gelman once faced a gunman. She threw herself across the cash register to stop him grabbing the money. He pistol-whipped her. But left with only a handful of cash.

This isolated incident was the talk of Baldwin Street for months. But considering the amount of cash in day to day use as prosperity on the street increased, guns and robberies were remarkably few.

One Friday night my mother called to me from the store. The tone of her voice was strange. I opened the kitchen door. And looked down. Two men, dressed like comic-book gangsters—grey

Stetson hats, wide-shouldered suits, dark shirts, light ties, gloves—were herding my mother to the rear of the store. One doubled back to the street door, closed it, put a hand inside his jacket. The other followed hard after my mother. "Lennie," she said, "tell your father his dinner is on the table!" Unseen by the man behind her, she could wink at me. My father was not in the house. Neither were any of my brothers. Only my sister Lorraine was upstairs. But it was impossible to see up the stairs from anywhere but the kitchen. "Lorraine!" I shouted, "Tell Paw to come down. And oh yeah, tell Syd and Ben I need their help. Now! Right now! And tell Solly to turn down that radio!" It was, as usual, at peak decibels. "And you'd better come down here too!"

From these weird instructions Lorraine, who couldn't have been more than eight years old, knew something was amiss. Street smart. Lorraine was street smart. "Syd, Sol, Ben," she shouted, "Lennie wants you." The radio went off. Lorraine clattered down the stairs making as much noise as she could. "Benny says he'll be here in a second," she told me, "ah, here he comes." The second man, who had delayed by arguing with Maw about sock sizes, looked at us. He shook his head at the man guarding the door. They both left.

"Do you think they were carrying guns?" I asked my mother at supper that night.

"Yes," she said. "That's what I get for letting customers in so late at night. And the Sabbath night, too. God's punishment."

That was as close as the Abelson store ever came to armed robbery.

BERNIE

"We'll grab us one of those sexy Jewgirls and bang hell out o' her. With big buzzooms. Stacked. Know what I mean, kid? We'll all give it to her. One guy after another. Even you, kid."

The teeth of a pocket comb disappeared into long straight black hair. Then a palm patted the coiffeur into roundness. This continued for some time. Combing. Palming. Combing. Finally Carlo D'Angelo turned from the mirror to face his younger brother. "So make up your mind, kid," said Carlo. "We gonna do it. Tonight. What d'ya say?"

Tony D'Angelo did not respond.

"C'mon kid. Answer. You comin' or not?" demanded Carlo.

Tony waited. A small shrug. "Yeah. Yeah. Okay. I guess so," said Tony finally. "I'll be with you."

—◦◦◦—

Ira and Eva Altman ran a small shop. Groceries. With a minimal amount of fruit and vegetables. No soft fruit. No berries. Too perishable. As were peaches, plums, grapes, and such. But lemons, oranges, grapefruits were to be found in the shop. As well as the occasional apple or pear.

The Altmans were early risers. The first hour or two after a simple breakfast—a hot drink, usually cocoa, into which a Kaiser roll was dunked—would be spent in the shop preparing for the day. Shelves were restocked. Cans polished. Displays dusted. Boxes with fresh supplies brought up from the cellar. Or from the back room. As they sorted the shop Ira and Eva chatted happily. Physically he was not a tall man. She was even shorter. Rotund. With a chirpy nature. Two little birds. Up ladders. Down ladders. Tins on shelves. Wrapping paper into roller. String into dispenser. Fresh fruit replacing old. Two little birds. Chirping at each other.

Marriage on Baldwin Street was not a conventional matter. The usual arrangement where the husband marches off to the working world leaving the little lady at home did not exist. Work was the store. Home was store. The marital twosomes spent twenty-four hours of each day side by side. At work. And at rest. Strain was inevitable.

But it hardly ever showed on Ira and Eva.

Both were toddlers when they arrived in Canada. His father was a tailor. Her father was a presser. Emigrants to the New World. Arriving in a city jammed with other emigrants. The children, as required by law, were to be educated. Ryerson Public School was nearest. Eva was two grades behind Ira. But he was aware of her even then. He had seen her before at the synagogue on holidays. A little girl with brown-blonde ringlets. Laughing. Chirping. Chattering. A noticeable little girl.

Ira tried the rag trade. A tailor. Failed. A cutter. Failed. He got a job in a corner shop selling candies, newspapers, magazines, cigarettes. He liked working in a shop. When he and Eva married, the two sets of parents pooled meagre monies to rent a store. On Baldwin Street.

Ira was not a pushy man. Not aggressive.

A constant running war existed on Baldwin Street between police and storekeepers. To do with the permitted size of out-front stands on which to display wares. The law stated that such stands must no more than eighteen inches deep. The storekeepers believed that in order to show potential customers what goods were available within the store the stands had to stretch from shop front to pavement. And beyond. And be crowded with a hodge-podge of items obtainable from within the shop. Every once in a while the police would swoop. Issue summonses. These were collected. Handed to Sam Abelson. Who took them to Alderman Nathan Phillips at City Hall. The summonses were quashed. Mostly. Once in a while it was decided to make a summons or two stick. A sign of good faith on both sides.

Ira Altman did not break the law. His stand was well within the permitted depth. Not that he was a goody-goody. But unlike his neighbours he could see little point in a vast exterior show of goods. His immaculate window enticed customers to enter. Not the stand. The stand was used only for lines he wished to discontinue or goods reduced in price for whatever reason.

The Altmans were comfortable. With themselves. With life. With their income. As with most stores in the market a liveable livelihood—coupled with long hours and hard work—could be turned over each week. Through the years the Altmans had built up a loyal clientele, mainly of older customers, who welcomed the shop's tranquillity compared with the din of the street. As neither partner was ambitious, Baldwin Street suited the Altmans. Soon the store was no longer rented but owned outright. The family's needs were small. No relatives leeched after money. No debts Damoclesed overhead. Small needs. Small life.

Ira and Eva Altman had no children. Unusual. The extra hands of children were a useful source of free labour to overworked parents. And other households on the street almost always consisted of father, mother, and a collection of children. But the Altmans were childless. After nearly twenty years of marriage Eva and Ira went through a series of medical tests at the Mount Sinai. Eva was asked to remain behind for further consultation. The night she returned from the hospital Eva wept. Bitter tears. The doctors told her to accept the fact that her marriage would be childless. "Never mind, doctors have been wrong before," said Ira. "And it'll be fun trying to prove them wrong."

Within a year it happened. Eva was pregnant. A bright-eyed beautiful boy was born unto the Altmans.

On the night of October 31, 1939, Bernie Altman was four years old.

———

"If the micks and the sheenies want to kill each other, let them." And then he laughed. The speaker was the Chief of Police of the city.

It was a laugh and a speech Marshall MacDonald recalled often in later years.

"Kikes and wops, communists and fascists, good ones and bad ones, who cares?" said the chief. "All heading for hell. And it's not my job to stop them. Is it?"

One night, six years earlier, the summer of 1933, Police Constable Marshall MacDonald had been in the force only a few months. A rookie. He and five other junior policemen were being assigned to Christie Pits. Six years ago. Six long years ago.

"Jews and Eyeties are cowards. Yellow bellies. The lot of them. There will be no trouble. Mark my words." The chief spoke with clipped consonants in what he perceived to be an English accent. But to PC MacDonald's more discriminating ear—he was born in Oban—merely sounded pretentious. "One sight of a blue uniform, one look at a swinging truncheon, and trouble will evaporate like ice off the back of an ice-wagon on a hot day."

Christie Pits was the name of an old quarry. Turned into a park and playground. And that night was to be the site of a baseball game. A re-match. For the softball championship of the city. Between St. Peter's School, mainly Italians, and Harbord Collegiate, mainly Jews. Harbord had won the first game. A large crowd was expected.

Subordinates of Police Chief Dennis Draper, Brigadier-General, were concerned that tension between the two ethnic minorities could escalate to violence. The Chief refused to take any dampening action. Instead he made the speech painting two of the city's largest minorities as mere cowards.

PC Marshal MacDonald disliked the uniform he was obliged to wear.

It was a replica, helmet and all, of the London bobby's outfit. He was told over and over again. And wrong for this climate. He told himself, over and over again. Too warm, too heavy, too thick. But when he saw the people arriving that evening at Christie Pits, Marshall was glad to be wearing a serge that could hide his trembling. Marshall put his hands behind his back. Rocked up and down on his toes. To hide the shaking. "Too hot for most folks to bother with a ball game," was one opinion as he left the police station. "Maybe a few dozen. Or a hundred or so, at most. You'll see." Hordes appeared. Wave after wave. Finally more than ten thousand lined the banks of the quarry. If this crowd turns into a mob, thought Marshall, there's just myself and five other policemen. Six men. "Shouldn't we call? Ask for reinforcements?" another recruit asked Marshall. Both knew the answer. "Stay calm," said Marshall. Corrected himself. "Look calm. Be friendly. Nod. Smile from time to time." "Good luck," said the other constable walking away. "That's what we need," said Marshall to himself.

And at first Marshall was surprised at how easy it was. He had found a shade tree well back from the throngs. He could be seen. But his presence was not ostentatious. All was well. But the viciousness of words between the two rival groups startled him. Venom. Hate. Scorn. Not like the heckling of a Saturday afternoon's football in Scotland. This was not good-natured banter. No sign of wit. No repartee. "Knock that fucking Jew's head off!" "Hymie, pitch it low, straight into that Dago's nuts." Kill. Murder. Die. Death. Murder. Kill. Kill. Kill. Exhorted the crowds.

Words, only words, Marshall told himself. He thought of his wife, Mary. A girl born in Canada of a good highland background. He thought of his son, Fulton. His baby son, three months old. Marshall looked skyward. Lord, he prayed, get me home safe tonight. Into my bed. Into my woman's arms. Please, Lord.

August 16, 1933, was the date. More than eighty percent of the population of Toronto was British. The ethos of Queen Victoria still reigned. My word is my bond. Fair play. Justice. Freedom for all. But no one who was not a member of the Orange Order and white and Protestant could get a job in City Hall. And in Germany, Adolf Hitler had taken control.

The Italian team won. Supporters erupted. Cheers. Shouts. Exultations. It might end this way, hoped Marshall, noisy but without violence. To his dismay on the far mound he saw a flag appear. A blanket really. Eight feet square. Onto which a Swastika had been painted.

A signal. Or was taken as a signal. For the Italians to start marching menacingly towards the Jews. For the Jews to attack the Italians and destroy the Swastika. Fights. Fists. Kicks. Blood. Noses bashed. Eyes bashed. Knees bashed. Blood.

Had Marshall been more experienced he would not have thrown himself into the fray immediately. Might have hung back. Picked off a leader or two. More effectively made his presence felt by talking, shouting, commanding. But such tactics were unknown to him. He was shoved. He shoved back. He was hit. He hit back. He was punched. He punched back. He did not use his truncheon.

Sticks, bats, iron bars, lead piping, brass piping, copper piping, metal lengths of all kinds, appeared when the doors of houses surrounding the playground disgorged their occupants. Kill the Jews. Kill the Jews. Word wild fired to the Jewish area. To the pool halls on College Street, the gambling parlours on Spadina, the boys on Baldwin Street. Trucks loaded. To Christie Pits. To fight.

The riot lasted from early evening until early next day. "Who's winning?" asked Chief Draper. A plainclothesman was reporting by phone. "The Jews, I think," said the detective. "Too bad," said Draper and hung up. Black-shirted thugs were met, possibly for the first time anywhere, by an equal number of opponents. And were losing. At the last moment, Chief Draper, pressured by politicians, reluctantly sent his men in. The riot stopped.

When one of his colleagues found him PC Marshall MacDonald was unconscious. A deep gash gouged his left temple. Probably from piping. He was in Western Hospital for three weeks. Comatose. Mary was told he might not recover. He might be brain damaged. He did recover. He was not damaged. But recuperation was slow and painful.

One day, flanked by flunkies, Police Chief Draper marched into the ward.

"Is this him? Is this the brave young lad?" projected Draper, coming towards Marshall, hand extended. "How are you, young fellow?"

I do not want to shake your hand, thought Marshall. I have no respect for you. You are a bad policeman. You are a bad man.

"I'm fine, sir," was all Marshall said. And with a wan smile took his boss's hand.

"Glad to hear it," said Draper, plonking himself on the bed. "You'll be up and about in no time. No time at all."

Go away. I do not want to talk to you. "Thank you for coming to see me, sir," said Marshall.

"We'll keep you off the beat for a while." Draper turned to one of his aides. Who nodded agreement. "Until you get your strength back."

What? Damn you! The beat is what I enjoy most. I won't. "Sir, there's really no need—" Seeing the look in Draper's eyes, Marshall flustered. *Why did you stop? Go on. Tell him.* "Yes, sir. Thank you, sir."

A few more pleasantries. A final shake of hands. And Draper exited.

"I'll be keeping a special eye on you, young fellow," was Draper's parting line. Marshall never saw him again.

Six years later, sitting in Dundas Street police station, Marshall looked again and again at the sheet of paper in his hand that had so provoked these visions of the past. He forced his eyes to scan the words one more time. Illiterate. Of course. But deliberately mis-spelled to put him off track? Or just the inability of a moronic mind? A crank? Or real? Addressed to The Polise, Ward 4, Toronno. Three lines. wHOT Hitler staRts, we finich. Death to Yids.

Marshall was now a uniformed inspector. The raging-red scar that seared his forehead had kept him away from the public for most of his career. He was a desk man.

It was the last day of October. Halloween. 1939. Marshall hated Halloween. Not for the ghoulies and ghosties. But because it brought out the worst in ordinary citizens who seemed to relish imitating the haunted spirits with a last fling at mayhem before the long nights begin. The American custom of children knocking on doors for shell-out had not yet—thank God, thought Marshall—crossed the border. Anyway there would be little point in children soliciting for goodies around here, he believed. Most people were starving. Short of food. Short of the basics. Salt. Meat. Potatoes. Who had candies?

Marshall considered himself to be fortunate. He had left a deprived home in Scotland. Was told things were not going to be much better in his new country. Yet he got a job almost instantly with the police force in Toronto. Met Mary. Was now blessed with a second child, little Mary. Not a lavish life. Secure. Stable. In unstable times.

"Who's on duty around Baldwin Street?" he asked the sergeant.

Both men checked the bulletin board. "Hamish and Mike in the vehicle, sir," said the sergeant. "George Untzmann on motorcycle is also available."

Marshall grunted. "Tell them to cruise by the market every once in a while. Check Kensington. Check Baldwin. Keep an eye open," said Marshall.

"Something up, sir?" asked the sergeant.

"Yes, it's Halloween," said Marshall.

"Yes, sir. I'll give 'em that hot news, sir." The sergeant smiled. "When they report in."

Marshall was back at his desk. Picked up the threatening letter. Too many fingerprints by now, he told himself. Not much use. Still, he would have it dusted. It was all he could do. Marshall placed the letter and envelope in the appropriate an out-tray. And turned to other matters.

To Harvey Willenski the riots at Christie Pits were folklore. Not much different to him than Moses parting the Red Sea. History. True, his eldest brother Tom fought at the Pits six years earlier. And on warm summer Saturdays, in the early hours of morning, when the shoppers had gone, the pavements in front of the stores swept clean, and the children of storekeepers, too tired from hours of work to contemplate bed, would gather to sit on a stand and urge Tom Willenski to tell and retell stories about the Christie Pits riot. Harvey's generation, boys and girls, mostly ten years younger than Tom, gathered to listen. And sigh. None sighed more than Harvey. Regretting that he had not been old enough to partake in such exciting events. Why not me? Why couldn't I have been the oldest? It's not fair, thought Harvey.

By now Tom Willenski had gone. Married. Living on Brunswick Avenue. Blocks away. Worlds away. No longer working in his parents store. A travelling salesman in sports goods. With a car. Sort of. A battered jalopy. But good enough to earn respect. Any occupation away from Baldwin Street tended to earn respect from those who stayed behind.

For some inexplicable reason the three eldest Willenski boys—Tom, Saul and Harvey—had bodies a Roman gladiator might envy. Wide shoulders. Thick necks. Small waists. Muscles, taut and tight, traversed their torsos. There were seven Willenski children. A daughter at each end, first and last child. The fourth son, Alan, was born with one leg shorter than the other. His mother, possibly in an overreaction to this imperfection, called him The Cripple. Where is The Cripple? Let The Cripple do it. She could be heard to say. Publicly. Not caring whether her unfortunate child heard or not. The last boy, Phillip, was of normal physical proportions but because he contrasted so much with the three older boys, was considered the runt of the litter.

Harvey was in the back of the store. Doing a job he hated. Sorting radishes. Bad radishes, beyond redemption, into one box. Those that could be saved by hulling into another box. A small knife removing rotting bits. Tedious work. Messy work. The deteriorating radishes smeared his hands. And stank. He had been assigned the radish task as punishment. For stealing.

From time to time Harvey's mother, guarding the front stand, glanced back to make sure her son was not shirking his work. If she had a favourite child it was Harvey. But earlier that day she had seen a two-dollar bill protrude from Harvey's back pocket. Theft.

All monies received in the store were to be handed immediately to either parent. No cash register. No till. The pockets of the parents sufficed. No one else serving in the store was to retain money. House rule. Store rule. Tradition.

"Where do you get this?" His mother held up the two dollars.

"I was gonna give it to you, Maw, honest," replied Harvey.

"Liar." She clouted his ear. She had to reach upwards to do so for in his middle teens, he was much taller than his mother.

"I wouldn't keep it, Maw. It's a deuce. Two-dollar bill. Unlucky," said Harvey.

"Unlucky for you." She hit his ear again. And again. A trickle of blood. "You're not going out. Not tonight. Not this week. Bastard!" Despite the blood she hit his ear again.

Every other member of the family was out that night. Halloween. Younger siblings played on the street. Older ones with friends. Or at the movies. His father, Shmiel Willenski, had sneaked off to the ice cream parlour on Augusta Avenue. Dominoes. His father loved the game. The clatter of the black rectangles on hard-surfaced tables exhumed excitement from a soul long dead with disappointment. A passion. Especially if a small wager were involved.

Fanny Willenski, Harvey's mother, despite a face framed in startling white hair, was an attractive woman. Correctly chiselled features perfectly proportioned. There was some conjecture among her neighbours why such a woman, who must have been beautiful in youth, married someone as schlocky as Shmiel. Gossip. Talk. Don't you know about the Willenskis? He had riches when younger but lost it all. Back in Europe she broke too many hearts and had to settle for what she could get. She was loose. Perhaps more than loose. Shmiel was the only one to offer marriage. Talk. Difficult to confirm. Difficult to deny. Talk. Only talk.

Harvey did not begrudge the punishment handed out to him that night. He had tried. And been caught. The two dollars was his entry to a dice game. If the maroon cubes with white dots had favoured him that night he might have parlayed the two dollars to twenty or fifty or more. But his Maw was sharp. Hard. And sharp.

He did not like stealing from his parents. But what choice had he? Maw never gave him enough money. Not enough for a crap game at any rate. So he stole. A guy's gotta do something to jazz things up. After all it's not like the old days when a punch-up on the street would break the routine of store work. Those days were gone. Over.

He cut away the rot from another radish.

———•••———

When the bad days were upon him Menasha had no recollection where he lived. In summer he slept in store doorways. In winter some merchants let him sleep on the store floors. Otherwise, fair weather or not, a child would be found to accompany him on the walk home.

Menasha was a professor. A lecturer. Part-time. He lectured at the University. Philosophy. On good days. When he was well. When his head was 'in order'. On other days a fog seemed to descend onto his front cranial lobes. A thick, relentless, insinuating fog. On those days he would retreat. Hide. Baldwin Street was his hiding place.

Menasha could foretell when the bad days were coming. He considered that to be fortunate. It gave him time to withdraw—reluctantly, for he loved teaching—from academic activities. To prepare himself. To warn himself. He had no one else to warn. The illness had made him a loner. But since he was a man who relished solitude, that was not a hardship. He had no family. Home was a tiny rented room with a narrow bed and a thin mattress. On Gerrard Street. Handy for the University. But blocks away from the market. A note of his address was always to be found in the inside pocket of his coat.

No one knows when Menasha first appeared. When seen on Baldwin Street he was always reading. A book. A paperback. Philosophy. Plato. Hobbes. Kant. Spinoza. Descartes. Sometimes a copy of *The Globe and Mail*. And, more rarely, *The New York Times*. He would sit on the curb, his legs tucked under him, bedraggled, occasionally lifting his eyes to the passing scenes before returning to his book. He would sit. Reading.

The words his eyes read sometimes spewed out in spasms through his mouth. Gibberish. Nonsensical. Silly. Or sensible. Orderly. Correct. He seemed unaware or uncaring of the sounds he uttered whether intelligible or not.

He was also, by some unusual route the mind is capable of taking, good with machinery. One day, when Toronto was hotter than Dallas, a delivery truck broke down in the middle of Baldwin Street. Chaos. Traffic blocked. Hooting horns. Voices raised. Tempers rising to match temperatures. A mechanic was sent for.

"Let me see, let me see," said Menasha, "I can do it. I can fix it."

The truck driver looked at this unkempt figure. "Go away," said the driver.

But Menasha pushed his way through to look at the open motor. Pulled a wire. Scraped. Twisted another wire. Used his shirt sleeve to wipe. "Anyone got a monkey wrench? I need a wrench," said Menasha. Then after a while, "Okay, try it now."

The truck started.

As night fell on October 31, 1939, Menasha knew his bout of illness was passing. His clothes stank. Which made him smile. For he remembered that an offensive odour assailing his nose was one of the first indications of recovery. He touched his hair. And nodded. Greasy. Yes. Matted. Ugh. When he was ill he was oblivious of his hair.

I must go home, Menasha said to himself. But where do I live? Church Street? No, I moved. It's not Church Street any more. Gerrard Street. Yes. Yes. But what number? Ah, here it is, written down. Good. He pulled the address from his pocket. But where is Gerrard Street? Which way? I must get home. Wash. Bathe. Clean. I must go home. If I can get to Gerrard Street I'll remember more. More about me. Yes. Yes. It will come back to me. It must. I'm getting better. I'm getting better.

Don't rush. Slow. Menasha cautioned himself. Easy. Sit for a while. Read. He went to squat on the curbside. A robotic reaction. But stopped himself. No, don't sit there. So dirty. He turned over an abandoned orange crate. Sat. And looked around. It's getting dark. Is it spring or autumn? One of those, I'm wearing a coat. Such a tattered coat. Where did I get it? Autumn. Yes. Look at the stands. Sweet potatoes. Corn. Squash. Pumpkins. The Fall. He instinctively dug into one of the coat's deep pockets. A book. *The Story of Philosophy*. Durant. What page was I on? Here it is. Read. Read. Calm. Find yourself.

"Hiya, Menasha. How y'doin?" A boy, no more than ten or eleven, passed by. And ruffled his hair as if stroking a dog.

Menasha? Oh, yes. Yes. That's what they call me. Menasha. *Meshugina* Menasha. Mad Menasha. Crazy Menasha. That's not my name. I'll call him back. Tell him. Look, kid, my name is— My name is— What? What? I can remember. Of course I can. He searched through the fog. Looking. Hunting. Seeking. To find his name. When the sound finally swept up from deep within his gut it was so loud shoppers and shopkeepers turned to stare. "Rifkind." A cry. A pained cry. An animal sound. Atavistic. Toneless. Without music. "Rifkind." He repeated more softly. Then again to himself. Rifkind. Maximillian Rifkind. I know my name. I know my name.

Tonight I will sleep in my bed. Tomorrow I will ring the University. But for a while I will just sit here. And read.

———•••••———

Leonard Abelson was the child usually assigned to take Menasha home. For many reasons. He was ten years old at the time. Malleable. Willing. And, most important, unlike most of his friends, easy to find. Leonard would be at the kitchen table grappling with school homework. Or minding the Abelson exterior stand. Or simply observing the antics of others in the market. Or playing softball in the schoolyard. When one of shopkeepers would approach. Mr. Kruger, Mr. Liebowitz, or Mr. Birnbaum. Adults. Therefore to a child always prefixed as Mister.

"Yes, Mr. Birnbaum, what is it?" Leonard would ask.

"Be a good boy," he would be beseeched, "take Menasha home."

Money for streetcar fares would be pressed into Leonard's hand. Plus a bit more. "Buy yourself a popsicle." In good weather. "Buy yourself a Neilsen chocolate bar." In bad weather.

Menasha did not always allow himself to be led away. If he resisted, pulling away from caring hands, on those nights he would be found shelter, in a doorway or on a floor.

"If he scares you, y'don't have to do it, y'know." Mrs. Abelson tried to intervene.

"It's okay Maw," said Leonard. "Menasha doesn't worry me."

Once on a rush-hour crowded College Street streetcar Menasha gurgled incoherent words while reading from his book. Other passengers backed away.

"Shh, Menash, shh!" implored an embarrassed Leonard, standing next to him. Menasha blinked uncomprehendingly at the boy. Leonard used his own mouth to demonstrate, forcing it to close. Menasha giggled. Forced his lips to close. Giggled again. Went back to reading.

After arriving at Menasha's room, Leonard would ease him onto the bed—fully clothed, shoes and all—cover him, and leave as quickly as possible.

One night just as Leonard reached the door, Menasha said to him, "Thank you."

Leonard turned. Menasha's blinking eyes stared at him, as if fighting to see through some mist.

"What's your name?" asked Menasha.

"Lennie," said the boy.

"No," said Menasha, "don't let them call you Lennie. Is your name Leonard? Good. Make them use the full name. Not the diminutive. You'll hate it when you're older. Goodnight, Leonard. Thank you."

"Goodnight, Menasha," said Leonard.

Leonard rarely used the money he was given for treats. He would buy books. Or at the very least magazines. *Time, Reader's Digest, National Geographic*. Once he saved enough to buy a book he had seen Menasha reading. *Crime and Punishment* by Dostoevsky. He soon put it aside. Too heavy. Leonard pondered for a long time after that as to how Menasha—sick Menasha, who could not even get home without assistance—was capable of reading such a book.

———•••••———

"I won't fight. I can't," said Ruby Waldman.

Carlo D'Angelo considered this statement with gravity befitting a leader. "Okay," said Carlo, "I understand. You're a Jew. You don't wanna fight other Jews. Okay. But you're also one of us. The Manning Avenue gang. You wanna stay in the gang, don'tcha?" He waited for Ruby to nod. "Okay. We do the fighting. You take care of our bikes. You can do that, can'tcha?" Carlo swung his bicycle onto the road. Under his breath he muttered, "Can't expect a Yid to fight, can ya?" Carlo laughed. Another member of the gang also laughed.

Carlo led the way. Eleven bicycles, some new, some old, a rainbow of colours, all CCC, Canadian Cycle Company, with footbrakes not handbrakes, all with racing handlebars upright, set off towards Baldwin Street.

———•••••———

Ira Altman decided to take in the stand early. The nights were closing in. Colder. Darker. He would leave the shop door open in case there were any late stragglers but he wasn't expecting any more custom. Winter was a mixed blessing. At least it meant shorter hours in the working day. Leaving him more time to be with Bernie.

Heinz Baked Beans. Small cans. Were in his hand. Dented. When the cans were first delivered he had complained to the van driver. The wholesaler discounted some of the cost. Ira lowered the price even more. He disliked selling goods damaged in any way. If they haven't sold by the weekend, he said to himself, I'm going to throw them away. He was stacking the few remaining tins into a box when he heard the cyclists approach.

With Carlo D'Angelo leading, the eleven bicycles sluiced through traffic on the street. The first run-by was an impromptu rehearsal. Boisterous. Catcalls. Whooping. Little notice was taken. Teenagers. Young men. High spirited. At Spadina, one end of Baldwin Street, the bikers turned back. On the second pass right arms were raised to salute and the voices of the cyclists repeated one cry. *Heil* Hitler. *Heil* Hitler. *Heil* Hitler.

"Harvey, come out here," Fanny Willenski ordered her son. Harvey gladly abandoned the radishes. And stood in the doorway next to his mother. Startled. Offended. Surprised. Hurt. Both watched the bicycled youths rode by. Saluting as Nazis. Heiling. The trouble-seeking intruders on wheels now had the attention of shoppers and shopkeepers. And rejoiced. Raising their voices. Shouting. Loudly. Defiantly.

"Bastards," said Fanny. Harvey said nothing. But was acutely aware of a tautness tightening the muscles of his body. How many? Eleven, eh? Too many for me. Even with a crowbar. Even with a hammer. Better to wait, he told himself. Until brother Saul comes home. And Danny and Muchel said they would be dropping in. Three or four. Better odds. "Bastards," repeated his mother. She was remembering other youths, descending on her village in Lithuania, when she was a child—how old? eight? maybe nine—also crude, also shouting, youths who destroyed and looted and bloodied and raped. Had she left Lithuania behind only to see it happen here? "Something should be done about those bastards," said Fanny. Harvey nodded. And smiled.

The eleven cyclists were now at the other end of Baldwin Street near the intersection with Augusta Avenue. Bikes were turned to face inwards. Abreast. Alongside one another. The bikers straddling their mounts. Like horsemen. The road was blocked.

"Hey, Ruby," said Carlo D'Angelo to Ruby Waldman, "can y' talk Yid talk?"

"Yeah."

Carlo reached into his jeans for a fistful of coins. "Thought so," said Carlo. "Go buy us some Cokes."

Ruby, resenting being put in a subordinate position, hesitated. "The storekeepers speak English," said Ruby.

"Y'call that English? More like Yinglish to me," said Carlo. "Do what I say."

Carlo watched Ruby go off. Then braked his bicycle on the curb. Shoulders swaying, Carlo strode towards the nearby Birnbaum fruit stall. Aggressively poised, he stood surveying the produce on display. Old Man Birnbaum was alone. Izzy, his son, was making deliveries. The old man was, unbeknown to him, dubbed Popeye by the children on the street. He had no teeth. And ate by masticating food—usually soft-breaded white sandwiches— with his gums, his jaw bobbing up and down as with the cartoon character. When Carlo approached the old man was perched on an orange crate behind the stand reading the Yiddish newspaper, the *Forward*. Another source of amusement for the children of the street. The *Forward* was read backwards.

"How much are these?" Carlo squeezed a peach. He was told a price.

"How much d'oranges?"

He was told.

He squeezed a pear. "Hey, these are no good." His thumb pierced the soft pear. He could hear the gang laughing behind him. "I should report you. Selling damaged goods." He threw the pear onto the pavement.

"Somethin'?" demanded Carlo.

Old Man Birnbaum knew better than to reply.

Carlo grabbed the metal container off the scales. "This is what I want," he said. He scooped up a pile of purple Victoria plums. "How much do I owe ya?" The plums were weighed. "Forty five cents," said the old man. Carol flipped a quarter at the stall keeper. "Here's twenty-five. 'S'all it's worth to me," he said.

Old Man Birnbaum nodded. "You'll pay me one day, when you can."

This puzzled Carlo. "Sure. When pigs fly," he laughed. "Naw. Naw. Better still. When pigs is kosher. Yeah. When pigs is kosher!" He laughed louder. And paraded back to his bicycle, shoulders once again swaying.

From his bedroom window Bernie Altman could watch the antics on the street below. He was in pyjamas. Waiting for Eva. He could hear pots and pans rattling in the kitchen. A comforting sound. And knew his mother was preparing dinner before she ascended the stairs to put him to bed.

Meanwhile he was alone. Observing. From the window. Watching from on high the behaviour of adults on the street was an activity he enjoyed enormously.

Bernie saw the one biker return from the Birnbaum stand to rejoin the group. Laughing. Then talk. And gestures. The cyclists spread their bicycles, flat on the asphalt street, from one curb to another. Blocking the street.

Even someone as young as Bernie realized this was unusual.

"What the friggin' hell is going on?" Muchel Brickhov demanded of Harvey Willenski. Muchel had inevitably been nicknamed "Brick" at school. A name he disliked. The brick shit-house. That's what the appellation conjured up in his mind. Muchel was short. His shoulder width appeared to be the same dimension as his height. He was afraid of no one. And at school had even got into scraps with a Negro boy or two—something almost unheard of—to prove his toughness.

"The street's blocked," continued Muchel. "Some Eyeties on bikes. No cars can get in or out."

"Where's Danny?" asked Harvey.

"Be here in a sec," said Muchel.

"We need a car," said Harvey. "To drive up to them. Can we get a car? Can we borrow your brother's car? Where can we get a car?" At that time a shopkeeper on Baldwin Street who owned a car or van was a rarity.

"We don't need a car," said Danny Givertz entering the Willenski store. "Use a bike."

Danny was tall and affable. A pudgy, rounded boy, with a big smile and a big nature. Later his physique would run to fat but for now he was plump. His weightiness impressive.

"Bingo!" said Harvey. He ran next door. The Abelson children had bicycles.

Leonard Abelson was carefully unpacking a tea chest of clover leaf cups and saucers from Japan. At the same time keeping a look-out for customers stopping at the outside stand.

"You? On a bicycle?" asked Leonard, "Harvey, what would you want a bike for?"

"Watch and you'll see," said Harvey. "Can I have it?"

"Sure," said Leonard. The family's bicycles were stowed between counters in the store.

"I'll take this old one." Harvey selected one of the older bikes. Outside he hopped on. Wheels splayed under him in varying directions. But he managed to drive up to his waiting friends.

Leonard called to his sister Lorraine. Asked her to mind the store. He wandered towards the blockade.

"You get on the bar," Harvey told Muchel. "I'll ride. Danny you walk along beside us. Okay? Let's go."

"Harvey do me a favour," said Danny. "With me around it may look like more, but there's only three of us. Remember that."

"Three's all we need," said Harvey. "It'll be okay."

Tony D'Angelo was the first to see the bicycle wobbling towards them. His older brother was busy cheerleading the gang.

"Carlo." Tony tapped Carlo's shoulder. Carlo turned. Followed Tony's head gesture. Saw the approaching bike.

"Where d'ya think yer going?" asked Carlo.

Harvey braked. Muchel hopped off the bike. "I'm going through," said Harvey, with a grin.

"Suppose I say yer not," said Carlo.

"I say you're wrong," said Harvey, still grinning. "Move those bikes. Or I'll ride over 'em."

"You want those bikes moved? Make me," threatened Carlo.

"No," cried a voice from the background. A crowd had gathered anticipating a fight. "No! Don't do this," said Menasha pushing his way through the watchers.

"Menasha! Come back!" Leonard Abelson tried to restrain the older man. "You'll get hurt Menasha. Don't. Come back!"

"I have to try," said Menasha to Leonard, "don't you see? I have to make them stop." Menasha easily pulled free from the boy and placed himself on the road between Carlo and Harvey. "Please, please. I beg you. Both of you. This is wrong! You must not do this!" said Menasha.

"Menasha, get lost!" said Harvey.

"Y'know this guy?" laughed Carlo. "One of yours, is he?"

"Violence only begets more violence. And ends in tragedy," said Menasha. "Talk. Argue. Debate. Use words. Not violence." He turned to Carlo. "Your forebears gave the world art and culture." Then to Harvey. "Yours, the law and hygiene." To both he said, "Force solves nothing." He closed in again on Carlo. "You are not Neanderthal. Not cavemen. Use your heads, not your fists. Think first and then—"

Carlo grasped a mess of clothing under Menasha's chin, lifted the would-be peacemaker off his feet, slapped his face back and forth, then hurled him back. The action ripped the front of Menasha's clothes. His nose trickled blood. Bystanders gasped. Murmured. Debated whether or not to intervene. Menasha's raised hand silenced them.

"Do what you want with me," said Menasha, still addressing the gang leaders, "but please, I beg you, don't fight." He lifted his arms to either side in supplication. The position on the crucifix. A Christ without a cross.

"Gee-zuss!" said Tony D'Angelo. Then softly, "Jesus."

"This ain't no Jesus," laughed Carlo. "This is some fruitcake. Some dirty Jew who comes here—"

"He too was a dirty Jew," said Menasha.

"Danny, get 'im out o' here!" ordered Harvey.

Danny scooped up Menasha. And deposited him beside Leonard. "Keep 'im here," ordered Danny. Menasha was on his knees, keening, weeping, he clutched at the hem of the boy's sweater. "Stop them. I beg you. Stop them," said Menasha.

"I can't," said Leonard, "I can't!"

Menasha nodded. "I know," said Menasha, "I know." He lowered his head. "A child. Helpless. As I am." Menasha rocked back
and forth.

When Danny rejoined him, Harvey again squared up to Carlo.
"Move the bikes," said Harvey.

"I bet you're as tough as that nutcase over there," said Carlo.

"Move the bikes," said Harvey again.

"You gonna make me?" asked Carlo.

"Yep," said Harvey, in best Gary Cooper fashion.

"You gonna fight us?" asked Carlo.

"Yep," repeated Harvey.

It was Carlo's turn to grin. "All of us?" he asked.

"If that's what it takes. Yeah," said Harvey. Carlo's grin broadened.

"That is if you're not brave enough to fight alone," said Harvey.
And waited for the slur to penetrate. Carlo stopped smiling. "You
strong? You got balls? Maybe you need all these guys. To help you
be Mister Tough Guy. Maybe on your own, you're nothin'. No guts,"
continued Harvey. Carlo's shoulders slid upwards. It's working,
said Harvey to himself. The schmuck is rising to the bait. "Why
don't we do that?" added Harvey. "Without the others. You and me.
Kosher. One on one. Okay? Or are you just chicken. A chicken in
chicken-shit. Chicken. C'mon chicken!" Harvey flapped his arms as
wings and added hen-like sounds.

Carlo's swing caught the side of Harvey's temple and would
have felled him if he had not swayed away. The two were well-
matched. Carlo was ten pounds heavier. But Harvey was more ath-
letic. Faster. Harvey's fists moved at a speed bewildering to Carlo.

"Okay, that's enough," said Tony D'Angelo dancing around the
two fighters. "That's enough," shouted Tony. He desperately wanted the fight to end. The vision of Menasha had raised eerie premo-
nitions within him. Meanwhile both combatants were bleeding.
Red slime oozed from Harvey's nose. And his teeth looked like pips
in tomato sauce. But Carlo was far worse. Blood gushed from
mouth, nose, and numerous cuts dotting his face, two of them
severe gashes above and below the right eye.

It wasn't Tony's supplication that separated the two fighters.

But the need for air. To breathe. As if a ringside gong had sounded, after a few minutes the two brawlers chose the same moment to break away from each other. And pause.

Carlo returned to his group. Who muttered a chorus of approbation. Not too convincingly. Tony appealed to his brother. "Let's go home," said Tony. "C'mon Carlo. That's enough. Let's go."

"He hurt me," said Carlo. "That Yid hurt me. Gotta hankie? I got no hankie."

"And you hurt him." Tony handed over his hankie. "So now let's go."

The handkerchief was soon a red flag.

Ruby Waldman struggled to hold the Coke bottles he had been assigned to buy in his embrace. Danny Givertz accosted him as he returned from his shopping mission. "Hey, don't I know you from somewheres?" asked Danny. "The Y? Or school? Harbord? You're that rabbi's son, ain't you? Waldman, right? What the hell y'doin' with these wops?"

"From the same street. I'm part of the gang." Ruby's head lowered. "I said I wouldn't fight."

Danny made a fist. Held it under Ruby's nose. "Y'can tell that to my knuckles," said Danny. "Later."

Tony was by now using the tail of his shirt to mop up his brother's blood. He and another gang member were doing their best to stop the blood flow, imitating professional corner men as seen at the movies, squeezing together the lips of the deepest gap . "That's a helluva cut," said Tony. "Call it a night, Carlo, it's over."

Carlo looked at his younger brother. Said nothing. Turned to see where his opponent was. A few feet away Harvey was sleeve-brushing his face as he talked to Muchel and Danny.

"Hey, Jew-boy," shouted Carlo. "No hard feelings. Right?" Carlo smiled. Hand extended he advanced towards Harvey.

Harvey shrugged, grinned, and said, "Okay."

When Harvey's fist was in his grasp, Carlo lashed out. A kick in the groin. Harvey crumpled. Carlo was about to kick him again when Muchel flew threw the air. Strong forearms encircled Carlo, pulling him onto the road. Muchel began banging Carlo's head against the curb. Cue the mêlée.

Initially most of the intruding gang had stood back convinced their leader would make short work of Harvey. An audience. Not participants. Who were then taken aback by the sight of Carlo's wounds. Muted conversation soon started. Let's get out of here. Leave. Tony was right. Go. Carlo's subsequent treachery caught his own supporters unprepared as it did his opponents. Two of them having decided to leave were stooping to pick up bicycles when Danny's balled fist toppled them like pins in a bowling alley. Danny was soon surrounded by several others. Half blinded by blood, Carlo had just managed to pull himself free from a now besieged Muchel. Who ignored the blows aimed at him and concentrated on a two-fisted punch-shove into Carlo's belly. Harvey was struggling to stand and restore himself.

"Hold my bike! Hold my bike!" said a gang member to Ruby Waldman. "Doesn't matter what happens to me. But if my bike gets scratched my Mama will kill me."

Harvey hunted for his prey. He was interested in only one man. Carlo. He pushed aside other challenges. And faced Carlo. Who was still in difficulty dealing with Muchel.

"Leave him," Harvey told Muchel, "he's mine."

"Kike bastard!" Carlo lunged at Harvey.

Again the first few blows sent Harvey reeling. But soon his fists were dominating the exchange. Harvey concentrated his punches around Carlo's left eye. The good eye. Blue bruises inflated the area. Affecting Carlo's vision. He was now in danger of being unable to see his tormenting enemy out of either eye.

Squinting, brushing aside blood, desperate and pained, Carlo managed to perceive Ruby Waldman standing close by. Loaded with Coke bottles. Carlo grabbed a bottle. To use as a weapon. A club.

What made Ira Altman intervene? It was a question he was to ask himself often. He was not a brave man. Not a *shtarker*, endowed with physical prowess. He had never been in a physical fight in his life. The idea of striking another human was anathema to him. So why? Perhaps he felt the fight was now in danger of progressing to another level, a serious level, where the effects could be permanent.

Knuckles bashing flesh were bad enough without involving another element, a tool, to inflict even more damage A sense of injustice.
Is that what it was? The unbalanced and unfair sight of one man
with a glass bottle in his hand while his adversary had none.

But intervene Ira did. He stepped between the two fighters
shouting, "No. No. No. No."

"Keep out of it," ordered Harvey.

Carlo used the distraction to wildly swing the bottle. Ira would
have been hurt badly if Harvey had not shoved him to one side.
The bottled-hand bounced off Ira's shoulder. The grocer fell to the
ground.

Watching from the window little Bernie Altman screamed. His
father was down. Hurt. Bernie ran through the store and out
towards the fray.

Bernie Altman did not see the motorcycle. Did not see the
policeman riding it. Did not hear the shouts. The screams. The
cries. Did not see Menasha's contorted face. The toddler ran
straight into the path of the motorcycle.

And was killed.

The Dundas Street police station never had a proper canteen. A gas
range reluctantly occupied a corner of the room set aside for relax-
ation. Against the wall a lonely table was surrounded by a disarray
of empty rickety hooped-metal chairs. An old woman with
unkempt hair and unkempt clothes, a Sweet Caporal cigarette forever hanging from her lower lip, supervised the coffee continually
percolating on the range. The coffee appeared as tired as the
woman herself. Not that that bothered Constable George
Untzmann. The beverage was free. Hot. And the break afforded his
ample ass escape from the motorcycle's saddle.

The serving woman placed a chipped white mug full of the
suspect brew—grains swivelling on top—in front of Untzmann.
He grunted as he took it away. He did not say thank you. He rarely

said thank you. To anyone. About anything. His thoughts focussed on being able to stretch this recess. Fifteen minutes was sanctioned. Tonight he hoped for twenty minutes. Perhaps twenty-five. As long as no one noticed. Untzmann was exhausted. He lowered aching eyes onto his fingers for a massage. He had spent the previous night with a McCaul Street prostitute whom he threatened with all sorts of blackmail if she failed to comply with his wishes. Yeah, let's have a good long break here in the warm, he told himself. It's getting cold out there. And nothing much is happening.

He found an abandoned *Toronto Evening Telegram*. Separated the pink sports section. And was nestling down when the desk sergeant approached.

"Inspector wants you to check the market. Baldwin Street," said the sergeant.

"Why?" asked Untzmann.

"No reason," said the sergeant. "He just wants you there." Untzmann's lips moved in silent protest. "Wanna argue about it? Why don'tcha go see the Inspector?" The sergeant turned away to get himself some coffee knowing that Untzmann would never challenge the Inspector.

The sergeant was right. George Untzmann was not the sort to face senior officers. Untzman was determined to make his way high up the constabulary ladder. You did not rise in the ranks by confronting the hierarchy. His ambition was clear to all.

Untzmann looked at his wrist watch. As a minor token of rebellion he would first read about the Maple Leafs. Finish his coffee. And then go. Nothing was happening on Baldwin Street that couldn't wait the allotted fifteen minutes. Or twenty. Or twenty-five.

The sounds of street fighting assailed Untzmann's ears as he approached the market on his motorcycle. Yells. Yelps. Shouts. Screams. Seconds of silence followed. Then thuds. Bangs. As flesh hit flesh. Around him people ran. Towards the tumult. Gathering to watch. A fight. A show. Entertainment. Baldwin Street style. Come and look. Free. No charge. Not a penny. Free.

As Untzmann rounded the corner from Augusta Avenue onto

Baldwin Street, he was behind the bicycles splayed out on the asphalt and almost instantly into the fray. The crowd circled the participants, dancing with them from one side of the road to the other, as if tied by some unseen cord. Through gaps in the herding audience Untzmann could see the fighters. It was when he saw the bottle swinging in one man's hand that he gunned the motorcycle. Straight at the crowd. Straight at the rioters.

He did not see young Bernie Altman cross his path.

Not until the last infinitesimal fraction of a moment. When it was too late. He braked. But the full weight of the Harley-Davidson and his own considerable bulk struck the boy.

———

"Then what happened?" Inspector Marshall MacDonald was questioning Harvey Willenski.

"I don't know what I saw first. That copper—" he pointed at Untzmann "—or the baby lying on the road." Harvey raised his head. The harsh lighting of the interview room accentuated the blood and bruises on his face. "I stopped. The Italians stopped. We stopped. Just stopped. Stopped fighting."

Another police constable was taking notes. Untzmann, having given a verbal report, was also present. Muchel and Danny were in a cell, waiting for Harvey's return. The D'Angelo brothers and the rest of the gang spread over three other cells. A few bystanders had also been brought in for questioning.

"Then what?" continued Marshall MacDonald.

"The father, old man Altman, took hold of the baby. Spoke to 'im. Cooed 'im. Rocked him. Back and forth. Kneeling on the road. Holding his kid. Out there. Like they was alone in a bedroom. Rocking. Back and forth. I thought, that kid's dead. For sure, dead. The way he was lying there. So still. Suddenly the old man starts to yell, 'He's breathing. Look, he's breathing.' Picks the kid up. Starts to run."

"Where was he running to?" asked Inspector MacDonald.

"Western Hospital. Where else?" answered Harvey. "I ran with 'im. I helped. So many people. Had to push away people. So many cars. From nowhere. Car. And trucks. Jammed. Jamming the street. I pushed through. I ran with 'im. I helped."

"Why didn't you get one of the cars to drive you to hospital?" said the Inspector.

Harvey blinked. "Dunno. Didn't think of it. Cars were jammed in. Faster to run. Had to do something. Had to move. Didn't think of it, I guess." He blinked again. "The old man running along the streets. Me yelling, 'Get outa the way.' The kid's hand kept hitting the sidewalk. Flopping. Loose. Wouldn't let me hold the kid, Altman wouldn't. And he's not a big man. Running with his kid. Running. Fast. For a little guy. Fast."

This time when Harvey raised his head he looked like what he was. Not a man, a teenager. "Holding his baby. Wouldn't let me do the carrying. Running. I think he knew the kid was dead. Must've known. Mustn't he? His kid was dead. But he couldn't stop. Had to keep running. Running." Harvey pinched one of his deep cuts. To feel pain. To stop himself from crying. He did not want to cry, not here, in a police station. "D.O.A. at the hospital. Dead on arrival. D.O.A. Just like in the movies. Only this wasn't a movie. All that running. For what? For nothing." The recollection of the image of father and son fleeing towards sanctuary, was too much. Tears escaped from Harvey's eyes. "On the slab, on the table, when the doctors looked, the back of the kid's head—yellow hair—was black. Blood. Thick blood." Harvey paused. "He was so still. The kid. So still. Dead. Dead."

<hr />

"Let the boy go." Menasha spoke to the sergeant. He bowed in Leonard's direction. "He's tired. He should be in bed.

Leonard's eyes were elongating saucers. He was yawning. Fighting to keep awake.

"You have his statement," continued Menasha "We can all confirm what happened. Send him home."

"I'll check with the Inspector," said the sergeant. A moment later he emerged from an inner office. "C'mon, son," he said to Leonard, "it's your lucky day. You're gonna ride in a police car."

Leonard forced a weary smile. "You gonna be okay? On your own?" Leonard asked. "I'll be fine," said Menasha. "I'll be around," said Leonard, "if you need me. On The Street. Or wherever. See ya." Menasha shrugged. "Not if I see you first," said Menasha. Leonard laughed, waved farewell.

———

Marshall MacDonald checked his notes. "It says here you're a lecturer, at the University. Is that right?"

Menasha nodded.

"Why were you on Baldwin Street?" asked the policeman.

Menasha stared at the Inspector. He took a long while before answering. So long that the policeman looking at the torn clothes and state of the man in front of him was about to rephrase the question in simpler terms when Menasha finally spoke. "Why were any of us there? Was it ordained? Meant to be? A profound question. Why were we there? Tonight. At that time. At that precise moment. All of us, why were we there? The antagonists, the protagonists, the watchers, the innocent lamb who was induced to his slaughter, why where we there? Can you tell me? A plan? A scheme we know not of?" He turned to Untzmann. "And you, the instrument of death, why were you present when you might have been—"

"The truth is, I was—" Untzmann interrupted aggressively.

"Ah, the truth!" It was Menasha's turn to interject. "Another profundity. Truth. 'What is truth asked jesting Pilate and stayed not for an answer.' I never before realized police stations were such havens of theoretical parlance."

"—I was instructed to check the market, and was obeying orders," said Untzmann. "That's the truth. As simple as that."

"Yes," said Menasha shrugging, "that is the truth as you see it."

Untzmann twirled a forefinger at the side of his head blatantly indicating his suspicions of Menasha's sanity. MacDonald looked fierce disapproval at the burly motorcyclist.

Menasha saw the exchange between the two policemen but ignored it. "I always go," said Menasha.

"What?" asked the Inspector.

"Baldwin street," said Menasha. "You asked me about Baldwin Street. I'm always there. It's a market. Full of life. Buying. Selling. Trucks. Cars. People. All kinds of people. Babies. Mothers. Old men in black yarmulkes. With long white beards. Old ladies in shawls. With stooped round shoulders. People. People mean sound. Noise. Car horns. Pushcarts squeaking. Horses clopping. Storekeepers shouting bargains. Hucksters. Chickens squawking. Children crying. Customers haggling. Full of life. Things to do. Things to see. Active. Love. And hate. Greed. And charity. And what else? Pride. Envy. Lust. Gluttony. Not forgetting sloth. Plenty of sloth around on The Street. 'And the greatest of these is charity.' If you want to lose yourself, it's a good place to go. Baldwin Street. If you have lost yourself, as I often do, it's a good place to be. You see, when I'm out of it, away, the people are kind to me. Strange, isn't it? Hard people. Being soft. Gentle. Kind. To me. Baldwin Street. Full of life." Menasha waited. "Tonight it also had its fill of death." He paused again. "What happened to that child was senseless. Useless. Tragic. Why did an innocent child have to die? For what reason? What good did it do?" Silence. "There'll be an inquest I presume?"

Marshall MacDonald nodded.

"A coroner's court," continued Menasha. "with the verdict predictable. Death by misadventure. An accident. Bound to be the judgment. Such judgments never answer the question. Why? Why did a babe die tonight?"

Another silence. Except for shuffling from the other three in the room. Menasha looked over at Constable Untzmann.

"Who is to blame?" asked Menasha. "No one. It happened. An accident. The finger of fate. No one is to blame. Not even you. But just think, if you had been looking where you were going—"

"I was looking," Untzmann again interrupted.

"Looking. But not seeing," said Menasha. "If you had looked and seen that child then I wouldn't be here. Sitting here. Babbling on. You would not be here. None of would be in this room. Think. Where would he be?"

After a while the Inspector said, "You may go now, if you wish."

"Yes, of course, I may go now. Without let or hindrance. No restrictions. Free will. Another subject for profound discussion. In a police station." Menasha rose. Stood in the open doorway. "It is a profound dilemma that we have in this instance. Do you know that? A policeman, an upholder of good, in trying to uphold that good, rushing to intervene in a crime, inadvertently kills a sinless victim, a child. Where is the right of it? Where is the wrong of it?" He swayed.

"There's a lot more to be said. A lot more. But I don't know what. A young life ended tonight. More should be said. What? Do you know? I don't." With that Menasha left.

The energy of Menasha's words seemed to fill the little room for some time after his departure. Untzmann was the first to speak. "Nuts," he said. "Off his rocker. Must be totally gone." No one else said a word. "Well he is, isn't he?" demanded Untzmann.

"Shut up," said MacDonald quietly but firmly, "do us all a favour, Constable, and shut up." Untzmann rose to leave. "I want a written report. And, Constable, be particular about what you write." MacDonald looked at the wall clock. "The chief will be here in a few hours. I'm asking for an internal police inquiry."

Untzmann paled.

Distant rumblings after the storm. Belches of sound signifying spent rage. Frightening darkness, sinister clouds, thunder, lightning, lashing rain, ear-splitting cracks across the heavens, all these having passed, leaving behind only threatless murmurs. Like the anticipation of settling sounds heard after a torrent.

So it was after the death of Bernie Altman. The funeral took place on a Friday. Mourners, returning to Baldwin Street from the cemetery, washing hands in portable water at the curbside as ritual demanded, formed into spontaneous clusters.

"Something should be done," said Pinya Gelman, fruiterer.

"What can be done?" asked Sam Abelson, general merchandiser. He found himself, as usual, chairing the discussion.

"March on City Hall," said Jack Kruger, grocer. The others stared at him.

"Make our Alderman, Nathan Phillips, make him lead us," said Manny Katz, fishmonger. "Pinya and I been talkin'. We think we should march, all of us, from here to City Hall. The whole street. To protest."

Mutterings of concurrence at this suggestion. Heads nodding. The voices growing louder in agreement.

"Y'know that on the front of City Hall," said Sam Lottman, baker, "a Star of David is cut into the stone? One of the three major religions of this city. The mayor and council would have to take notice of such a delegation. Well they would, wouldn't they?"

Shouts of approval. A march. Yes. Yes. That's what is needed.

"But what are we gonna ask for when we get to City Hall? What do we want changed?" asked Sam Abelson.

"The police," said Joseph Litvak, dry goods retailer.

"The police were here," said Abelson. "Pity they were. One of them killed the boy, remember?" That pierced the bubbling agreement. "Maybe without the police the fight would have fizzled out. A black eye or two. Bones broken. A lot o' cuts. But not end with this, a child's blood, a child's death."

A pause.

"If the police had been here, a cop walking the beat, the fight wouldn't o' started in the first place," said Pinya Gelman.

"Yeah, that's right," said Manny Katz, "we need the police around here more. Patrolling. Lookin' after us."

More mutterings of agreement. "Awright," said Sam Abelson, "we'll send a letter to—"

"We'll send a committee," said Manny Katz.

"We'll send a letter and a delegation," amended Sam Abelson, "to speak to Alderman Phillips. About the police. And ask for more police protection for the area. Right?"

This resolution seemed to meet the unanimous approval of the impromptu meeting. But, returning to living quarters behind the stores, the storekeepers knew this to be only a token protest. Little could be achieved. Little was achieved.

"Yeah, they listened. At City Hall. They listened," said Sam Abelson wearily to his wife, stripping down to long underwear as he prepared for bed after the agreed visit to various officials. "It ain't gonna bring back little Bernie is it?"

"Sam," said Pearl Abelson, "it coulda been one of our kids."

"I know that," sighed Sam. "Don't ya think I don't know that?" He was annoyed with his wife, pregnant with another child, for reminding him of the vulnerability of their lives. "Go to sleep," ordered Sam curtly.

The death of Bernie Altman was scarcely noted by the newspapers. A small two-column item in the *Daily Star*. One column in the *Evening Telegram*. Listing the bare facts. A comment, in both papers, by Alderman Nathan Phillips on 'this tragic event.' A photo, in both papers, not of the victim but of Constable George Untzmann. The articles ended saying there would be an inquiry. Newspapers had more pertinent stories to print.

The war in Europe was progressing. Anti-Semitism was a feature of the enemy's politics. Discerned as being vaguely unpatriotic. Not that it disappeared. Hardly that. But it was suppressed. Making life a little less fearful for the people of Baldwin Street.

Throughout the ordeal of burying their son, Ira and Eva Altman were as stone. Not only to outsiders. But to each other. At the funeral parlour, Benjamin's on Spadina Crescent, they were oblivious of the numbers packing into the benched room. At the synagogue the rabbi's words became a jumble of sounds all without meaning. Only at the cemetery, when clothes were rendered as tradition demanded did Eva's hands force the attendant's scissors to cut, not the symbolic black ribbon worn for the purpose, but across the breast of her coat. A sharp incision ruining the coat forever.

From the graveside Ira and Eva went to a darkened home. The

store was lightless to discourage prospective customers unaware of the events of the week. The dwelling behind the store was also dark since orthodoxy necessitated someone else to switch lights on and off during the seven days of mourning. Eva and Ira sanctioned being left in the dark. Street lighting from windows being more than sufficient.

Alone, neighbours having gone, friends having gone, distant relatives having gone, Eva and Ira sat for some time in the unlit kitchen. Wordless. Motionless. Still. Eyes blank. As stone.

"Something to eat?" Some wifely compulsion made Eva utter the first words she had said to her husband in days.

Ira shook his head. "No," he said.

On the table was food. Lockshen pudding from Mrs. Kruger. Cheese and celery and crackers under a tea towel from Mrs. Abelson. The mourners, not allowed to cook for the seven days of sadness, would be catered for by neighbours.

Eva mounted the stairs. Ira followed.

On the bed they lay, backs to each other. Not weeping. Not speaking. Not sleeping. As stone.

A week to the day of Bernie's death, a Tuesday night, the two Altmans were again in bed. Back to back. Apart. The few inches of space between them a chasm. When Eva began to weep. And weep. And weep. As the sobbing increased her tiny body racked with spasms. Shaking her. Uncontrollably. Ira rolled over to look at Eva. Raised a gentle hand tentatively. Tripped tender fingers across his wife's shoulder. She shrugged away from his touch. Ira's tears fell softly on the pillow. Through her misery Eva became aware of her husband's weeping. She reached behind her. Took the hand she had rejected in hers. Held it to her chest. They lay side by side. Husband and wife. Man and woman. Throughout the night. Crying.

"I want you to kill me," said Eva to Ira the following morning.

Mrs. Berman had brought in cocoa and Kaiser rolls for breakfast. Ira, forcing himself to eat, had just chocolated a portion of the white-breaded roll, when Eva made her request.

Ira stared at her. Pushed the food aside.

"I can't go on," said Eva simply. "I don't want to go on. The *shiva* ends today. Seven days. It's over. What am I supposed to do? Open the store? Talk to customers? Cook meals? Eat? Drink? Laugh? Make jokes? I can't. I can't. I can't. I want to die. Help me to die."

Ira bowed his head. He could not speak.

"Help me. Help me. Please," pleaded Eva. "I can't do it alone. I need you." Ira looked up at her. "You're my husband. You give me what I want. Give me this. Please. Please. Please."

A long pause. Eva waited. "All right," said Ira.

Eva's body slumped. "Promise?" she asked.

"I promise," said Ira. "We will go together."

"No, no! You can stay," said Eva, "let me go. Just me."

"Together" said Ira, "As always. Together."

Eva moved to kneel before her husband. She grasped Ira's interlocked hands. Raised them to her face. Kissed his hands.

Anger appeared to be the chief emotion of those exiting from behind the locked and guarded room that housed the police inquiry into the death of Bernie Altman. The police Commissioner, who presided over the investigation, was angry that the death of a small child caused by a policeman, however inadvertent, had come just at a time when he and his colleagues were trying to raise the image of police work to new heights of civic appreciation. The war was coming closer. The force was soon bound to feel the effects of losing some of its best men to the armed services. Public support for the police was essential at all times. But never more than now. Strangers swamping the city. The halls at the exhibition grounds being converted into emergency barracks. Fathers and brothers leaving the city. Posted to barracks elsewhere. Unrest. Unease. Uncertainty. Always precedes social changes such as occur at the beginning of a war. What was needed, the Commissioner believed, was a vigilant police force. Not an inquiry to rationalize one policeman's unfortunate action.

"What has the committee decided?" asked a flush-faced

Telegram reporter, confronting the policeman in the echoing corridor.

"Hello, Pete," said the Commissioner, "nice to see you again. A statement is being prepared. Just let me add my personal sadness regarding the tragic circumstances that led to Motorcyclist—" he searched to remember the name "—Untzmann's involvement in the death of—"

"Why was the inquiry held behind closed doors?" a cub reporter from the *Star* interrupted. "Why wasn't the public allowed to be present? If not the public, then us, the public's representative?"

"Sometimes it is easier to ascertain the facts in private," said the Commissioner, "away from the public and—"

"Are you hiding something?" continued the reporter.

The Commissioner visibly struggled to control himself. "There is nothing to hide. As I said, a statement will soon be issued. G'day, gentlemen." He strode away.

The reporter shouted after him. "If it had been a baby from north of St Clair, would it've still been a police whitewash? Answer me that, Commissioner?"

But the Commissioner did not answer.

George Untzmann was also angry as he left the inquiry. Hell, anyone would think I deliberately killed the little kid, he said to himself. It was an accident, ferchrisake! Can't they see that? Anyway what was the kid doing out that late? Bloody Jewkid. The thoughts jumbled in his head. Gonna go on my record, they said. Bastards. Let it go on my record. See if I give a damn. 'Doesn't show the force in a good light.' Well, o'course it doesn't. Stupid thing to say. Did I have full control of the vehicle? Another stupid question. Yes, mother dear, I was driving with due care and attention. You're not gonna get me on that one. It was an accident! Six months. Six months off the bike. Back on the beat. Six months! Bastards. It was an accident!

Inspector Marshall MacDonald was also angry as he marched down the corridor towards a waiting police car. On the pavement outside, George Untzmann hovered near the car hoping for a lift back to the station. But the stern look on MacDonald's face clearly indicated that the constable was not going to be invited to share the ride.

"Can I ask, sir, what happened in there?" asked the driver.

"A reprimand," said MacDonald settling into the back seat.

"Is that all?"

"And six months of foot patrol," said MacDonald. The car moved off.

MacDonald's thoughts reflected back to the inquiry. Untzmann had played it clever, he told himself. No. Not clever. Cunning. The fat slob. Devious. Using all the tricks. Smiling. Agreeing. Appearing calm and rational. Loquacious. Using words to good effect. Using veiled, and sometimes not so veiled, anti-Semitism to emote responses and prejudices from the others sitting round the table.

"You did not, either before or after the incident, question the people around you?" the Commissioner had asked.

"No, sir," Untzmann had replied. "I took names. As you can see from my report. A lot of names, of everyone involved, as well as witnesses. But no questions. Perhaps that was a failing on my part. I must admit to that. But to be honest, sir," here Untzmann had smiled, "I don't know how much good questioning would have done. The accents and dialects those people have. I can't always understand what they're saying."

This evoked a snigger or two. And a smile or two. Like an actor playing to the gallery, Untzmann signalled his gratitude towards those who had sniggered and smiled.

"Yes, I could hear some sort of commotion as I approached Baldwin Street," Untzmann had answered another interrogator, "I thought it might be the hubbub of prayers. Another one of their holidays. Those people have religious holidays at all kinds of different days, don't they? I thought maybe Halloween was—"

"You say you heard a commotion," Inspector MacDonald cut across the policeman's testimony. "You also saw people running, saw crowds gathering. Weren't you alarmed? Apprehensive? Feeling a need to be cautious?"

"Tell you the truth, sir, I thought they might be running towards a bargain," said Untzmann, "for potatoes. Or rotten apples.

Those people are good at bargains."

"How do you know, Constable," asked MacDonald, "have you ever shopped on Baldwin Street?"

"Well, no, sir. I—"

"What's that to do with this inquiry?" asked the policeman who had been assigned to help Untzmann's defence. "Hardly salient, sir."

"Might be salient," rejoined MacDonald, "to Untzmann's attitude to 'those people.'"

A reprimand. The Commissioner would have let Untzmann off with merely a reprimand, MacDonald reminded himself. Fortunately others insisted this was inadequate. Six months off motorcycle duty with subsequent loss in salary. Not enough. You fat hairy toad. Not enough.

After the hearing, the Commissioner had taken MacDonald to one side. "Don't let your personal feelings cloud your logic, Marshall," said the Commissioner.

"No, sir. I won't, sir," MacDonald had replied. "But I do believe George Untzmann should—"

"Forget Untzmann," said the Commissioner. "I'm talking about you. And Christie Pits. Those race riots. All those years ago. Could be affecting your judgment. Don't let it."

"No, sir. I won't, sir," MacDonald had said.

Of course it affects my judgment, you old turd, MacDonald was telling himself in the car. "I am part of all that I have met." As we all are. I was at Christie Pits. Not you. I must think of a punishment to fit George Untzmann's crime. I wish I had one drop of Jewish blood. I would think of something. Something rabbinical. Something sage. Talmudic. Hah, yes, that's it!

The chortle from MacDonald startled the police car driver.

"You okay, sir?" asked the driver.

"I'm fine. Just fine," said MacDonald. "Get me back to the station." The Inspector laughed once more.

"Keep away from me, Tony," said Ruby Waldman through the minimally opened door. "If my old man sees me with you it'll start all over again."

"Geezus," said Tony D'Angelo, "what the hell's happened to you?"

He pointed to cuts and bruises on Ruby's face. Tony had called round to the Waldman house on Palmerston Boulevard. The Edwardian porch with squat pillars at each corner confirmed this to be a home of some substance. As he mounted the steps Tony could smell cooking. So someone must be home. But he had to press the buzzer for some time before Ruby appeared to inch open the door.

"My old man did this." Ruby indicated his face.

"Your old man's a rabbi," said Tony.

"Doesn't mean a fart," said Ruby. "First he used a stick. A branch or something. It broke. He went for the razor strap. Beat the shit out o' me. 'You went with the *goyim*?' he kept saying. 'To Baldwin Street? And a child died?' Then wallop. 'I'm not raising a *Yiddishe* anti-Semite'. Then he'd wallop me again. That black strap really hurts, y'know."

"I'll bet," said Tony.

"You tell the guys, I'm not goin' with 'em anymore," added Ruby. "The old man won't let me. Anyhoo, it's better that way. I'm not one of you guys. Never was. I'm better on my own. From now on."

"Sorry, Ruby. Look if there's anythin' I can do, tell me," said Tony.

Ruby paused. "They came here, y'know. Those guys from Baldwin Street. One of them knew who I was. The one called Danny. I've played basketball with him at the YMHA. He knew me. Came looking for me. Wanted the names of all the guys who were on that bike raid. So you watch it, Tony. They're gonna beat the crap out o' all of you."

"Did you tell 'em?" asked Tony.

"I'm no Judas," said Ruby. "I'm not goin' with you guys anymore. But I'm not with them either. I didn't give 'em any names."

"Good," said Tony.

"Don't know if it's good or bad," said Ruby. "Don't care. They can go to hell for all I care and you guys can go to hell too. I'm on my own." With that he closed the door.

———•—•—•———

I hope he objects, Inspector MacDonald said to himself. The more he protests the better. Then he would be out of line and I could make it stick for more than six months. Insubordination. C'mon you fat slob, say something.

But Constable Untzmann only blinked his eyes several times on hearing the news. "Yes, sir. Whatever you say, sir," he said with subdued simplicity.

"Fine. You start tomorrow." With that the interview was over. MacDonald rose from his desk to hold open the door. Untzmann shuffled to his feet. Extended a hand towards his superior. MacDonald was wondering how best to avoid the proffered handshake, when, looking over Untzmann's shoulder he saw the answer. Menasha was sitting in the waiting room.

"Ah, professor. Good morning," said MacDonald. "You've met Constable Untzmann, haven't you? You'll be seeing a lot more of him in the next six months. I've just assigned him to a new beat. He's to concentrate on foot patrolling one area. Baldwin Street."

Untzmann barely recognized Menasha. A soft brown tweed jacket, leather elbows, coordinated with a contrasting pair of slacks was startlingly different in apparel from the tattered man he had first met.

"Baldwin Street, eh?" said Menasha.

"I'm looking forward to it," said Untzmann, supposedly unctuously, but then added, "except of course, for the smells."

"Well," said Menasha, "it's a market place. Cabbage and sprouts going off does—"

"I'm not talking about rotten cabbage," said Untzmann. "Old Jewish ladies smell."

All eyes in the large centre office of the station where the conversation took place turned to look at Untzmann.

After a beat Menasha said, "You're wrong."

"They do smell," said Untzmann.

"Presuming that your highly unlikely statement is accurate and that elderly Jewish women do give off offensive odours," said Menasha, "you are still wrong. Wrong. Wrong. Grammatically. They would stink. It is you that smells."

A slight titter could be heard from the listening members of the police force.

"They do smell," repeated Untzmann.

"And Negroes? Does the negroid race also offend your olfactory senses?" asked Menasha.

Untzmann's eyes blinked. "Y'mean niggers? Sure. Everyone know niggers smell. Or stink. Or whatever. Well they do, don't they?" He turned for support to his fellow policemen in the office. But received none.

"Man's stupidity about his fellow man is boundless," said Menasha. "Exceeded only by man's cruelty to his fellow man. Think of what we did to the Indians in the last century. Or what the Turks have done to the Armenians this century. To say nothing of what is going on in Germany now. Boundless cruelty. Symbolized by this officer here. What did you say your name was?"

"Untzmann. Constable George William Untzmann. Do you want my number too?"

"Five thousand years of civilization," said Menasha. "Five million years of life. And what have we achieved? This!" He gestured towards the policeman. "Constable George William Untzmann."

Untzmann marched out of the station avoiding eye contact with any others.

"Come in, come in," said MacDonald indicating his office to Menasha. "What is it you wanted to see me about?"

—•••—

"You owe my father twenty cents," said Izzy Birnbaum.

"What the flippin' hell you talkin' about?" asked Carlo D'Angelo.

On a porch on Manning Avenue, enclosed by rusting screens with frayed edges and many slashes, useless against any insect invasion the following summer, but certain to be patched to last yet another season, the two sized each other up. Izzy was larger than Carlo, a man, twenty-two years old.

"I'm talkin' about plums," said Izzy. "Lovely, juicy, purple Victoria plums. Delicious to eat. Y'bought some. But didn't pay. Remember? You pay me now."

Izzy held out his hand palm up for the money.

"Screw you," said Carlo.

The two punches Izzy threw were so fast Carlo never saw them. Neither did Tony who was lingering in the background. Carlo toppled. Izzy lifted him by the ankles. And shook him. Coins clattered out of his pockets onto the wooden porch floor.

Izzy addressed the upside-down head of Carlo. "Pick up twenty cents. Nothing more. Nothing less." Carlo hazily selected two dimes. Izzy dropped him. And again held out his hand towards the crumpled figure. The coins dropped onto Izzy's palm. "Thank you," smiled Izzy. And helped Carlo to his feet. "Y'know my father always says to customers 'Pay me when you can.' He's such a softy my father. I'll tell 'im you could afford to pay now." Izzy slammed the screen door behind him. "One other thing," Izzy turned back to say, "we specialize in free home delivery. Anytime you want another free delivery like this, you just let me know."

<hr>

Friday. This Friday it will be done, Ira told himself. A good night. The Sabbath. If there is a God then He will be so busy receiving the prayers of the devout he won't notice two sinners escaping. More important, Baldwin Street was quiet on Friday nights. Customers gone. To houses. To prepare for the holy night. To wash cupboards. To wash floors of wood and linoleum and to carpet them with newspapers. *Balabustas* busy. Housewives hurrying home. To light candles. To chop liver, to chop herring, to mince gefilte fish, to grind horseradish, mix hardboiled eggs with onions, boil chicken, prepare salad, slice some pickles. And get dessert ready. Strudel or lockshen pudding or cottage cheese blintzes with cinnamon and sour cream. The storekeepers also kept to themselves on Friday nights. Resting. In anticipation of the Saturday onslaught. Yes, thought Ira, Friday night is a good night.

Life without Bernie would be eating potatoes without salt. A mush. A mash. Flavourless. He could think of no reason to prolong his ability to throw a shadow on this planet. It was a meeting with Constable George Untzmann that changed his mind.

Untzmann patrolled the length of Baldwin Street with the measured tread of a policeman. Flatfoot. The name accurately described his walk. Foot up. Foot down. Flat. Deliberate. Slow. Stately. Unhurried. A copper on the beat.

When he first started his duties, and the tradesmen whispered animatedly to identify him as the motorcycle cop who had struck down little Bernie, his presence was acknowledged only with deliberately turned backs. No storekeeper stooped to talk to him. Or greet him. For his part, Untzmann did not try to ingratiate himself with the community. He was not liked. Fine. He would never like them. Snap. Untzmann was also aware, though in no way wary, of the youths of the Street. Two or three would often gather on the pavement as Untzmann approached. When Untzmann saw the bunched young men he would simply cross the road. Avoiding confrontation. Avoiding incident. Better that way, he told himself. "Y're not there to measure the size of the stands. Y're there to keep the peace!" Inspector MacDonald had roared down the phone at him when he reported the shops were breaking the law with their outside displays. So he knew he could expect little support from superiors. Untzmann did make a note, however, of MacDonald's reaction, including date and time, in case it should ever be needed for some future tribunal. Stories circulated, confirmed and unconfirmed, that the Italians who had initiated the bicycle mêlée were being sought out and beaten by the Baldwin Street youths. Again Untzmann noted that MacDonald was turning a blind eye to such lawlessness. Y'never know, he told himself, could be useful one day, I won't always be a lowly patrolman. In the meantime let this six months end, he thought, as smoothly as possible. And so he walked. Along the north side of Baldwin Street, along the south side, east on Kensington Avenue, west on Kensington, back to Baldwin. Over and over again. Time after time. Day after day. Without incident.

Ira was putting out a metallic Salada Tea sign to indicate the shop was open— a habit he seemed incapable of breaking—when he saw Untzmann. He had been told that the man whose machine had killed his son now patrolled the area. This was the first time he had seen him. Ira planted himself in Untzmann's path.

Untzmann blinked when he saw Ira. Who is this little man blocking my way? One good puff, and he's gone. Oh, Kee-rist! He remembered seeing Ira at the inquest. It's the father.

He came close to the grocer. Only inches separated them. Untzmann wondered what to do next. He touched his helmet. "Good morning," said Untzmann.

What else? Ira asked himself. *What else are you going to say? "Good morning." Is that all? Are you going to say you're sorry, you didn't mean it, it was an accident, a mishap, a calamity, or even a pity? I'm sorry, I'm sorry, I'm sorry. Anything? Say it!*

"I said, 'Good morning,'" Untzmann repeated.

Ira still did not reply.

You mamzer, *thought Ira. Devil. Evil man. You took the light out of my life. You killed my only child. My wife is waiting for me to tell her what day will be her last day. Then I must kill myself.*

Untzmann looked around. It was too early for the teenage boys to be on the Street. "You are in my way," said Untzmann.

Ira did not move. One good puff, thought Untzmann, and I could blow you away little man. One good puff. And you and your clean white apron would be rolling in the gutter. Where you belong. I can't. Not today. Not for a few months. It's your lucky day. Untzmann sighed, stepped around Ira, continued on his route. Ira watched the policeman's departing figure.

Not a word. Not a word from you. Just one word, thought Ira, would help me. And maybe help you. One wounded animal to another. But no. Nothing. Not a tear. Not a whimper. Not a moan. Nothing. Leaving me with the pain. Leaving me with the hurting.

"Before I kill myself," vowed Ira, "I must do one other thing, Constable Untzmann. Kill you."

———◆◆◆———

"Coffee, please, Sergeant. Hot, black, in two containers that are not chipped, and without cigarette ash floating on top," said Inspector MacDonald.

The sergeant whistled.

"Well, they tell me miracles still happen. Let's see if it's true," said MacDonald. He closed the office door and turned back to Menasha. "When are you going back to teaching?" he asked.

"In a few more days," said Menasha, "I need a few more days to make sure I'm settled, when I'm sure my head is clear, then I will call the University."

"Good." MacDonald settled at his desk. "What are you reading?"

Menasha produced from his breast pocket a protruding paperback. "Bertrand Russell," he said. "Lord Bertrand Russell. British. He says something that's relevant to us."

"What?"

"That Naziism is a scourge that must be stopped," said Menasha.

"Hardly need a genius to tell us that," said MacDonald.

"Russell is a pacifist. He went to jail because of his pacifist beliefs. He's now sanctioning the war. A volte-face. He's saying he now approves of force. That at times it provides the only solution," said Menasha. "It's a tremendous change for him and his followers."

"Well we're going to need all the help we can get," said MacDonald, "including you philosophers."

"A lot of innocents are going to die while we stop that scourge," said Menasha. He looked out of the window. "Bystanders. Not warriors. Victims."

"Like little Bernie," said MacDonald.

"Yes."

A knock on the door. The sergeant entered with two coffees. One was in an enamel mug with a blue rim, chipped. The other was in a white ceramic mug, chipped.

MacDonald shook his head, stood, reached for his coat. "There's a new Chinese place around the corner," he said. "Let's have lunch."

"Was the assignment you gave Untzmann wise?" asked Menasha.

"I hope one of two things happens to Untzmann on Baldwin Street," said MacDonald. "He either gets his hide thrashed. Or he learns tolerance," he opened the door. "I suspect neither will happen."

"Suppose he gets killed?" asked Menasha.

"Unlikely," said MacDonald. "Bad guys only get shot in westerns." They exited. "Do you like sweet and sour?"

——•◦•◦•——

His abundantly tailored camelhair coat coordinated beautifully with chestnut brown skin. He was in Ira Altman's store. And could not believe what he had just been asked by the proprietor.

Ira had decided to put his request to the first coloured customer to enter the shop.

"Hey, man, I'm a singer," said the man in the coat. "What do I know about guns?"

"Sorry," said Ira.

The customer hurriedly settled his bill and left the store behind.

That night Ira went to visit what to him was another world. Spadina Avenue. Not Spadina near Baldwin Street. He vaguely knew that area. But further away. Below Dundas Street. Foreign. Unfamiliar. Strange. He eventually found what he was looking for. The Spadina Ice Cream Parlour proclaimed the window's lettering. He entered.

A smoke-filled room. Mostly men. A spray of women. On

hoop-backed metal chairs in front of round marble tables. Dominoes clattered. Cards shuffled. Raucous laughter. Talk. In a range of accents. And tones. From guttural to soprano. Coffee and cake, Coke and pie, sat before the few who were actually eating. Ice cream was not to be seen.

Ira looked about. Saw the rear door. And entered another room. Smokier than the first. Three large tables covered loosely with green baize. Card games only. Coins, some stacked neatly, others splayed sloppily, before each player. Here and there dollar bills mattressed the coins. Cash. No chips. The lighting, in contrast to the glaring bare bulbs of the outer room, was focussed. The tables lit. The surrounds dark. A more serious atmosphere. Except for the conversation.

"If you had three kings in there, then I'm my own grandmother."

"Then make me a potato latke, *bubele.*"

From one table, as cards were being shuffled.

"Deuces are wild. He's got two deuces showing. And you raise him! How could you raise him?"

"It's my money, right? I play it my way. Forty cents more to you. You in or you out?"

"I'm out. I don't play with madmen!"

"Y'mean y'don't play with yourself?" came from another table.

It was a milieu unknown to Ira.

"Ya want somethin'?" A face with a nose that had seen better days loomed in front of Ira.

Ira refused to speak out. He crooked a finger. The man's head bowed. Ira whispered into an ear that matched the nose.

At first the ex-pugilist's face registered incomprehension at what he was hearing. After listening more carefully, his eyes popped.

"Hey, boys, listen t' dis! Dis guy wants t' buy somethin!"

"Yeah? What?" "This ain't Eaton's." "Ain't even Simpson's!"

"If he wants a broad, tell him to try Maggie on Vanauley Street."

"Does he have money?"

"Money isn't everything."

"So who wants everything?"

"Money can't buy ya the love of a loyal little lady, can it?"

"Y'mean for five thousand dollars I couldn't have your wife?"

"For five thousand dollars, I'll throw in her sister."

"Luck. Y'can't buy luck. Does he know that?"

"Sure y'can, with enough gelt, y'can buy anything. Even luck."

"No, y'can't!"

"Yes, y'can!"

"Y'wanna bet?"

"No! Not me. I'm not lucky. I got no money!"

"He wants to know where he can buy a gun!" shouted flat-nose above the din.

The talking ceased. Activities ceased. Abruptly. A pause. Before one of the players said, "If he gets one bring it here, so I can shoot this *potz* who bets against wild deuces."

The laughter followed Ira as the bouncer showed him out of the back door. He slumped away miserably. Clumping back up Spadina Avenue thinking about his failed mission. After several minutes a hand restrained him.

"Mr. Altman." It was Harvey Willenski. "I was in the parlour. I heard you. What ya want a gun for?"

Ira looked at the brawny young man. And told him.

"Not you, Mr. Altman," said Harvey. "You couldn't hurt anyone."

Ira considered this for a moment. Then turned to continue his walk. Harvey again chased after him.

"Leave that copper to us," said Harvey. "Don't get involved."

Ira kept walking.

When he was in the darkened store later that night, Eva asleep upstairs, Ira mused over the evening's events. That boy, Harvey, was right. I can't shoot that fat bastard. I can't shoot anyone. The Bible says the meek shall inherit the earth. How? Unless they learn to fight for it. I can't. I can't help. I can die—that I can do—and I'll take Eva with me. That's not the same as killing. That's merely ending. A weak ending for a weak man. Ira began to weep.

On the counter was a tin of Heinz Baked Beans. Misplaced. Ira picked up the tin to return to its allocated spot. A conditioned response. He stopped. Looked at the shelves in the store. Row upon row of cans. Neat. Tidy. Clean. Dust free. In place. As he once was. As Eva once was. As life once was. Until the death of Bernie. He threw the tin in his hand at the shelves. More tins toppled. He collected them. To throw. Other cans collapsed onto the floor. Not enough, he thought. His arms scooped a row of cans from a shelf. Then another row. And another. He kicked over a sack of lima beans. Upset a burlap bag filled with barley. Scattered dried mushrooms. Lashing out. Kicking. Destroying. He was now weeping. Uncontrollably.

————

George Untzmann went to the movies on his night off. Always. Tonight was no exception. As he came out of the cinema his chubby cheeks were set in a smirk. He was recalling images from the film he had just seen. Tonight he had visions of himself as Clark Gable, whom he was convinced he resembled, smothering Vivien Leigh with kisses. Despite the cold November blasts his windbreaker was open, his bulk making him impervious to winter conditions. Untzmann cut down the alleyway next to the cinema.

Danny, Muchel, and Harvey were waiting in the Birnbaum delivery truck, borrowed, at the other end.

"Here he comes," said Muchel.

"Big sonofabitch, ain't he?" said Danny. "Bigger than I remember."

"'The harder they fall,'" quoted Harvey.

"Y'sure y'want to take him alone?" asked Muchel. "He won't fight fair."

"Neither will I," said Harvey, leaving the van.

Harvey hurried forward. He wanted the confrontation to be at the bleakest part of the alley. Away from street lighting.

"Hello, Untzmann," said Harvey.

The big man came to a standstill. "Yeah? Oh, you. What the hell do you want, kid?" said Untzmann.

"You," said Harvey.

Untzmann started to stride past Harvey. "Go away, kid," he said, "I don't want no trouble."

"You got no vote in this matter," said Harvey. To provoke his opponent he aimed a kick at the policeman's groin. For a man of his size Untzmann was surprisingly agile. He sidestepped the kick. Taking most of the impact on his hip.

"You little kike shit," said Untzmann. "I'll murder you." He hobbled forward. Decoyed to make it look as if he too was about to kick. A ruse. He threw a hook that carried the full weight of his body behind it. That punch changed Harvey's nose forever. "I'm gonna teach you a lesson," said Untzmann.

The brick wall of the cinema supported Harvey. He saw Untzmann reach into a back pocket and pull out a police blackjack. "And if you had your gun, would you use that too?" said Harvey. From around his waist Harvey removed his belt. Thick, black, studded with rivets and ending with a weighty metal buckle.

As the blackjack swung towards him, Harvey whipped his belt into action.

At the police station the next morning, Inspector MacDonald listened to Untzmann on the phone. And smiled.

"I was fixing the roof. Fell off the ladder," said Untzmann.

"Fixing a roof at night? Sounds pretty feeble to me, Constable. You claim you are ill. You say you won't be coming in for a few days. I will report that. For the record. I know you believe in records." Then the Inspector added, "And Constable, don't forget to get your clothes cleaned." MacDonald hung up. And laughed. He knew the truth. Menasha had told him about the fight earlier that morning. Harvey had thrashed the big man. And then pissed on him.

From a drawer Ira took a stack of aprons. White aprons. Pristine. Laundered. Ironed. Folded. Made from sugar bags he himself had carefully selected at Abelson's. He manipulated the soft cloths into the crack under the door leading to the store. Then under the back door. The windows were next. Gaps stuffed.

Eva descended the stairs into the kitchen. Not a word had been said. No designated hour had been appointed. But she knew. And he knew. It was dusk. On a Friday night. The Sabbath was about to commence.

Ira closed the door to the stairs after Eva entered. Crammed more aprons into slits. Went to the stove. Turned the handles on all four burners. Turned the oven to its maximum release. Gas fizzled into the room.

Bedding had been placed on the floor. Ira held out his hand, to help Eva. She took it. Eased herself down. Ira lay down beside her.

Eva was wearing her best outfit. An elegant cream suit, trimmed with narrow floral edges. A gloved hand, held the other glove. She smiled at Ira. With her free hand touched his face. "Thank you," she said.

"You look a bride," said Ira.

Eva snuggled into her husband's arms.

—◦•◦—

The evening that started off so well was ending badly. A few laughs. Were turning to frowns.

"Do you eat pork?"

"Only if it's cooked, " said Menasha. Marshall MacDonald laughed, as did his wife, Mary, as did the two children, all gathered around the family dining table.

Fulton MacDonald, age six, thought it particularly funny. "You can't eat it raw!" declared the child.

"I could if I was a lion," said Menasha. With that he roared, turned his hands into claws about to pounce on the boy.

Fulton shrieked with delight. His younger sister, Mary, joined in the shrieking.

"Do we call you Menasha or Maximillian?" asked Mary.

"Call me anything. As long as it's not late for dinner," replied Menasha. The diners giggled.

During the course of the meal, Menasha asked the Inspector, "How are you getting on with the book I left you?"

"I'm reading it," answered MacDonald, helping himself to more potatoes.

"How far have you got?" asked Menasha

"I started. I'm into it."

"How far?" chuckled Menasha.

"It's good. I'm enjoying it," said MacDonald.

"How far?" insisted Menasha.

MacDonald, appearing to concentrate on his food, did not reply. Mary did. "Page three. Until he fell asleep. Last night," she said.

More laughter. MacDonald had alleged he wanted to increase his knowledge of philosophy, to study man's thinking, and coerced Menasha into leaving him a prescribed text book. Menasha had given him a copy of Plato's *Republic*. After the laughter subsided, Menasha told him that studying was always more difficult for those other than full-time students. Especially adults with a demanding occupation.

"You've got enough to keep you busy," said Menasha.

"I wanted to talk to you about that," said MacDonald. Menasha wondered what he meant. It wasn't until Menasha was being shown out that MacDonald clarified his thoughts.

"I could use someone," said MacDonald leaning on the door, "who could keep his pulse on the Baldwin Street tom-toms."

"Mixing metaphors," said Menasha.

"Sorry."

"Someone who would let you know what's going on?" said Menasha. "Tell you the latest?"

"Yes. Exactly," said Macdonald.

"A squealer. A rat. A stool-pigeon. A two-timer," said Menasha, "that's what you're asking me to be."

"No! Hey, now wait a minute. I just thought—" said MacDonald.

"Good night, Inspector," said Menasha. "Thank you for the dinner. I've already thanked Mary but you can thank her again for me. And I enjoyed the children. You have a lovely family. Good night."

MacDonald watched Menasha depart, wanted to call him back, but knew better than to try.

Once a policeman, always a policeman, thought Menasha. He can't help it. He is what he is. It was a cold night. But clear. He wanted to walk. Too early to go back to his dismal room, he told himself. Baldwin Street. Back to sanctuary. Yes, good idea.

He almost always walked on the south side of Baldwin Street. Something impelled him this night to cross to the north side.

In front of the Altman store, Menasha got the first strong stench of gas.

He realized he had read the same paragraph three times. The inner lids of his eyes were sandpaper. But just once more, he told himself, you'll get it next time. Marshall MacDonald was in bed, a light glowed on the book in his hand.

"We could offer him a room," said Mary MacDonald. To shield herself from the light, her back was to him.

"Who? Menasha?" he asked. "Might not want it."

"A man like that shouldn't be on his own. And we have the space," said Mary. Since her husband did not answer, she stretched her hand behind her and forced the book downwards onto the bedding and glanced at the top of the page. "Page three!" she chortled, "you're still on page three!" After a moment MacDonald also began to giggle. "Come along, Einstein, put the book away," she said. Which he did. Lowered himself into the quilt. Snuggled against his wife's back. She murmured. He murmured in return. She murmured more. He put the light out.

"How dare you! How dare you!" Menasha was shouting. Furious. Oblivious of the retching of Ira and Eva. "You are suffering? I am suffering. We all suffer. Suffer! Suffer! Suffer! We creatures of this earth. We suffer. None of us escapes." When he had first broken into the kitchen, Menasha used a chair to smash the window. He dragged the Altmans, Eva first then Ira, into the backyard. The front of the store might have been airier but Menasha wanted to avoid prying eyes. He propped Eva against one fence. Ira across another. Moving from one to another. Slapping backs hard. Shouting.

"You are in pain? Use your pain to help others. Use your pain to understand others." Eva was choking. Vomiting. Gasping. "The Catholics are right. Suicide is a sin! Not against God. He'd be too busy to worry about you. It's a sin against you! You're saying your life was nothing. No life is nothing. It all counts. Make it count." Ira wheezed fresh cold air into his lungs. "Every good man who kills himself is letting a bad man win. An evil bastard smiles. One more out of the way. You helped him win." Slap. Slap. "Who's going to remember Bernie? Who's going to light a candle for Bernie? You are. You must." Slap. Slap "Years ago a sperm and a egg met. And created you. You. To love. To hate. To laugh. To cry. To know anger. To know serenity. To rejoice in achievement. To know frustration. To revel in success. To regret failings. To know for certain. To be unsure. To be bad. To be good. To be wrong. To be right. To be generous. To be mean. To be forgiving. To be demanding. To be faithful. To be fickle. To know magnanimity. To know jealousy. To be healthy. To be sick. To think, to reason. To be silly and unreasonable. To live!" Menasha was tiring. He was no longer addressing the Altmans. He was speaking to himself. "You have been given the gift of life. You are given it only once. Only once. Don't throw it away. Use it."

Still choking, Eva began to sob. Ira, also gagging, took her in his arms.

"Live. Live. Live," said Menasha faintly.

MacDonald's hand groped for the ringing telephone.

"Yeah?"

A patrol car cruising on Baldwin Street had spotted a broken store door. Upon further investigation became aware of a strong stench of gas.

"Which store?" asked MacDonald.

"The Altman's," said the patrolman. "The folks of that child, Bernie." That's why, despite the hour, I thought you should know, sir."

"Obviously an accident, isn't it constable?" said MacDonald. "Gas burners left on inadvertently, right?" MacDonald was waking rapidly.

"If you say so, sir," said the voice on the phone.

"I do say so. And that's what I expect to see on your report," said MacDonald. "Secure the store. Help the Altmans to settle. And leave."

"Yes, sir, I will, sir."

"Who found them?" asked MacDonald.

The constable could be heard rustling through his notes. "A man they called Men-a-shaw. I think that's how you pronounce it."

"And where is he now, this rescuer?" asked MacDonald.

"I don't know, sir. He slipped out. Sorry, sir. Must be nearby. Shall I search for him?" asked the policeman.

"No," said MacDonald.

———————

Half an hour later Menasha was sitting on a bench in Dennison Park and looked up to see the dark overcoated figure of Inspector MacDonald coming towards him.

"Good evening." He looked at his wrist. "Sorry. Good morning, Menasha. Or should it be Maximillian?" asked MacDonald.

Menasha stared at him. Continued to sit in silence. "What was there before the universe began? What existed in space? Was there space?" said Menasha. "What was there before the amoeba crawled out of the sea? Did the amoeba crawl or was he pushed? Maybe dumped on the shore? Why was I there tonight? Why did I stray from my usual route tonight? If I had not strayed, been on the other side of the street, would I have smelled the gas? Suppose it's all pre-ordained? Suppose it's all written in some book that we never get around to reading. Like you with Plato? Suppose the answers are in front of us but we don't know the alphabet. Can't translate the words. Why were we given such powers? To paint the Sistine Chapel, to fly into the sky, to create canons. Why?" Menasha paused. "I won't lecture. I'm not quite strong enough yet. To return to lecturing."

"Sorry to hear that."

"Suppose God is a child who treats us like toys. We're God's playthings. Ever think of that? God is a spoiled child? Nothing we do is enough for him? Ever think of that?"

"No, never," said MacDonald.

"Presbyterian?"

"Yes."

"No, God wouldn't be a child to you then. An old man, maybe. Of course that might be more accurate. It would explain why the seasons are all wrong these days. God is getting old and forgetful. When it's summer, He gives us winter. All wrong. God is getting old. Ever think of that?"

"No. Never."

"Or better still, God is a Stage Manager, like in the theatre, not good at his job. We pray to Him. Please God let it be sunny for my wedding. And the result? He gets it wrong. It rains on the wedding. He's bad at his job. He should be fired. I'm all for getting God fired." Menasha paused, looked up at the Inspector. "At the moment, I am Maximillian. But sometimes when I turn, I can see Menasha. Advancing. Towards me." Another pause. "He's on his way. He'll be here soon."

"Come home with me, please," said MacDonald. "Mary would like you to stay with us."

"Yes, yes," said Menasha softly. "I would like that." He rose from the bench. He let MacDonald lead him by the arm.

Some were arrogant. Most were humble. Some were tall. Most were short. Some were fair. Most were dark. Some were loud. Most were quiet. All needed care. All were in rags. Refugees. Rescued from the hordes of hell that had swept across Europe.

The first such batch to arrive in Toronto. Displaced Persons. Jammed into a welfare hall on Beverley Street. Where relatives, established citizens of the city, searched among the newcomers hoping to find relatives, or relatives of relatives, or news of relatives, or any fragment of information about the town, the village, the hamlet that had been left behind.

"Which shtetl are you from?"

"Where?"

"Is that near Ludsk?"

"Do you know—?"

Eva and Ira Altman sat to one side. Watching. Among the many arrivals being ignored, she had seen a little girl, eyes rimmed with tears and tiredness, huddling against her parents. Eva approached. Ira hesitated, then followed. From a paper bag Eva took a red shining apple. Held it out. The child took a dummy nipple out her mouth. Looked up at her mother. The mother nodded. The child snatched the apple.

"Do you speak English?" asked Ira.

"Hello. Yes. Hello," said the father eagerly. He was in his twenties, thought Ira, as was his wife.

"Where are you from?" said Ira.

The father's face frowned, shoulders shrugged. "Hello," he said again. His command of the language was limited.

"*Kenst redin Mama Loshen?* Do you speak the Mother Tongue? *Du redst Yiddish?* Do you speak Jewish?" asked Ira.

"*A bisel.* A little. *Nor ein bisel.* Only a bit," said the father.

Before the conversation could proceed further, a welfare worker approached. She checked the tag flapping from the mother's lapel. "Their name is Berclov. From Romania." She spoke to the father in Russian. "They know no one in this country," she said.

Ira took the welfare worker to one side while Eva busied herself with the little girl. "We have room, in our house," said Ira, "if they want to come." The lady welfare worker pointed out that the mother, although not apparent yet, was pregnant. Ira nodded. "We have room," he repeated.

Ira and Eva and the immigrant trio left the hall. To begin a new and different life, for all of them, on Baldwin Street.

George Untzmann was subjected to a further two months beyond the original six as a foot-patrolling policeman. After three years he left the motorcycle division and rose in the ranks of the force to become a Detective Chief Inspector. He was never liked. But his diligence was rewarded and respected. His star seemed limitless. He could possibly have become Chief of Police had he not assaulted a teenage girl in the cells one night. He denied the charge. Four deep scratches down his left cheek plus a graphic description of the attack convinced his superiors that the girl was not lying. The incident never made the newspapers. Untzmann resigned from the force with a full pension. He began a security firm and was soon prosperous.

Marshall MacDonald retired to a small house in the Florida Keys. In summer he alternated visits to Toronto, to see family and friends, with visits to Scotland, to rejoice in the highland countryside. He was particularly fond of visiting the Edinburgh Festival. Where for a fortnight he attended every play, every concert—jazz and classical—that he could. Much to Mary's chagrin.

Tony D'Angelo became a priest. He moved to Chicago and joined the American army as a padre. He saw service in Vietnam. And his bravery under fire—administering last rites, consoling the wounded, etc.—was noted. After returning to Chicago he was crossing a quiet suburban street when a car killed him. The driver was never found.

Carlo D'Angelo also went to the States where he disappeared into the maw of the mafia and was never heard from again.

For ten years after the Halloween affray, Menasha was one of the most successful lecturers in philosophy at University College. He was popular with students. His lectures were always packed. His bouts of illness diminished in both intensity and duration enabling him to work long and hard. Until one bright spring day, crossing the campus towards Hart House, he had a stroke. And died instantly. He lived with the MacDonald family until his death.

Ruby Waldman, much to his rabbi father's pride, became a doctor. He decided to practice, much to his father's annoyance, not on Bloor Street but in Malaysia.

Harvey Willenski opened a fruit and flower shop on Eglinton. He was successful both in business and with many lady customers. Muchel Brickman died young from an infection from which there was no known antibiotic at the time. Danny Givertz became an insurance salesman, changed his name to Gibson, married out of the faith, had four children, and lived in a large house in Etobicoke.

In the Altman store the immigrant family, the Berclovs, took over most of the heavy work. And domestically a pattern was soon established with Eva willingly helping in the rearing of the two children. One day, with both families gathered for lunch in the tiny kitchen, Eva was feeding the youngest child, Chiam, a toddler still in a high chair. He was managing to speak his first words.

"All gone," said Eva, tipping the spoon into the boy's mouth.

"All gone," repeated Chiam.

"Say 't'ank you,' Chiam," said Mrs. Berclov, still struggling with English. She turned to her daughter. "You too, say 't'ank you,' Malke."

"Thank you," said Malke, the little girl, carefully. And as an afterthought added, "Bubba."

Chiam repeated the last word. "Bubba," he said triumphantly.

Eva looked at her husband and smiled. Ira smiled back. Mrs. Berclov laughed. And Chiam's father, filled with pride and joy, laughed even louder. Encouraged by this response, the child said the word again and again.

"Bubba. Bubba. Bubba."

From that day Ira and Eva were "Bubba" and "Zaideh." Grandma and Grandpa.

When they died, the Altmans left all they had to the young family. Including the store on Baldwin Street.

———•••———

"I hear you want to be a writer," Menasha said to Leonard Abelson one day as they were having lunch at Hart House. Leonard was by then an undergraduate at the University. He had enrolled in Menasha's philosophy course.

"If I can ever find anything to write about," Leonard replied.

"That's easy," Menasha said. "Write about Baldwin Street."

A Note on the Type

The text was set in 12 point Minion with a leading of 15 points. The display font is Minion Pro Bold. A 1992 Adobe Originals typeface, Minion was designed by Robert Slimbach, and was inspired by classical, old-style typefaces of the late Renaissance— a period of elegant, beautiful and highly readable type designs. Created primarily for text setting, Minion combines the aesthetic and functional qualities that make text type highly readable while remaining versatile with digital technology. The uses of this adaptable font range from limited-edition books, to newsletters, to packaging.

Composed by Jean Carbain
New York, New York

Printed and bound in the U.S.A.